SUZANNE FERRELL

An Edgars Family Novel
VANISHED

Copyright © 2014 by Suzanne Ferrell
Cover Art by Lyndsey Lewellen
Formatting Libris In CAPS
Release date: February 2014
Ferrell, Suzanne (2014), Vanished,
A Romantic Suspense Novel.
Suzanne Ferrell.

All rights reserved to the Author

This book and parts thereof may not be reproduced in any form, stored in a retrieval system, or transmitted in any form by any means - electronic, mechanical, photocopying, or otherwise - without prior written permission of the author and publisher, except as provided by the United States of America copyright law. The only exception is by a reviewer who may quote short excerpts in a review.

Dedication

For Jim, the hero who has always been by my side. Thank you for the love, laughter and support throughout this long slow road to and through publication. Having you as my sounding board and cheerleader helps more than you can ever imagine. Your pride in everything I do or attempt to do keeps me going.

Acknowledgment

It takes a lot of people to make a book complete, especially so with independently published books.

I'd like to think my cover artist, Lyndsey of LLewellen Designs. The whole series is so cool, and this one is PURPLE!

My beta reader Melissa Kelley and critique partner, Sandy Blair who kept this story following the right path and my sanity on just this side of the narrow line into crazyville!

My formatters at Libris in CAPS. Mitch and Alison have done such a great job!

CHAPTER 1

Cleveland, Ohio

The acrid odor of liquid copper hit Abigail Whitson as she pushed open the condo's unlocked door. The smell roused memories of pain and dread.

Her heartbeat leapt into double-time.

She dropped her overnight bag just inside the doorway, and pushed the condo's door open farther. The parking lot's light lit the entrance, casting shadows down the length of the long hallway in front of her. Reaching into her purse, she pulled out her 9mm Glock and gently clicked a bullet into the chamber. This was the first time she'd used the thing outside the firing range since she finished her training five years ago. She fought to control the trembling in her arms and hands as she held the weapon.

"Brianna?" She called from the foyer.

Silence.

Where was she? Her oldest friend had called, asking

her to fly from D.C. to Cleveland. Brianna wanted to meet with her here at her townhouse to talk about some irregularities she'd found at the company where she worked. As self-centered as most of Brianna's faults were, tardiness wasn't among them.

As Abigail's eyes adjusted to the shadows, she glanced down to see a rusty trail smeared over the hallway's expensive Italian-marble tiles. It led from the doorway farther back into the townhouse toward a dim light.

She inhaled deeply, sucking in the cool spring air. The sweet scent of hyacinth from the flowerbed just outside the door mixed with the lingering metal one in her nose. A wave of nausea washed over her. With a trembling hand, she covered her nose and mouth. She inhaled and exhaled slowly in an effort to stop the threat of revisiting her bad airline meal.

Don't lose your lunch here, Abigail. You're a Treasury agent, and it wouldn't be good form.

Technically that was true. Even if she'd never spent one day in the field away from her accounting and support duties, at least her government-issued license said she was a trained agent for the United States Treasury Department.

Now she wished she'd followed protocol and waited until the lead investigator for the department's Columbus division had contacted her before heading to Brianna's home. At the time, however, she'd assumed her friend needed her expert skills in investigative accounting, but was in no physical danger. Seeing no need to wait at the airport for the field agent, she'd simply left the address on the cell number she'd been given and grabbed a taxi.

Now she had no choice but to proceed on her own. Carefully, she stepped farther into the condo's hallway and along the side of it to avoid disturbing what she suspected was dried blood on the tiles.

As she moved past the darkened kitchen and great room in the condo's front, she pressed herself against the hallway wall, pointed her gun into the darkened area and tried to see if anything moved. Nothing did. She moved to the other side and slid further down the hall, passing one bedroom, then another. Her arms ached from the effort to control their trembling.

She supposed she should check out every room, but for her first building search she might as well start with the already lit one.

Coward.

Not really. She might be inexperienced but she wasn't stupid. It was a practical move. If nothing jumped out at her on the way to the living room, she'd just begin there and work her way back out.

"Brianna?" she called again, hoping to get an answer as she neared the room at the hall's end.

None came.

The hum of a computer modem broke the eerie silence. Abigail stopped just inside the doorway.

The room lay in shambles. The stuffing erupted from

the deep knife slashes in the couch cushions. Drawers of the desk and built-in entertainment center stood open, their contents strewn about like an indoor tornado had whipped through the room. The lamps lay in shattered pieces on the floor, except for the one in the corner, which lit the mayhem.

Abigail expected to find a body, either injured or dead among the mess. Thank God there wasn't one. Her relief was short lived as she saw the large pool of congealed blood that had soaked into the room's handwoven Persian rug.

What on earth had Brianna gotten herself into this time?

A click sounded behind her.

Abigail froze in place. Her heartbeat pounded in her ear.

"So, Abby, what have you gotten yourself into this time?" said a distinctly familiar, taunting voice from behind her.

Abigail swallowed the scream she'd been fighting and stiffened her shoulders.

Great. Just what she needed. The last man on the planet she ever wanted to see again.

Her eyes narrowed as she slowly turned, pointing her weapon at the man behind her. The light from the parking lot cast an intimidating silhouette of him as he stepped farther into the room so she could see him, then he leaned casually against the wall. He hadn't changed in the last five years. He still moved with the grace of an expensive sports car on a clogged freeway. Sleek and dangerous, just waiting for the opportunity to pounce on an opening and hit its top speed.

"Hello, Luke." She fought to keep her voice neutral. "Let me guess. *You're* the district field agent."

* * *

Luke Edgars ground his teeth. Pissed didn't even begin to describe his current mood. His mission to Southeast Asia had yielded no new information on his current military espionage case. The trip home had been long and boring, and the man seated beside him had smelled of five-day-old body odor and bad cologne, giving Luke a nagging headache just behind his eyes. Then, at his layover in St. Louis, his boss had ordered him to divert to Cleveland, instead of his home base of Columbus, to baby-sit a desk agent who *might've* stumbled onto a federal tax fraud case. And at the airport, instead of finding a nervous novice, he'd received a text message telling him to meet the agent at this address.

He hadn't thought his week could get any worse. Boy, was he wrong.

Seeing this particular woman—looking very much like the accountant she was, dressed in her loose-fitting blue suit, white blouse, and sensible shoes—holding a gun pointed right at his chest didn't do anything to improve his mood. "You want to put that thing away before someone gets hurt?"

"I do know how to handle a gun," Abby said, pointing the gun at the floor.

He pushed himself away from the wall. No longer a target, he walked into the room, careful not to disturb any possible evidence, his own weapon pointed at the floor. "Whose place is this?"

"Brianna Mathews. My college roommate."

A slight catch in Abby's voice drew his attention away from the chaotic mess in the room and back to her. In the dim lamp light he saw the glistening tears in her green eyes.

Dammit. He didn't want to see her cry. Not again. Distraction. That's what he needed. Distraction for both of them. "Did you secure the other rooms?"

The embarrassment that crossed her features, followed quickly by the firm set to her lips told him she hadn't, even before the word no escaped her lips.

"Dammit, Abby. Did you forget all your training?"

"I was going to work my way back out."

He gave her a skeptical look then edged back into the hall, signaling her to stop when she moved to follow him. "Stay there. And try not to touch anything. Remember it's a real crime scene, not an exercise we played back in Georgia."

Her eyes narrowed and her lips pressed into a thinner line, but she didn't move a muscle.

Luke turned away and lifted his weapon out in front of him, pausing a moment. Tension gripped his neck, back and shoulders. He waited to see if she'd put a bullet between them. Wouldn't blame her if she did.

When no deafening sound blasted through the night and no searing pain ripped through him, he exhaled and inhaled. Apparently, Abby had learned to control that temper of hers in the past five years.

Slowly he stepped back into the hall to the first doorway. This was probably overkill, since all the noise she'd made on entering the premises and their own conversation would've alerted anyone still in the place, but he needed to be sure they were alone. He also needed some distance between them.

Of all the people he expected to find standing in the center of a crime scene, Abby Whitson wasn't among them. Hell, she hadn't even been on his radar, let alone on his short list of possible agents. Seeing her again slammed memories into him of the last night he'd seen her. For nearly five years he'd managed to put the horror-stricken look on her face into a neatly closed compartment in his memory's deepest recesses. Now he'd have to face what happened between them again.

However, first he had to secure her safety. Then he'd deal with the wrath of the one woman he'd never wanted to hurt.

His gun extended, he reached into the first room with the other hand and flicked on the light. It took a moment for his eyes to adjust to the sudden bright light reflecting off the huge mirror nearly covering the opposite wall of the wrecked bedroom.

Nothing moved.

The mattresses had been slashed just like the sofa pillows in the living room. The satin coverlet and silk sheets lay in shreds. The dresser drawers had been emptied, their contents strewn across the floor. Whoever had taken Abby's friend had searched every corner in here.

He moved farther into the room, checking out the closet. The cloying scent of an Asian perfume, probably worth thousands of dollars, clogged the air in the tiny space. Silks, satins, furs—all lay scattered across the floor. Boxes of letters tossed on the pile's top. Even the suitcase lay emptied, the sides slashed open.

Whoever they are, these guys are thorough.

Framed pictures of a strikingly beautiful blonde littered the dressers and nightstands next to the bed. Abby's friend liked men. Lots of them. Each picture had her posed with a different man—old, young, white, black—never the same one twice.

How had prim and proper Abby gotten a friend like this?

* * *

Abigail's trigger finger itched to tighten and take aim at the center of Luke's back as she watched him retrace his steps down the dark hallway. She clenched her eyes shut and counted to ten, then counted to twenty.

I will not kill a fellow agent. I will not kill a fellow agent.

She repeated her old mantra several more times. After five years of extreme professionalism, two minutes in Luke's company and she'd reverted right back to the insecure trainee, easily goaded by his arrogant confidence.

Opening her eyes, she watched him stalk away. His leather jacket stretched tight across his shoulders, his gun arm stretched out in front of him. The black linen pants clung to his buttocks and thighs, and even in the dim light she saw the details of his powerful muscles as he moved.

She let out an exasperated breath then turned back to the living room's chaos once more. Admiring Luke's back side and wishing to kill him at the same time were not her priority. Finding out what happened to Brianna —why, how, and who did it were important now.

Abigail forced herself to concentrate on the disarray in front of her. Her body stilled, and she studied the room, inch by inch. Just like a crime scene photographer, with her eye as her camera, she divided the room into sections, starting closest to her and sweeping in a clockwise fashion. Her mind clicked off mental pictures, cataloging every detail, no matter how innocuous. Later, when she was alone, she'd review each scene in her mind for details.

Finished, she edged her way through the mess on the floor, careful not to step on anything—especially the pooled blood and blood splatter patterns—making her way to the desk in the far corner where Brianna's day planner lay open, a finished Sudoku puzzle on top of it. Abigail slipped her gun back into her purse and pulled out a pen. Using the capped end, she carefully edged the puzzle off the day planner. She turned the pages one at a time, her brain again working like a camera, quickly reading and filing every entry, along with phone numbers, notes and odd symbols. Were they doodles?

The number of men's names on her friend's itinerary surprised her. She knew men were attracted to Brianna, but she had no clue just how many her friend dated at a time. One name, Dylan, popped up more frequently than the others.

A noise behind her alerted her that Luke had exited the first bedroom and was moving further down the hall. She quickly flipped the pages back to the original spot. No need to let Luke know she'd been snooping in there. Her ability to photographically remember any image she wanted was a closely guarded secret. One she didn't intend to share with an adversary such as Luke Edgars. Once she was alone, she'd look for a pattern in all the information.

Hoping to find something useful on Brianna's computer, Abigail used the end of her pen to wiggle the mouse to stop the screen-saver pattern of fake fish floating around.

Great. The first window open was a screen full of

head shots on an adult dating site. *You couldn't leave me some clue or file, Brianna? Something more helpful than pictures and statistics of young women? And why women, not men? Strange research for such a heterosexual as Brianna.*

Tucking the odd thought in the back of her mind, she minimized the screen. A map with pinpoints on them, but no tags. Behind that screen she found one with shipping dates from her company. *What was Brianna doing? Did any of this have to do with the phone call asking—no, demanding—she come to Cleveland today?*

Next Abigail opened the browsing history, scanning it for URLs over several days, then closed that screen and enlarging the others in the orders she'd found them.

She squatted beside the desk, pulled out a pair of tweezers from her purse and used them to lift some scattered papers off the floor. Most were bills, some receipts from restaurants and a few personal correspondences, all from men. Didn't Brianna have any other female friends besides her?

Quickly wiping away the tears that had somehow slid down her cheeks, she stepped away from the computer just as Luke's footsteps on the hallway tiles announced his return to the living room. She never cried, and she'd be damned if she'd let him catch her in a weak moment. Not again.

"I told you not to move."

His arrogant tone grated on her nerves.

"Despite what you think, I *am* a trained agent. I

know how to investigate a crime scene without destroying evidence." She didn't try to hide her own indignation. She knew she hadn't disturbed vital evidence the crime scene investigators might need.

He pulled out his cell phone. "Anything on the computer?"

She shook her head. "Who are you calling?"

He flipped open the phone. "The local police."

Panic surged in her. "Wait! Can't we look around a little longer before we call them?"

He lifted an eyebrow, his finger paused above the buttons. "The longer we wait, the longer it'll take them to find your friend."

"Look around us." A shudder ran through her and she let out a long sigh. "Do you really think whoever did this hasn't killed her already?"

Luke closed the cell phone. "If they haven't found what they wanted here, then they still have need of her. We have to proceed as if she is still alive."

"I pray you're right, with my whole heart, I do." Why did he have to sound so sensible? "But if you're not, once there's an official local investigation, the red tape to look at the evidence alone will be a mile high. I need to look around a bit to see if she left me a clue as to why she needed me."

"She didn't tell you on the phone? Exactly why did your friend ask you to come here?"

Abigail ground her teeth. She didn't know which she hated worse from this man, arrogance to rival an NFL quarterback, or the condescending patience equal to Sister Compassionatta back at the Sisters of the Sacred Heart orphanage.

Closing her eyes, Abigail recalled the conversation she had the night before with Brianna. "She was scared. I could hear it in her voice. Brianna has never sounded scared the entire time we've known each other. There wasn't a hesitant bone in her body." *Unlike me.* Abigail opened her eyes and looked directly at Luke. "You would've liked her."

"I doubt it," he said, looking around the room.

For a brief second, something odd crossed the hard lines of his face—contempt? Then it disappeared, replaced by an intensity that sent a shiver running over Abigail.

"So what exactly did she say to you that made you think this was more than just boyfriend troubles?"

"Brianna was a beautiful woman, but she also had a great head for math. Her beauty hid her passion for crunching numbers from any man pursuing her. They rarely looked past her blonde hair and chest size." She smiled, remembering the conspiratorial wink her friend would give when some guy tried to tutor her in math. "Brianna called it her secret weapon. On the phone last night she said she'd run across some irregularities at her job."

"And she didn't tell you what they were?"

Abigail shook her head. "She said she didn't want to give details over the phone. I assumed it had to do with money. Otherwise why call me?"

"Sounds like she was paranoid."

Abigail gestured at the mess around them. "Apparently with good reason."

"Did you at least ask where she worked?"

Okay, now he was pushing her buttons. Alright, she'd just push back.

"No."

He let out a curse. "Even a rookie would've asked that."

She gave him her most saccharine smile. "I didn't ask because I already knew. Hollister-Klein Exporters."

The name of the international import/export firm registered recognition in his eyes, but he quickly hid it. The muscles in his well-chiseled jaw flexed. He pulled out his phone once more and dialed. Holding the phone in one hand he dug into his pockets with the other and threw her a pair of latex gloves. "Put these on so you don't leave any fingerprints behind. You have until the police get here to search for information. But leave everything where you find it." He spoke the address into the phone then waited. "By the way, was there a disk in the A drive?"

Dammit. Why hadn't she considered that?

Abigail pulled on the gloves as she opened the A drive slot on the ancient hard drive Brianna refused to update then shook her head. He pressed his lips into a thin line and nodded.

When he spoke into the phone again, she squatted to

study the papers on the floor once more. Bills and letters. What had she hoped for? Spreadsheets? Files? Those would've been the first things taken.

There had to be something useful in this mess, something the killers had missed.

Killers, not attackers.

A pain filled her chest. Despite Luke's optimistic words earlier, he couldn't possibly believe Brianna had survived this attack. Lifting a paper, Abigail paused to blink back tears once more.

As sure as she knew today was Thursday, she knew her friend was not simply missing.

CHAPTER 2

"You want to tell me why the feds are interested in this missing woman, Agent Edgars?" asked Detective Jeffers, the local cop who'd caught the case. A tall, older man in good physical shape, Jeffers sported a close-to-the-head military cut of his dark hair and a serious expression that would rival his own brother Dave's.

Luke gave Jeffers his I-mean-you-no-harm smile. "We're not officially here. Ms. Whitson and I came to see her friend and found this situation."

"So you expect me to believe there was no reason you two came here, except to visit an old friend?" Jeffers eyed him with a no-way-am-I-buying-that-crap look.

"You know how it is, Detective," Luke laid on the charm. "The little lady wants to visit a friend, we come and visit her friend." He pulled the detective to the side. "I'd appreciate it if you could keep our names out of your official report."

"If I need more information about the victim?" Jeffers left the comment up in the air.

"You'll have our full cooperation. Believe me, we want her friend found as quickly as possible. We'd also like to be apprised of any progress your department might make. Unofficially, of course."

"Then you won't be keeping any leads from us?"

Luke smiled again, the smile that usually got him out of trouble with his superiors. "If anything comes our way we'll be only too happy to share it." He'd promise to sell his soul if it kept Abby's name out of official channels.

Moments later Luke watched Abby repeatedly thread her fingers together as she stiffly sat on the edge of the white leather chair talking to Detective Jeffers. After he'd placed the call to the police, she'd asked him not to inform them why she'd come to visit her friend. It went completely against protocol, and they both knew it.

Although he'd made a career of bending the rules to the breaking point in order to solve a case, for once he'd been tempted to play by the rules, ignore her request, and insist she tell the detectives why her friend summoned her. That would've been the easiest way to get Abby off this case and to the safety of her desk back in Washington.

However, he had his own agenda for not giving away her secret, and it had little to do with the shadowed plea in her green eyes, the fine tremors that shook her elegant hands, or the catch in her smooth-as-honey voice when she spoke of her friend. When she'd informed him her friend worked for Hollister-Klein his internal warning bells went off. For the past year he'd been secretly looking into the life of one of the founders of the company, Senator Howard Klein. If Abby's friend was missing, he'd bet his new laptop-tablet there was a connection to the company. He didn't believe in coincidences.

He studied Abby a moment, remembering all the times he'd teased her during training. Touchy as a wounded hedgehog on the outside, sensitive on the inside.

As she talked to the detective, she slipped her long fingers into the blunt cut of her dark bangs, pushing them off her face. The rest of her thick hair was knotted behind her in some sort of professional, boring sort of bun. Despite her attempt at professionalism, the benign action showed just how frightened she was.

Luke turned his attention away from her and the feelings her vulnerability set off deep inside him. He looked out the window at the dark parking lot behind the condo. Oh yeah. He had his own reasons for suppressing information from the local cops.

If Abby's friend survived the torture—and by the looks of this place she'd been beaten beyond endurance—she'd already told her abusers what it was they wanted to know. If she hadn't, every possibility existed that she'd at least let them know she'd called Abby for help.

Abby could've innocently walked into a trap. Instead of just her friend's blood on the floor, Abby's could've been there, too. At the thought, Luke's gut tightened with white-hot anger.

Any way he looked at it, naive Abby was now a target. A target he had to protect at any cost, even if meant pulling rank on the local cops like he had with Jeffers.

A hand tapped him on his shoulder. Luke turned to see Abby standing right behind him. God, he'd forgotten how tall she was. If she ever wore a pair of sexy heels instead of sensible shoes, she'd be nearly eye level with his six feet two inches. "Done talking to the locals?"

She nodded. "I hate to ask this, but could you give me a lift to a hotel? I don't want to wait for a taxi at this late hour."

Dammit, there was that catch in her voice again.

"You don't have a rental car?"

She shook her head. "No, I just had a taxi drop me off."

Great! Beside himself and the police officers, now the taxi driver could identify her as the first person to arrive at the condo to whoever took her friend. Just great.

"Do you have a hotel reserved already?" He tried to keep the anger out of his voice, but she flinched and pulled her hand away as if he'd slapped her.

"No. I'd thought I'd be staying here." She took a retreating step, and looked around the room. "I'll have one of the officers give me a ride—"

"No." Luke grabbed her by the elbow. No way was he letting her leave here with anyone but him, certainly not some young yahoo beat cop who was more interested in getting home than securing her safety. "I'll take you."

Not releasing his grip, he led her back to the detective, pulled out a business card and handed it to him. "My cell number's on there, Jeffers."

The officer took the card. "Ms. Whitson is a material witness, Edgars. How do I reach her?"

Without waiting for him to answer for her, Abby rattled off her cell phone number for the detective.

Luke fought the urge to growl at her. He didn't want every police man in the place to know her number. "Use mine first. She'll be with me. If you need to talk to her I'll see that she's available to you. Otherwise, I'd appreciate it if no one else knew of her whereabouts for now. And let me know when the crime scene analysis is ready. Put a rush on it, if you can."

He shook the other lawman's hand, then led Abby away from the bloody mess, hearing several murmurings of "damn feds" as they passed the officers milling around.

At the bedroom door, they nearly collided with a wet-behind-the-ears officer holding several pictures of Abby's friend. The top one was Brianna with a man about forty years old and signed, *For Abigail*.

"That's for me." Abby reached for it, only to have the young man step back.

"Sorry, ma'am. For now it's evidence."

Abby nodded and blinked back tears. "Oh, yes, I almost forgot. It's just...well, I don't really have a recent picture of my friend."

"Sorry ma'am." Sympathy washed across the officer's face. He glanced at Detective Jeffers, then back at Abby. "Maybe, if it weren't vital..."

She smiled at the young man, a half smile, the kind that said she was disappointed, but wouldn't make a big deal out of it. "It's okay, officer. I understand."

Luke hated to see Abby hurting, especially over a picture of a woman who had so little regard for her friend she'd dragged her blindly into a dangerous situation. He glanced out the front door. TV trucks had set up their lights and cameras, reporters peppered the lawn, a crowd of neighborhood gawkers milled on the far side of the street.

Dammit, could this night get any better?

"Officer..." he glanced at the man's badge. "Wilson. Could you loan us a police hat and jacket?"

The rookie glanced around nervously. "I don't know..."

Luke pointed toward the front. "See all those reporters out there?"

Wilson and Abby both glanced out the door.

"If they see us leaving here, they'll assume we're

witnesses, plaster our faces on the news, and point whoever did this straight for us. But if they see a female cop leaving with a detective, then no one will even notice."

"I don't need to hide," Abby said, her chin going up stubbornly.

"If you want to help your friend, you need to keep a low profile." He didn't add that her life might already be in jeopardy. What he needed from her now was cooperation, not panic.

She pulled her lower lip through her teeth, and nibbled on it, as if she were calculating the benefits of arguing with him. The action sent heat through him, and made him want to nibble on her lip himself, just to see if it tasted as soft as it had five years ago.

"My overnight bag and laptop are in the foyer."

Her words drew him back to the here and now. "And?"

"How do we explain taking them with us, if we're just cops doing our job?"

"They'll just be more evidence we're collecting," added Officer Wilson, getting into the act.

Luke could've kissed the guy as he removed his coat and hat, and gave them to Abby. "Get that picture dusted for prints, too, kid, and we'll carry it out with the rest of her stuff." Luke held up his hand when Wilson started to protest. "If Jeffers needs it back, he'll call me. The evidence will be in federal custody, so he won't have a problem with us taking it."

As the young officer went to have the picture dusted, Abby slipped on the coat then pulled the hat onto her head. "I'm ready."

Looking at her, Luke shook his head, pulled the hat off then shoved the loose strands of her dark hair up inside it before pushing the hat back onto her head. The bun at the base of her neck faded into the collar of the coat. "Let's not give anyone a chance to get an accurate description of you."

She rolled her eyes. "I really think you're making too much out of this. No one will notice me."

I did.

"Listen, I'm the senior agent on this case now. You do what I say, no matter how over the top you think it is, *capisce*?"

She threw him a salute. "Yes, sir!"

Wilson returned with the framed picture, freshly covered with powder, and handed it to Abby. "Detective Jeffers said he doubted they'd find any prints other than the vic's on anything. And he'd like nothing better than to cooperate with the feds, but he's still holding you responsible for the evidence, sir."

Luke looked into the living room at Jeffers. They exchanged nods. Both of them understood the situation. If anything happened to Abby or the evidence, the local cop wouldn't hesitate to lay the blame on the federal agent.

"Ready?" Luke led the way to the front door. "Keep your face turned slightly from the reporters, Abby, just in case they film the general scene."

She rolled her eyes again and thrust her friend's picture at him. "Wait. You take this."

He lifted a brow, but took the picture. "Why?"

"You're the big bad detective. I'm the lowly beat cop. You'd expect me to carry the cases, while you took the victim's picture."

Wilson actually laughed behind them then coughed to cover it up when Luke shot him a glare.

Abby thrust her hand at the guy and smiled. "Thanks for all your help, officer."

The kid actually blushed as he shook her hand. "The pleasure...was all mine, ma'am."

It was Luke's turn to roll his eyes. Then he opened the screen door, holding it long enough for Abby to pick up her bags and exit behind him, both of them careful not to brush the outside frame where a CSI member dusted for latent prints. Luke walked beside her, talking quietly, hoping everyone would think he was giving her instructions and not stop them for questions.

"No matter what happens out here, keep walking toward that gray BMW halfway down the block," he said.

She nodded.

They had to step past two more CSI people who were scanning the sidewalk and street with UV light. They'd sprayed the area with Luminol to find hidden blood splatter, which was glowing like a fluorescent polka-dot trail. Luke glanced down the path which led to the east, away from his car about five yards, then stopped. He'd bet anything there were tire tracks at that spot, and that's where the culprits stashed Abby's friend into their getaway vehicle.

Too bad he couldn't stay and get some firsthand information on the case. Right now, his priority was to get Abby to his car and away from the reporters.

They were halfway there. *This just might work.*

Suddenly lights and people approached from the right. "Detective! Detective, could you tell us what's happening?" asked a female voice.

Shit.

Luke thrust the keys into Abby's hand. "Keep going and get inside the car. I'll try to distract her."

Abigail took the keys and kept walking. She'd just bet he'd distract the pretty blonde reporter.

Behind her Luke changed his voice to smooth-as-silk. "What can I do for you, Ms…?"

His voice drifted off and Abigail couldn't hear the woman's reply, but wouldn't be surprised if she didn't ask him to take her home and have his way with her.

Disgusted, Abigail put her bags in the back seat, taking a moment to look at the scene near the house, her mind taking quick snapshots. There must be five news crews. She looked across the road at the spectators watching the police and reporters. Old and young alike. Had they known Brianna or were they just out to see the macabre sideshow?

With a sigh, she settled in the passenger side to watch Luke's performance with the lady reporter. After a few minutes they were both laughing, and with his hand on the small of the woman's back he propelled her toward Brianna's condo and away from the BMW.

"If we wanted to keep a low profile, we put the wrong person in a disguise," Abigail muttered.

Five years ago, she'd watched him flirt the same way with every woman in their training class and any female training officer he came into contact with for nearly six months. She had to admit, he hadn't been the one doing the pursuing. The man seemed to attract women like rednecks to beer.

Everyone but her.

From the moment they'd met they'd managed to act like flint on stone, sparks flying every time they were within ten feet of each other. For some reason he'd decided she had no business training for field work, and she'd been determined to follow her goals no matter how much he'd tried to goad her into quitting.

Out on the lawn, he disengaged himself from the crowd and was sauntering back toward the car. As he moved toward her in the dark, she felt her pulse quicken. No matter how much he irritated her, something about him set her blood to boil. Just being near him heightened her senses. Her skin still tingled where he'd gripped her arm.

She sighed and looked away.

No use wanting what you can't have, Abigail. You

threw yourself at him once and he turned you down. No matter how tempting the man, she wasn't into humiliation and wouldn't go there again.

The sisters had been right. She was a plain woman and might as well accept that. No matter what Luke believed, she was as safe as could be. Even in a crowd of two, she was invisible.

Abigail gave herself a mental shake. Enough self-pity. She needed to concentrate on the problem at hand —Brianna was counting on her.

With resolve she shoved images of Luke and memories from the past back into her filing cabinet mind. Then she lay her head back on the seat, closed her eyes, opened another drawer in that mental storage unit and pulled out the first image she'd seen in her friend's home.

Just like a crime scene photograph she could see every detail in cold clarity. The rust stains on the tile floor had a tread in them. Probably some sort of soft-soled shoe. Which means they carried Brianna out and stepped in her blood. Possibly two of them. Smearing the blood as they walked.

"Is she still alive?"

"Probably."

Abigail slammed the mental picture of the hallway back into its drawer and sat straight in her seat. She hadn't realized she'd been talking out loud or that Luke had gotten into the driver's seat. "Excuse me?"

He turned in his seat, set her friend's framed picture

into her lap and studied her with those hazel-colored eyes of his. "Until we know otherwise, let's just go with the assumption your friend is still alive, okay sweetheart?"

Surprised by the actual tenderness in his words, Abigail could only nod. He started the car and she swung her gaze out into the night, blinking at the fresh tears stinging at her eyes.

After a few minutes she felt she could speak. "Don't call me sweetheart."

He laughed. "That's my Abby. All guts and spirit."

"I'm not your *Abby*, or anything else for that matter. Just get me to a hotel, and I'll take care of myself."

"You're doing a great job so far," he muttered as he turned onto the main thoroughfare.

Abigail ignored the sarcasm in his voice and stared out into the dark night.

She already knew his opinion of her. He didn't think she could do this job, that she belonged behind a desk far away. Well, that was too damn bad. He could stick his opinion in his...tailpipe. Brianna didn't call him, she'd called her. Short of the second coming, nothing and no one was keeping her from helping her friend—especially not Luke Edgars.

They traveled in silence until they came to The Compton Inn—a modest, three-story hotel just a few miles from Brianna's home. The whole area retained an upscale appearance.

Luke pulled into the eave-covered entrance. Abigail

waited until he'd put the car in park before hopping out, still hugging Brianna's picture to her chest. Luke lazily exited the driver's side then came around to get her bags from the backseat.

She claimed them from him, pulling her laptop carrier onto her shoulder, then held out her hand. "Thank you. I appreciate the lift."

He shook her hand, the corner of his mouth lifting in a half grin, as if he thought her words amusing. "No problem."

Hefting her overnight bag, Abigail turned and marched through the lobby's front sliding glass doors to the reservation desk. "I'd like a room."

The gangly African-American man, probably a grad student working the night shift, tugged at his grey vest and started clicking the keys to his computer terminal. "And how long will you be staying with us, ma'am?"

"A week."

"Make it two rooms," came the all-too-familiar sound of Luke's voice from behind her.

She glared over her shoulder at him. "What are you doing here?"

"Same as you. Getting a room."

"Why don't you go home?"

"That would be a bit inconvenient, since the three-hour commute from Columbus is a real killer."

The desk clerk snickered.

Abigail swung her glare at him a moment. "I'd like a room before breakfast, if possible."

The kid swallowed his grin and once more fixed his eyes on the computer screen.

"Make it two rooms, with connecting doors, and I'll throw in a twenty dollar tip." Luke set down his own travel bag, pulled out his wallet and handed the kid the bribe.

The desk clerk smiled, took the money and typed faster.

Abigail counted to ten again before speaking. "I do not want a connecting room with you. I don't want to even be in the same hotel."

"Too bad, sweetheart. You're stuck with me until you decide to give up this crazy idea of yours and head home." He reached over and stroked her cheek with his knuckles, holding her gaze with his for a moment.

Lost in the heat of his nearness, Abigail's pulse jumped. Then she realized what he was doing. He was intentionally giving the impression they were a couple having a spat, instead of working colleagues—a very loosely fitting term for their relationship.

She tried to kill him with her stare. "I'm not going back until I've finished my *job*."

"Fine. And I'll be at your side the entire way." He pulled out a credit card, flipped it to the desk clerk. "Two rooms, connecting doors, put them both on this card, and list them only in my name."

Abigail set down her bags and reached for her own wallet. "I'll pay for my own room, thank you."

Luke gripped her arm while her hand remained

inside the big black bag, and dragged her out of hearing distance of their audience. Moving closer until barely any space existed between them, he fixed her with a commanding stare of his own and lowered his voice to a tight whisper. "You want to stay, then you stay. But we play by my rules. I want your name so far off the radar you'll look like a stealth bomber. Got it?"

Abigail nodded.

"Good girl," he said, then winked at her and returned to the registration desk.

Oh, she so wanted to take him down a few pegs. However, the kid behind the desk now watched them with complete fascination. If she made any more of a scene, he'd tell everyone he knew. Seeing as how she also wanted to stay, as Luke put it, *off the radar*, she'd let the arrogant lout have his way—for now.

* * *

"Home, sweet home," Luke muttered as he set his overnight bag on the bed closest to the door, looking around at the standard two double beds, cheap veneer desk, semi-comfortable chair, television and DVD set-up of his hotel room. The same room, complete with English fox-hunt picture, could be found in countless hotels across the North American continent. He should know. In the past few years he'd seen more than his fair share in one way or another.

His stomach rumbled. He glanced at the clock.

Almost midnight. Too late to order pizza, and he was too damn tired to drive out and go get a burger. They'd passed a pancake house on the way to the hotel. Now he wished they'd stopped to eat before getting rooms.

No use thinking about it after the fact. At the time all he'd wanted to do was get Abby away from the crime scene and into a safe place for the night. Somehow, he needed to convince her to let him and the local police take over the investigation. It was only a matter of time before someone leaked the information that her friend had contacted Abby before she'd been abducted.

He kicked off his shoes and walked to the window.

Abducted. Like hell.

To keep her thinking on the positive side, he'd told Abby they'd work as if her friend were still alive, but they both could read the evidence. Given that much blood loss, if her friend wasn't dead already, she probably wouldn't last out the night.

With a frustrated groan he pushed himself away from the window and strode over to the connecting door. Dammit, he couldn't send Abby away. There was only one person who had any useful knowledge as to what happened to Brianna Mathews and she sat in the other room.

He opened his door, and knocked on Abby's side.

No answer.

Why wasn't she answering?

He pounded on the door.

Still no answer.

Panic rising inside him, he raised his fist to really pound on the damn door. Suddenly it opened.

"What?" She stood there, her hair hanging wet about her face, dressed in a T-shirt that gave just the impression of her breasts and a pair of flannel pajama shorts. Her long, shapely legs seemed to go on forever. Her feet were bare and her toenails were a shiny, deep crimson.

He swallowed hard. He couldn't help it. She looked—sexy. Sad and cute, but sexy nonetheless.

"Why were you pounding on the door?" She gazed at him with a curious look in her eyes.

Struggling to keep his mind off her long legs, he cleared his throat. "You didn't answer when I knocked."

"I was in the shower. Did you want something?"

Yes, those legs wrapped around my hips. He shook off the image of a wet, naked Abby in his arms and focused on the question. What had he wanted?

"I wanted to ask you some questions about your friend." He pushed his way into her room and sat on the edge of the nearest bed. When she walked past him, her breasts bounced slightly beneath the T-shirt. He nearly groaned.

"Ask away. I don't know what I can tell you that will help." She sat on the other bed, drawing her legs up and wrapping her arms around them. "Before yesterday, we hadn't talked in nearly six months."

"What did she do at Hollister-Klein?"

"She was the assistant to the Chief Financial

Officer."

"So she was a secretary."

She shrugged her shoulders. "No. She handled accounting duties same as the other members of her department. I already told you that. And since I work for the Treasury Department, I assumed her phone call had something to do with some sort of government fraud."

"What do you know about Hollister-Klein?" He loved the game of twenty questions. You discovered the most interesting details when you played it—like how Abby curled her toes when she was thinking.

"Just that they're a major importer and exporter and have defense contracts to move equipment throughout the world."

Standard public information anyone could glean from the news or internet. He reached for the television remote, tracing his fingers over the keys. "And your friend gave you no hint what the irregularities she found might pertain to?"

"She told me something didn't add up on a new project she was working on." Abby yawned.

"I don't suppose I could talk you into going home and letting me handle this?"

She shook her head. "No. Brianna called me. She and I have known each other since the day she came to the orphanage. I want to help her."

"You were in an orphanage?" He couldn't hide his surprise. He'd never thought of Abby's past, but he'd assumed it was like his—mother, father, siblings.

"My mother died when I was three and I went to live at the Sisters of the Sacred Heart orphanage. Brianna came along about a year later, and we became friends. Even after she'd been adopted a few years later, she always wrote me."

"I thought you said she was your college roommate."

"We stayed in touch all through school. When it was time to go to college, we planned it together and ended up at MIT, me on scholarship, her on her adoptive parents' Money. Brianna is the nearest thing I have to a sister." Tears formed in Abby's eyes, and she blinked hard at them. "So, no. I'm not going home until I find her or find out what happened to her."

Uncomfortable with her pain, Luke pushed himself off the bed. "Then get some sleep. We'll start searching for answers in the morning."

He stopped at the connecting door. "Leave this open. Just in case."

"I'm a big girl, Luke. I don't need the door open just to feel safe."

He grinned at her. "Maybe it will make me feel safer."

* * *

The two men relaxed in leather chairs opposite each other across the polished mahogany desk in the century-old library. They sat in silence for a few moments, sipping their cognac. Smoke rings from their cigars wafted above their heads, filling the room with a spicy Indonesian aroma. The firelight in the river-stone fireplace flickered off the dark panels of the walls.

"Did she tell you where it was?" The gray-haired man asked.

"No. I'm afraid our men were a little too enthusiastic in their efforts." The younger man took a sip from his crystal snifter. "All she mumbled before passing out was something about it being with an Abby."

He pulled out his phone and played the recording he'd made of her interrogation.

"Tell us what you did with it, bitch."

Smack.

"I don't know what you want."

"The flash drive. We know you made one."

Smack. Thud. Crack.

"Uhm," she moaned.

"That's when they broke her nose," Dylan interpreted the sound before her moans started.

"Tell us and we'll stop. Don't and I can do this all night."

"Sister Compassionatta," she whispered.

"A Sister? You left it with a nun?"

Another thud as fist met flesh. More cracks as they'd broken her cheek and eye socket.

"Abby, Sister."

Then nothing as she'd passed out.

"An Abbey." The first man swirled the golden liquid

in his snifter and studied the fire for a moment. "Did she go near a church after she left the office?"

The other man shook his head then ran his fingers through his dark hair. "We tailed her from the minute she left the building until she got to her condo. She made two stops along the way, the dry cleaners and the grocers, then home."

"See if there are any Catholic churches near those businesses she might've dropped the information off at when we weren't looking." The older man held up his hand to stave off any protest and fixed his lieutenant with a cold stare. "Have them check out the businesses, too. This time, insist they leave no trace we've been there. Her disappearance in tomorrow's news will be bad enough."

The younger man swallowed hard, but didn't let his gaze drop. He'd gotten this far by being cool in a crisis and thinking ahead. "Once I realized she didn't have the item with her, I sent someone to watch the condo to see if anyone had arrived to contact her."

"And was there?"

"They reported the police and news crews were already there, but I've instructed to continue their surveillance until further notice."

"Good."

"And the woman? She is quite a beauty."

"When she ceases to be of use to us, make her disappear in whatever manner you see fit."

CHAPTER 3

A light snoring came from the other room.

Abigail lay in her bed, curled on her side, her heart pounding in her ears as she waited in the dark to be sure the snoring continued. For the past half hour she'd resisted turning on the light. She could hardly breathe in a dark room, much less sleep, but she'd never give Luke the satisfaction of knowing how scared she was of the dark.

What kind of field agent would she make if every time she needed to work in the dark she had to spend half the time fighting off panic attacks?

If Luke knew that information, he'd have her on the first plane back to Washington.

She sighed, then strained to listen to the sounds from the other room. The snoring sounded steady.

Thank goodness. Her hands shook as she clicked on her light and took a deep breath.

Great. It would be hours before she calmed down enough to sleep. Might as well get some work done.

She retrieved her laptop from the desk then scooted back under her covers to stay warm in the cold, drafty room. Sitting with her back against the headboard, she bent her knees and used them as a prop for her laptop. Before she started, she listened once more for sounds from Luke's room.

Still snoring.

Some bodyguard. If someone slipped into the room, he'd never hear it.

Then her gaze drifted to the hallway door. A chill ran over her skin. She reached beneath her pillow and pulled her service weapon out from where she'd hid it for the night and set it next to her right hip.

Even if you had an experienced field agent asleep in the next room, it never hurt to be prepared. You never knew when a monster would invade your life and change it completely.

"Poor little thing. You say she was there when her mother was killed?"

The kind looking lady in the black-and-white outfit reached out a hand to her. Still clutching her mother's pink sweater, she released the policeman's hand and took the lady's.

The big policeman in the dark blue suit nodded. "We're not sure how much she witnessed, Sister. We found her hiding in the closet. She hasn't said anything but 'Mommy' since."

The lady in black smoothed her work-roughened hand over the little girl's hair. "And there's no father?"

"Not that we've been able to find. In fact, there's no family at all." The policeman handed the sister a box with her clothes in it. *"If you can get her to tell you anything, we'd appreciate you giving us a call."*

He turned and left.

The lady smiled. "You're safe here, little one. I'm Sister Rose Thomas. Won't you tell me your name?"

She stared into the Sister's gentle, wrinkled face and compassionate eyes. "I'm Abigail."

Sister Rose Thomas was the first to notice her unusual abilities.

"Your mind is like a huge filing cabinet, Abigail. Whenever you want to remember something, you reach in, pull out the image, and it's as if you're seeing it again for the first time, isn't it?"

Abigail managed a smile. Other than her mother, Sister Rose Thomas had been the only other gentle person in her life. Her death had left another hole in Abigail's world. One she doubted would ever be filled again.

Abigail swiped at the moisture in her eyes and shoved the memory back into the corner of her mind. Good lord, she was maudlin tonight.

The framed picture on the bedside table caught her eye. Brianna loved to have her picture taken. And why wouldn't she? Her blonde good looks rivaled any movie star. So why would someone want to put out that light?

Abigail drew in a deep breath. She couldn't help her

mother, and she couldn't bring back Sister Rose Thomas. But she could help Brianna.

Opening her laptop, she pulled on her reading glasses and started a new file. Then she closed her eyes and reached into her memory for the pictures she'd stored of Brianna's townhouse. For now she'd avoid the bloodier ones. They'd have to wait until she could better handle seeing them. Blood always reminded her of the first pictures she'd ever stored in her brain—those of her mother lying dead on her bed, bloody and broken.

Instead, she'd concentrate on the datebook. She snagged those images from the pile, shoving aside the one with the Sudoku puzzle and moved to the actual pages of the datebook. She typed every date and time for the past six months into her laptop.

Finished, she sat back to study the pattern of her friend's life. Brianna was a high-maintenance woman. She had weekly standing appointments for her hair, nails, pedicures and massages. Numerous men's names filled the datebook, mostly for evening dates, but some for afternoon meetings and lunches.

A set of dates were marked with asterisks and appeared on a six-week cycle. What was that all about?

Then there were all the odd markings in the margins. Weird symbols that repeated, but at no constant interval. Was it some sort of code Brianna had developed or a shorthand? If so, what did they mean?

Only three sets of initials appeared more than twice

throughout the pages.
D. K.
P. H.
R. B.

Were they all business associates? Or was one of them the man in the picture with his arms around Brianna? And which one was responsible for her friend's disappearance?

All these questions, so few answers. Now her head hurt. Probably from frustration more than anything else. Exercise always seemed to help her focus.

If she were at home back in Washington, she'd go to the gym and work out, or throw on her Nikes and run a few miles. But she wasn't at home, didn't know the area well enough to go for a run, and she was pretty sure her self-appointed bodyguard in the next room wouldn't take kindly to finding her missing. She'd just have to find an alternative plan.

Practicing her Kata might help. Performing the series of movements used in karate always cleared her grey cells and let her brain focus on a plan.

She set her laptop on the side of the bed and lay her glasses on the bedside table. Moving as quietly as possible, she set the lamp and generic chair away from their standard position by the window to the far side of the other bed. In the center of the empty space, she stood, inhaling and exhaling slowly. Eyes closed, she cleared her mind of the evening's events and concentrated on stretching. First her whole body, then each group of muscles.

At home, she usually gave herself an imaginary foe—some criminal element or a mugger—a faceless attacker she could defend herself against. This time, however, she had two very real foes to give herself motivation as she practiced her skills. If she wanted to, she could imagine Brianna's attackers. But that still gave her a faceless opponent. The other choice lay snoring on the other side of her wall.

Abigail opened her eyes, a grin on her face.

With Luke's arrogant face in mind, she raised her foot in a high kick. It felt good. She forced herself to concentrate, and began the series of movements that would take her through the Kata.

* * * * *

In the colorless room the woman's body lay sprawled facedown in the blood pooling beneath and around her on the hardwood floor. His pulse raced and his hands shook as he reached to turn her over. Her dark hair covered her face. He didn't want to move her, didn't want to touch her cold, lifeless body, but he had to know.

A branch tapped on the window.

He pulled her onto her side.

The tapping continued.

He brushed her hair off her face.

The tapping grew rhythmic.

Abby's dark eyes stared at him, lifeless and cold.
The tapping stopped.
Then her lips moved, and she whispered, "Why didn't you help me?"

Luke shot up out of the covers, panting hard. Sweat pouring off his brow, his heart pounded in his chest. He shoved the blankets free, sat on the edge of the bed and tried to get his bearings.

With great effort he sucked in air and forced his heart rate to slow down. He wasn't in the shadow-filled room of his dream anymore. Even in the dark, he could see the colorful bedspread and the picture on the wall of his hotel room.

This dream had haunted him for years. The first time he'd had it was the day he met Abby. It was always the same. Her inert body lay on the floor, covered in blood. Each time he prayed he'd turn her over to find her still alive. However, it always ended the same—Abby dead and him helpless to stop it.

Only this time the dream was different. This time she spoke. She wanted him to help her. Never before had she spoken to him. And something else was different.

The damn tapping.

Where had that come from? What did it mean? And where had it gone?

His breath coming at a less frantic pace, he listened to the silence in his room. Then he heard a sound. Not tapping. Something altogether different.

A soft grunting came from the next room. A light

shone through the cracks around the partially opened door. And a thudding sound, like someone hitting something.

Visions of the blood pool at the condo and Abby dead in his dream still fresh in his mind, Luke untangled his body from the sheets and pulled his gun from its holster by the bed. He didn't know what was going on next door, but if someone was hurting Abby, they weren't escaping with their lives.

With his back pressed tight against the wall, and the urge to rush in firmly pushed deep into the back of his brain, he inched his way toward the connecting door. The grunting and thudding continued in an odd sort of stop and start fashion. Inhaling deeply, he pushed the door open with his foot, and wedged himself into the narrow opening between the door and the frame.

Silently counting to three, he turned, moved through the doorway, and crouched. His gun extended in front of him, he growled out, "Freeze!"

He followed his own command.

Abby stood frozen in mid-kick. A light sheen of sweat covered her long slender legs and arms stretching from beneath her T-shirt and shorts. A few of the dark strands of her hair had escaped her ponytail to lay wet against her neck and cheek. In the dim light he could see the light flush of pink in her cheeks. Her eyes widened even more as she watched him from across the room. Then she parted her lips, her tongue darting out to moisten them.

"Can I put my leg down now?"

He swallowed hard, nodded, lowering his weapon as she lowered her leg.

She bounced on the balls of her feet a few minutes, then began slowly stretching down toward her toes. Mesmerized, Luke watched her T-shirt fall forward, revealing the soft curve of her lower back and the stretched shorts over her hips and ass.

Still feeling the effects of his dream, he fought the urge to make her work up a sweat for another reason. Then the red glowing numbers of the bedside clock-radio caught his peripheral vision.

3:15 in the morning.

"What the hell are you doing?" he asked, not trying to hide his irritation.

"Stretching. What does it look like I'm doing?" she asked as she straightened.

Besides torturing him?

"I meant the kick boxing routine in the middle of the night." He laid his weapon on the edge of the credenza.

"It's called a Kata. Since the space is so limited I've had to modify the steps a bit. I needed to think. Some sort of physical activity clears my brain."

She stretched to the side, her T-shirt sliding up and revealing more of her creamy skin, this time on her waist and abdomen. And visions of them both participating in another activity filled his sleep-deprived brain.

He bit back a curse. She had to be doing this on

purpose.

"It's the middle of the night, Abby. You're supposed to be sleeping. Or do you do this all the time—exercise in the middle of the night?"

She shrugged, grabbed the towel from the bed and mopped at the sweat around her face and neck. "If a problem bothers me I usually go for a run, but I didn't know the area here, so I thought this was a better solution."

He couldn't believe it. White-hot anger coursed through him and he advanced, until he stood less than a foot from her. "You go running in the middle of the night by yourself?"

She looked at him as if he were the crazy one.

"Well, no. If it's late at night, I usually go to the all-night fitness club near my apartment. There's an indoor track and a security guard." The towel in one hand, she thrust her fists onto her hips, her cheeks red and her eyes narrowed. "Despite what you think, I'm not stupid or irresponsible."

"I've never thought you were stupid or irresponsible, Abby. Just a little out of your element, sometimes."

"What is that supposed to mean?"

He folded his arms over his chest and gave her a once-over exam from head to toe. "Let's face it, Abby. Give you a set of numbers or data to analyze and you're a whiz. Out in the field? You're a disaster waiting to happen."

"How would you know? I haven't had enough field

experience for my superiors, let alone a fellow agent to know how I handle myself during a case."

"I've seen you in action today. You walked right into a crime scene without waiting for backup."

"Give it a rest, Luke." She looked briefly at the ceiling then fixed him with a determined stare. "I've already explained. The whole situation took me off-guard. I arrived at my friend's townhouse thinking I'd be spending a quiet night with an old friend. I didn't expect to find her place in shambles, blood on the floor, and no sign of Brianna."

"And what are you going to do if someone attacks you like they did your friend? Scare them with karate moves?"

"I'm not defenseless." She stepped back, dropped the towel on the bed and raised her arms in a defensive posture. She motioned him to attack.

If she didn't look so earnest, Luke would've laughed. "You can't be serious. The last time we tried this during training, you couldn't take down anyone in the class, Abby."

"What? You afraid I *can* do it this time?"

Luke shook his head. "I don't want to hurt you."

"This isn't a joke to me. Attack me, dammit."

He held up his hands. "I'm sure you've been practicing a lot. But this is the real world, not some karate gym. Even if you have been practicing, you could still get hurt."

She whirled, kicking at his head.

Instinctively, he grabbed her leg, then lifted her by the other one, turning and landing them both on the bed. She lay trapped beneath him, his hips wedged intimately between hers. Her arms stretched above her on the pillows and rumpled covers.

Anger replaced his humor. "That's what I'm talking about. If you seriously mean to use karate as self-defense, then don't go showing off."

She gulped, panting, her breasts rising and falling beneath the T-shirt now pulled tight across them. Her eyes widened and her lips parted.

He pressed his body closer, slowly lowering his head towards hers. God, he wanted to taste her again. It had been too long since the last time.

"Luke," she whispered when his mouth was but a fraction away.

"Yes, Abby?"

"Don't."

"Don't call you Abby? Or don't do this?" He closed the space between them, pressing his lips softly against hers. Lingering. Tasting. Warm honey. That flavor had lingered in his mind for the past five years. A man could die wanting more of it.

Cold metal pressed against his side.

He went still as a statue. Slowly he lifted his face, their lips parting.

"I...said...don't." Abby panted out each breath, pushing the gun into his ribs for emphasis. "Now, get... off me."

Luke eased his body away from hers and rolled onto his side. He flopped an arm over his eyes, inhaling deeply. Then he shoved his other arm over his head, hitting her laptop. "I'm sorry, Abby. I shouldn't have…"

"That's right. You shouldn't have." She released her grip on her weapon, lying beside him. "I told you. I can take care of myself. You seem to think I'm that same naïve kid right out of college you knew five years ago. Believe me, I left her on a sidewalk outside my hotel back in Georgia."

"Abby." He reached for her hand only to have her shove herself off the bed.

"Don't. Just don't say another word." She stood straight and walked past the bed with her head held high, back straight. At the bathroom door she stopped. "I neither need nor want your pity. But you're right. I probably can't do this by myself. What I need is your help to find Brianna or whoever hurt her. Help me do that and I'll go back to Washington and we'll never have to see each other again."

Before he could answer her she stepped into the bathroom and closed the door.

"Argh." Luke pressed the heels of his hands to his eyes until he saw stars. Dammit. What was it about this one woman that drove him crazy? He couldn't make the right move no matter what he did.

The sound of running water in the shower filtered through the bathroom door. Visions of Abby naked, standing beneath the jets, water running over her long, lithe frame, steam rising around her, flashed into Luke's mind.

With a groan, he rolled to his side and came face-to-face with Abby's laptop. She'd left it open to a file titled *Brianna's schedule*. Had Abby taken evidence from the crime scene? He glanced around the room. Nothing looked like her friend's datebook. He studied the computer screen again. Apparently Abby had reconstructed it from memory.

Interesting.

The water stopped.

His imagination working overtime thinking of every inch of skin Abby toweled dry behind the bathroom door, Luke tried to concentrate on the screen in front of him and not the rustling coming from the bathroom.

Get a grip, Edgars. There's a missing woman out there depending on you to find her, and all you can do is lust after Abby—naked, hot and willing for you. The memory of her pushing the gun into his side quickly cooled some of his ardor. For both their sakes he'd best remember she was armed and knew how to use her weapon.

He focused his attention on the open file. Abby definitely had her friend's daily activities listed for the past six months. From the pattern, the missing woman was a very busy lady. So, how had Abby reconstructed her friend's schedule? Who were the three sets of initials she had highlighted?

"I'll bet one of them has something to do with Brianna's disappearance," Abby said, coming out of the bathroom, rubbing her hair with a towel.

"What makes you think our man is one of these?"

She pulled back the cover on the other bed, climbed in and turned on her side to study him for a moment. "Because each one..." she yawned, then closed her eyes "...had a meeting with Brianna yesterday, before she called me."

"How did you get this copy of Brianna's datebook?" Luke studied the computerized itinerary and waited for an answer. None came. He glanced at the other bed. "Abby?"

Her eyes remained closed, her breathing easy and regular. She'd finally exercised herself into exhaustion. He closed her file and the laptop, setting it on the bedside table next to a pair of black-framed glasses. Had he ever known she wore glasses?

Before leaving, he turned off the light. Tomorrow he'd get an answer to his question about the datebook. Only he had a feeling he wouldn't like what he heard.

* * * * *

Even with her eyes swollen shut, Brianna knew the room was dark. If her captors thought to frighten the information out of her, they'd miscalculated. Darkness didn't scare her.

The familiar metallic taste of blood filled her mouth.

Ignoring the reflexive gag, she swallowed. Her parched throat needed something fluid down it, even if only her own blood. The last time she'd had anything to drink was when she'd gotten home from work today. Or was it yesterday? How long had it been? She couldn't remember.

Throughout her life she'd had her share of beatings—at least before she'd been adopted. This one ranked as the worst. She hadn't told them where the disk was, had she?

Her mind was fuzzy. How much blood had she lost?

She forced herself to take a deep breath. It hurt to breathe. That couldn't be good.

Voices murmured in the distance.

Were they in the room with her? No, there wasn't anyone in the room. She didn't know how she knew, she just did.

She strained to hear what they said.

"Did you get her cell phone?" a raspy voice asked.

"No, I left it on the table with the rest of the junk from her purse. It doesn't matter anyway. She's tied up," a deep voice answered. "Besides, she'll be dead soon. No one can survive that kind of beating. Especially not a broad."

A click sounded, followed by a pause in the conversation.

Brianna's heart jumped two extra beats, skipped one, then jumped two more. *Please don't let them come back.* She just couldn't take anymore.

Fresh-burning tobacco tickled her nose.

A man coughed. "Yeah, I guess you're right. By tomorrow she ain't gonna be a problem to no one," raspy voice said.

The words changed to a muffled murmur as they moved away. Finally, in the distance a door closed.

Brianna struggled to take several breaths. Their words rang in her ears. She'd be dead tomorrow. Did that mean they'd be back to actually kill her? Or were her injuries so bad she'd just slowly bleed to death here tied to a chair in the dark?

What a disgusting way to die. Helpless. Restrained. Broken. A sticky-gooey mess. Worse, she'd dragged Abby into this, and had no way to warn her.

Abby. Poor frightened-of-her-shadow Abby. The image of a gangly, rail-thin girl sitting on the bench outside Sister Compassionatta's office with her dark brown hair hanging down to her shoulders and almost covering her face flashed into Brianna's mind. They'd both been sent to see the principal of the orphan school that fateful afternoon. Abby for crying when one of the boys teased her, Brianna for talking to the boys too much.

"You know it's silly to cry when the boys tease you," she'd said in her snootiest voice. *"It only makes them tease you more."*

The frightened mouse turned her big green-and-gold-flecked eyes on Brianna. There was no malice in them, only an honest stare. "At least they aren't nice to my face and talk mean behind my back."

In that moment, Brianna found the one thing she'd never had in her life. Someone she could trust to always be honest with her. They served detention together that day and until the day Brianna was adopted, they were inseparable.

She shook her head to clear her thoughts. Everything seemed fuzzy. She wasn't sitting on the bench outside Compassionatta's office. Her ears rang again. She struggled to inhale. God, her chest hurt.

What had she been thinking about?

Oh, yeah, Abby. She needed to warn Abby.

How?

The cell phone. Didn't they say they left her cell on the table in the room? It might as well be ten miles away as just across the room. Tied to this chair, she had as much a chance of getting there as she did going to the moon.

She struggled to inhale once more. The trickle of blood rolled down her arms.

Abby needed to know…

Brianna shook her head again. Maybe if she tried, the ropes would give. She lifted her right shoulder. Her arm extended and her wrists pulled on the ropes binding them together behind her back. She slumped in the chair. The effort forced her to inhale and exhaled deeply.

She wiggled her wrists. Had the ropes loosened? All the blood was making the bindings slip a little.

How long would it take to get free? How much time did she have? It was impossible.

She closed her eyes.

"You can't conquer the world all at once, Brianna." Abby's voice filled her head in the darkness.

"Oh, and you have all the answers, Ms. Perfect?"

"No, it's like a giant cookie. You can't eat it in one big bite. You have to nibble it a piece at a time."

"What do you want me to do, gnaw at the ropes?"

"Try to loosen the ropes a centimeter at a time. You can do it. You can do anything you put your mind to."

"I don't think I can this time, Abby."

"Just try."

Brianna sucked in air. She leaned to the right and lifted her left shoulder this time. Her arm tightened and she tugged on the ropes again. Her wrist slid slightly past the rope.

"Okay, Abby. I'll call you."

CHAPTER 4

The ringtone erupted from Abby's cell phone. Jumping nearly out of her skin, she struggled out of the pile of hotel-issue blankets and sheets wrapped around her body to snatch the phone from the bedside table.

"Brianna?" she asked hopefully as she squinted through the mid-morning light to read the time on the bedside clock. Quarter to noon. How had she slept so long?

"No, Ms. Whitson," a slightly familiar, deep voice said on the other end. "This is Detective Jeffers. We spoke last night."

"Oh, yes. Detective Jeffers. What can I do for you?"

"I wanted to ask Agent Edgars a few more questions, ma'am. I've tried the number he gave me, but he isn't picking up. I'm sorry to bother you. Is there any chance you can contact him for me?"

Luke wasn't answering his phone? Had Brianna's captors found them? Images of his body lying in a pool of blood on the other side of the wall flashed through her mind.

Abby swung her legs out of the bed, and hurried over to the slightly ajar door joining her room with Luke's. Across the opening she saw the closed bathroom door and heard the shower water running.

Thank goodness. She leaned against the doorframe and heaved a sigh of relief.

"Ms. Whitson?"

"Uh, yes, Detective. I can get him a message. What did you need me to pass on?"

"I'd like to meet with you both today."

"At the police station?"

There was a pause on the other end of the line. "I believe Agent Edgars wanted to keep a low profile while you were in town. I'm thinking we should probably meet someplace away from the station. Maybe for lunch? Say in an hour?"

Abby glanced at the clock again, quickly calculating how long it would take her to throw on some clothes and be ready. "I would imagine we can meet you. Where did you have in mind?"

"A place called Flannery's Pub. It's about five miles from where your friend's condo is and they've got great fish and chips. Do you have a pen and paper?"

Abby spied a pen and pad of paper on Luke's beside desk. "Yes. Go ahead." She bent over the desk writing down both the address and directions from their hotel. She paused, swallowing before continuing. "Detective?"

"Yes?"

"Have you...has anyone...Brianna..." She swallowed again, blinking back the tears.

"No, Ms. Whitson. I'm sorry, there's been no word from her, but we are actively looking for her. Perhaps you or Agent Edgars will be able to help me search in the right direction after we talk."

Abigail mumbled an agreement and hit disconnect on her phone. Fighting hard not to cry, she stared out the window at the just budding trees of spring. She'd decided last night that tears wouldn't find Brianna.

"Who was that?"

Abigail tore her gaze away from the street to find Luke standing in the bathroom door with only the hotel's cheap white towel wrapped low around his hips.

All moisture in her mouth disappeared.

His wet blond hair was slicked back and last night's stubble still clung to his face. Her gaze wandered down his body, taking in the well-defined muscles of his shoulders and arms, the pale hair over his sculpted chest and down over his abdomen. He didn't have the overdeveloped six-pack body builders had, but what he did have heated her blood.

"Abby?"

Startled, she jerked her gaze north, only to see the corners of his mouth rise in a smile and a bit of a twinkle in his dark gaze. Damn, she didn't want him laughing at her. Not again.

Quickly, she turned back to the desk and lifted the

note. "Detective Jeffers has been trying to get in touch with you. He wants to meet us for lunch to talk about the case."

"Lunch?"

"Yes, he said you wanted to keep our presence out of the official reports. He wants to meet us at this address in about an hour."

Serious now, Luke strode over, his bare feet thudding softly on the carpeted floor, and took the note from her. "I know this place. It's down near the baseball park. My brothers and I usually stop in for dinner when we come to town to watch the Indians play. Damn good fish and chips, not to mention the beer."

His body heat warmed her skin as he stood next to her. The scent of the masculine hotel soap tickled her senses, setting her nerves on high alert.

What was she doing? Hadn't she learned her lesson, that any desires she had for him weren't reciprocated?

Get a grip, Abigail.

She'd wanted more from this man once before and it had ended with her humiliation. The last thing she needed to do was get distracted by his nearness. This time Brianna's life depended on her focused attention.

Ignoring the heat rushing to her face, she fled the room before he could comment on her awkwardness. "I'll be ready in a few minutes."

After washing her face and brushing her hair into a serviceable bun at the back of her head, she put on the navy-blue suit she'd hung in the closet last night and hoped it wouldn't look too wrinkled. She smoothed her hands down the skirt as she stepped out of the bathroom.

"You're not wearing that, are you?"

Jumping at the sound of Luke's voice, she turned to find him leaning against the doorframe between their rooms. Thank God he'd dressed. Although the hip-hugging jeans and red Henley shirt stretched over his muscular chest was almost as sexy as his near-nakedness in only a towel.

She was pathetic.

"Yes, it's this or my pajamas," she said, a bit more peevish than she meant.

"That's all you packed for a visit with Brittany?"

"*Brianna.* If you must know, she left me the message when I was on an out-of-town audit. I never went home to get more than my work clothes. So, yes, this is all I have to wear."

He looked at his watch. "Okay, we should have time to stop and grab something before we meet with Jeffers."

"I don't see why, this is a perfectly acceptable suit for a meeting with the detective." She grabbed her laptop bag and slid the strap over her shoulder.

"Yes, it would be if we were auditing the man in his office. We're meeting him in a pub outside a sports facility." He opened the room door for her.

She inhaled as she passed by him—a little tremor of heat ran through her again, and she swallowed the sigh that threatened to pop out at the masculine scent of spice and hotel soap.

Pathetic.

* * * * *

Luke pulled into the parking lot of a strip mall down the road from their hotel. The chain store should have just what they needed.

"We really don't have time to be shopping," Abby complained even as she climbed out of the passenger side. "We should be worrying about what's happened to Brianna, not what I look like."

"Until we have a clue as to what happened to your friend we need to not attract attention. Right now you scream Federal Agent," he said as they headed into the store.

He held the door for her again, hiding the smile that threatened. Every time she got too close she blushed. If getting her cooperation in hiding her identity from anyone who might be searching for her wasn't so serious, he'd love to tease some of the starch out of her.

"Everyone in the bar will be relaxed and casual. We want to blend in, not stick out as an easy target."

"You're a little paranoid, don't you think?" She turned her back to him and marched toward the women's section of the store.

Not when it comes to keeping you safe.

Growling under his breath, he counted to ten before

stalking after her. In the first aisle of clothes, she stood considering a pair of dark, stiff jeans that said *brand-new-just-went-shopping*. She really had no clue how to fit into her environment, or relax for that matter.

"Not those." Before she could stop him, he snatched them out of her hand and hung them back on the rack.

"Hey! I thought you wanted me to get jeans," she said, getting that stubborn-Abby look in her eyes and her chin rising.

"Yes, but we want these to look like you've worn them for years, not that you bought them today to look like a tourist." Grasping her elbow, he led her farther down the aisle to the pre-washed jeans. "This is more what I was thinking." Releasing her arm, he pulled out several pairs—one with some well-placed, frayed rips—checked the sizes and thrust them into her arms.

"You don't know what size I wear."

He sized her up from head to toe and gave her a grin. "Trust me. After last night I have a very good idea of just what size you are, sweetheart. Check the tags and see."

She did, muttering a curse under her breath about arrogant asses.

Could he help enjoying the way she narrowed her eyes at him?

Without waiting, he moved around the aisles until he came to the sports fan section. "I don't see you as a basketball fan, so baseball or football?" When she started to answer, he held up his hand. "Wait, I know.

Baseball."

"Why baseball? Don't you think I can understand football or like looking at all the muscle-bound men in tight pants like other women?" Her lips had pinched tight and the urge to kiss them loose hit him.

"No. I'm more than sure you'd love all that violence and sweat, but baseball is a thinking-person's game. Given your love of numbers, the game's stats alone would probably give you an orgasm." With a grin he held up a baseball jersey proudly proclaiming love of the Cleveland Indians.

"Screw you, Edgars," she muttered as she grabbed the shirt and stomped away toward the changing room.

"Take off the tags and save them. You're wearing these out of the store."

Over her shoulder she flipped him the eternal symbol of brotherly love and kept walking.

This time he laughed at her disgruntlement. In the past five years he'd forgotten what fun it was to aggravate Abby. The more she fussed about it, the stronger his urge to tease her.

Picking out a few more nondescript items—one black sweater, a black skirt, a dark grey hoodie pullover and some sneakers—he refrained from getting her underwear. As much as he wanted to, she'd draw the line in accepting him buying her those items. He handed them to the petite little brunette attendant, asking her to deliver those to his girlfriend, then wandered over to the men's section. Abby wasn't the only one who wasn't prepared for a long stay in Cleveland.

As he chose a few items for himself, his mind kept focusing on Abby. Why was he so damn attracted to the only woman who had more prickly sides than a cactus? Had been since the first day at the Federal Law Enforcement Training Center down in Glenco when she'd rolled her eyes at him. She saw right through his charm-boy act, which both thrilled and scared the crap out of him. The youngest of three brothers and only older than their sister by a year, he'd always been able to sweet-talk his way out of any situation. Not even his family saw the real him as well as Abby did.

His clothes selections made, he moved away from the changing room and stood in a corner, watching everyone milling about in the store. No one seemed to be paying him any unwarranted attention or looking for Abby. Perhaps their presence on the case was still unknown to the people responsible for her friend's disappearance.

Then he remembered his dream and a cold chill ran through him.

He hadn't had it since he'd been with Abby on that disastrous night of FLETC graduation—not until last night. If he could just ship her back to Washington, maybe the dream would go away. But she was right. Her friend had called for her help. Either Abby subconsciously knew something or had the ability with that magnificent brain of hers to find her friend and unravel this mystery. Which meant until they found her friend or solved the problem, Abby was in danger and his to protect.

Thank God with all her wallflower tendencies, she flew under the radar of most men. He didn't need *that* complication.

"What do you think? Will I do now?"

He turned at her voice and stared.

Oh hell! Things just got very complicated.

His wonderfully geeky Abby had transformed into a supermodel.

Starting at her feet, where her red-tipped toes peeked out of a pair of open-toed sandals, he let his gaze travel north. Her trim ankles showed just below the hem of the jeans that hugged every inch of her long, slender legs—legs that seemed to go on forever—and accented the curves of her thighs and hips. The baggy jersey should've hidden her curves, but the way the team's name clung to the tops of her perky breasts made his mouth go dry. As much as the bun she'd had her hair in said, *I'm all business*, the ponytail she now wore announced, *I'm young and fun*.

This was not good. Not at all.

"What's wrong? Did I forget something?"

Yes. You forgot to be Abby.

He swallowed his irritation. "No. You look fine."

She stepped back into the changing room to retrieve her old clothes and the other items he'd sent in to her, including a pair of running shoes the sales girl must've gotten her, too. "This is going to cost a bit more than I meant to spend."

"Don't worry about it. We'll put it on my credit card and the government can pay for it." He grabbed her elbow to steer her toward the front of the store. We just need to get moving."

"I can walk by myself," she said, jerking her arm from his grasp. "Besides, if we're late, it's your fault, not mine. You insisted we go shopping."

Following her to the checkout, he cursed his own suggestion. The whole idea had been not to draw attention to them. Now every man in the pub would have to be blind or stupid not to notice Abby. If anything happened to her now, as she'd just said, it was his own damn fault.

* * * * *

Luke parked around the corner from Flannery's Pub. They locked her laptop and their other purchases in the trunk. He insisted Abigail put her hand through his crooked elbow so they'd look like a couple as they walked up the street. She'd never admit it to him, but she was thankful he was there to steady her as they walked. Unused to even the small heels of the sandals she'd bought at the store, she'd wobble more if it weren't for the support of his strong arm.

The pub sat on the corner of the street in the lower part of a refurbished building that looked like it dated from the turn of the previous century. They strolled past the outdoor patio with umbrella-topped tables and flowerboxes full of spring flowers. It was still a little too chilly for diners outside yet, but Abigail imagined what a lovely spot it would be in summer for lunch al fresco.

"After you," Luke said with a wink as he held the wood-and-lead-glass door for her.

She gave him a slanted look of irritation then stepped into the warmth of an Irish pub, complete with Celtic designs etched into the glass panels throughout the space. Rich, dark wood covered the bar, the paneling and all the booths. Numerous televisions mounted around the area marked it a sports enthusiasts' haven. Luke was right, her new attire helped her relax and blend in with the lunch crowd, many of whom looked like they were going to the baseball game later in the day.

Detective Jeffers sat in a corner of the pub, a heaping plate of fish and chips and a glass of something dark in front of him. As they approached his table, he scooted out of the booth, focusing his attention on her. Even she would be hard-pressed to miss the sudden male appreciation in his face.

"Ms. Whitson," he said, shaking her hand.

Abigail liked his firm handshake. Sister Rose Thomas always said, *You can tell a lot about a person from their handshake.* Jeffers' grip said *I'm someone strong and trustworthy.*

Abigail smiled at him before sliding into the booth.

"Edgars," the detective said as he shook Luke's hand too. "Glad you two could join me."

"Jeffers." Luke slid in beside her, muttering under his breath.

She swore he said something about damn supermodels. When she peeked at him, his mouth was set in a firm line and he stared down at the beer menu. Ever since she walked out of the changing room, he'd been as grumpy as a bear with a burr up his butt.

Too bad. He'd wanted her in this outfit and he'd just have to get over whatever was bothering him. Putting Luke's surliness out of her mind, she leaned a little closer to the policeman. "Is there any news about—"

Luke grabbed her hand, startling her. He stared into her eyes, giving his head a little shake.

The waitress, dressed in a green T-shirt promoting the pub and jeans stepped up to their table. "Can I take your order?" she asked, smiling sweetly at Luke.

Flashing the girl his best smile as if nothing in the world was bothering him seconds before, he pointed to the beer section of the menu. "I'll take a Black and Tan and we'll have two orders of fish and chips."

Abigail swallowed her own sudden irritation. "I'll just have water, please," she said when the waitress quit grinning at Luke. "And make that one order of fish and chips, I'd like the Reuben instead."

"Don't know what you're missing." Luke winked at the waitress who actually blushed before turning away.

Did the man know how to do anything but flirt with women?

Once the waitress brought their drinks and were alone again, Detective Jeffers cleared his throat, drawing their attention back to him. "To answer your unspoken question, Ms. Whitson, no we haven't gotten any closer to finding your friend."

"If you have nothing new, then why did you want to meet with us?" Abigail asked, her irritation with Luke spilling over to the policeman.

"Simple, sweetheart," Luke said, sliding his arm onto the back of the booth, once more giving the illusion that they were a couple. "Jeffers wanted to make sure we hadn't left town."

Jeffers shrugged. "I was hoping that after a night's rest you could give me some more information."

"I told you everything I knew last night. I have nothing to hide." Which wasn't the truth. While she'd answered his questions honestly, she'd kept her suspicions from him. Luke knowing them was problem enough.

"I understand you've been friends with Miss Mathews for quite some time."

"Yes, since childhood." She took a drink of water and filled him in on meeting Brianna at the orphanage and the years of their friendship.

"You've remained close? Even after college?"

"We went in different directions after school, but doesn't everyone? She went into the corporate world and I found work with the government." She gave a little shrug, not liking the twinge of guilt that nibbled at her brain. Even though they'd talked several times a month by phone or internet, she and Brianna had drifted apart more the last year or so. She should've kept in closer contact, known more about what was going on in her friend's life.

Their waitress returned, saving her momentarily from further questions. While they dug into their food, Luke and Jeffers chatted amiably about baseball and the Indians' chances this year against the rest of their division. Despite how good her sandwich tasted, Abigail picked at her food, idly listening to the two men.

What was it about men and sports? A woman is missing and they can focus on the earned run averages of starting pitching as if there were no crisis going on. Of course they didn't know Brianna, hadn't held her hand after they'd both had their tonsils removed, hadn't stayed up and listened to her heartache when her first college boyfriend dumped her.

Burning started behind her eyes and in her nose. Abigail set her Rueben back on the plate then clutched her linen napkin in her lap with both hands, biting her upper lip and staring out the window, willing the tears to stop. She was a professional. She shouldn't be crying in public.

"Hey, come here, sweetheart," Luke said as he draped his arm around her shoulders and pulled her into the side of his body.

It was an act for the detective, keeping him thinking they were a couple, but she couldn't help how good being held and comforted against Luke's strong warm body made her feel. Even with her eyes closed tight, tears slipped out to slide down her cheeks, but after a few minutes, she'd managed to get her control back. With a little sigh, she dabbed at her eyes with the napkin and blinked back the remnants of her tears.

"I'm sorry about that detective," she said with an embarrassed lift of the corner of her mouth.

"Quite understandable." He wiped his mouth, set the napkin on the table and pulled a notebook out of his pocket, indicating he was finished with his meal and the question period had started. "So exactly what branch of the government are you working for?"

"The Treasury."

A lift of his brow was the only indication he was surprised by the news. He looked at Luke. "You, too?"

Luke gave a quick nod.

"And Ms. Mathews? What function did she have at..." Jeffers looked at his notes. "...Hollister-Klein Exporters?"

"Brianna was..." Abigail paused and swallowed the lump in her throat. "She *is* the assistant to the Chief Financial Officer for the company."

"A secretary then?"

Luke snorted beside her. She cast him a narrow-eyed look, then smiled at Jeffers. "No, sir. Brianna was the

A/P manager."

"A/P manager?" he asked making a note in his small notebook.

"Accounts Payable. She reported directly to the CFO. Despite what you see in her pictures, she was probably smarter than most of the men in her department, if not all of them."

Jeffers had the grace to look embarrassed. "Did she ever talk about anyone she had a problem with at work?"

"Not that she ever mentioned to me."

"Any particular boyfriend or lover?"

The question and his tone suggested he believed Brianna was a loose woman. Abigail wanted to defend her friend, but given the number of pictures of Brianna with so many different men Jeffers had obviously seen in the condo the night before, Abigail didn't argue the point. "We hadn't talked in a few weeks, but she hasn't mentioned anyone special in her life."

"Did she ever use any on-line dating services?"

The question caught her so off-guard she choked on the sip of water she'd taken. "Excuse me?"

"The last page she had open on her computer screen last night was to an on-line dating service. Do you know if she was a member or if she'd been a member of other sites like it?"

Her mind quickly retrieved the first page Brianna had left open. She hadn't been logged in as herself. *Guest.* That's what had been on the login bar and what she'd been browsing under.

"No. As far as I know she's never used any online dating sites. Besides, Detective, you've seen how stunning Brianna is. She wouldn't need to advertise for a date. She got them by simply walking into a room."

"I didn't think so, but it I wanted to be sure it wasn't connected to another case."

"You've had more women disappear like this?" Luke asked, the edge in his voice surprising Abigail.

Jeffers finished off his drink before answering. "No, just covering any possibilities."

"I can assure you, Brianna wasn't part of an online dating service. At least she hasn't ever mentioned one to me." Could her friend have been part of this? If so, why would Brianna have been so insistent that she come see her this weekend?

"And you just came to town for a visit?" Jeffers asked as if reading her thoughts.

"That's right," Luke answered before she could, his hand lightly rubbing her shoulder. "Like I said last night, when the lady wants to visit an old friend on a whim, we hop on a plane and come visit."

"Right." Jeffers locked gazes with Luke and for a moment Abigail was reminded of two gunslingers in an old-time western movie—the first one to blink lost.

The hair on her neck lifted and a chill ran through her, not from the tension between the two men, but something else in the pub. She slowly looked around the room. The lunch crowd had thinned out. A family of four sat at a table near the window. Two different couples sat in cozy booths, talking intimately.

No one was near the bathrooms, but the wait staff filtered in and out of the doors to the kitchen. She let her gaze slowly slide over the few men seated at the bar, then studied them a little closer through their reflections in the mirror behind it.

There. The younger man with the baseball cap and hoodie, his body turned away from them, seated closest to their table—near enough to keep an eye on them, but not close enough to hear their conversation, his fingers flying on the phone in his hands. Caucasian by her best guess, although he might have some Hispanic features, she couldn't quite tell. Possibly mid-twenties to mid-thirties. Something about him was familiar, but at this angle she couldn't get a good view.

"If you'll excuse me, please." She gave an apologetic smile to Detective Jeffers and a light elbow nudge to Luke. "I need to go to the ladies' room."

As she scooted out of the booth, Luke gave her a worried look and whispered, "Everything okay?"

His warm breath against her ear startled her as much as the concern in his voice. "Yes. I'll be right back."

Focused entirely on getting to the bathroom, she kept her gaze straight ahead, even though the urge to stare at the man seated at the bar ate at her. She was sure she'd seen him somewhere before. As she turned to enter the women's room, she took one hard look at his face in the mirror, then went through the door.

Inside the stall, she sat and closed her eyes, letting her mind pull out images and work backward over the past two days. He hadn't been on the street outside the pub, nor at the shopping center. She scanned the images from the hotel and the parking lot this morning. No. Not there.

She switched further back to their arrival at the hotel. No one had been in the lobby except the guest registration boy and the man mopping the far end of the lobby. Both had been African-American, the housekeeping man much older than the man at the bar.

Further back she went to the walk from Brianna's condo to Luke's BMW. She pulled out the mental pictures of the crowd that gawked from the opposite side of the street. Two elderly couples huddled together. An extremely tall man and woman, with an equally small dog. Several young teens.

There. Just off to the side. Same hoodie, same hat, same muscular build. Adjusting her mind's camera lens, she zoomed in on his features. Dark brows, dark eyes, straight nose, mustache and goatee. Even the same pock marks from uncontrolled acne.

It was the same man. He'd been outside Brianna's condo watching the police. Had he been looking for Brianna? Had he been observing to see who'd come to find the condo in such a mess and Brianna gone? Had he followed them to the hotel, then here?

Taking a slow breath, she willed her heart rate to slow to a normal pace. She was a professional agent.

She'd been trained to handle situations like this and right now she had the advantage. The man at the bar didn't know she'd identified him. First thing, she needed to warn Luke.

Gathering herself together, she exited the stall and washed her hands, then splashed a little water on her face. Once she dried everything, she took another steadying breath and studied the near stranger in the mirror.

Slow, deep breath. You can do this. Calm, casual. Blend in. Concentrate on getting to the table. Do not acknowledge the suspect.

She opened the door and let her gaze focus on her own table—on Luke. As if he knew she needed his strength, he looked up, his gaze locking on hers. Pasting on a smile, she concentrated on his face and headed straight for him.

"Everything okay?" he asked when he stood.

She leaned in and gave him a quick kiss, murmuring against his lips, "Of course, darling."

The hand he'd laid on her hip tightened slightly and she knew he'd gotten the message from her endearment that something was entirely wrong. Then he stepped aside to let her slide back into the booth, his eyes promising they'd talk as soon as they were alone.

Detective Jeffers looked at the time on his watch before reaching for his check and sliding in cash to pay it. "I'm afraid I'll have to cut this short, but if you think of anything your friend might've said that will help us, please don't hesitate to contact me, Ms. Whitson."

"Of course. And you'll let me know if you find..." She swallowed hard and blinked back the sudden burn of tears that threatened. "If you find anything."

"Edgars," he said, shaking hands with Luke again before sliding out of the booth.

Slipping his arm around behind her shoulders, Luke drew her into his warm side once more as they watched the detective leave the bar area and head for the men's room. Once they were alone, Luke leaned in and whispered in her ear, "What's got you spooked?"

She tried not to jump at the shiver of awareness that shot through her as first his breath then his lips caressed her ear. He was in character, a lover indulging in a public display of affection. She needed to remember that and keep up her part in their cover. Turning her head so her lips were mere millimeters from his, she murmured, "The guy at the bar in the hoodie."

"Ohio State cap? His body turned slightly away from us?" Luke kept his gaze locked on hers, the warmth of his eyes drawing her closer. He never even glanced at the bar.

"Yes. I saw him before."

Luke lifted his hand and smoothed a stray lock of hair behind her ear. "Where?"

"Outside Brianna's townhouse last night. In the crowd across the street."

"Have you seen him anywhere else we've been today?" he asked without questioning if she was sure and how she knew she'd seen the man before.

"No. I only saw him the one time before now."

Luke leaned in and kissed her ear, tugging slightly on her earlobe, sending more shivers of heat through her. Then he whispered, "Can you get out your phone and get a picture of him, but make it look like you're taking pictures of the bar for some reason?"

She pulled away slightly and turned her head to look at him, her gaze going immediately to his lips that were just a few inches from hers. Quickly she lifted her gaze to his eyes, which had deepened even more to a darker jade. "Um, I don't need a camera to remember what he looks like."

"I've figured that out, sweetheart," he said with a grin, his words surprising her. *How had he known*? "But," he continued, "I do need the pic to run background on him on my laptop."

"Oh. You can do that?"

He leaned in closer, he lips brushing hers once more. "You'd be surprised what I can do. I have mad skills."

Swallowing hard at his implied sexual prowess, she blinked and turned to fish her phone from her purse. He moved slightly away, giving her a little space and she took a steadying breath.

"Why do you want pictures, sweetheart?" she asked just loud enough to be heard by the people near the bar as she started clicking pics at the entrance, away from their suspect and working closer, one picture at a time as if she were taking random shots.

"This place could give my brother some ideas for his pub in Cincinnati when he opens it. Don't forget to get some photos of the bar and pool room." Luke pointed around, giving her an excuse to get a picture of the hoodie guy.

After a few more views of the pool room, she focused her attention on Luke, who had slipped cash into the check sleeve to pay for their meal. "What a great idea. Your brother is going to love these pictures."

A moment later Jeffers walked out of the men's room and headed for the pub's front exit. Almost immediately, hoodie guy slid off his barstool and followed the cop out of the pub. She'd been right. He was following someone, just not them.

She lifted her phone and snapped another picture of hoodie guy as he walked past, hoping to get a better angle for Luke to use.

"Come on," Luke said, sliding out of the booth and grabbing her hand, nearly pulling her out with him. Cursing whatever insanity had caused her to buy the heels instead of just sneakers, she stumbled along beside him as he hurried out the bar to follow their suspect.

"Dammit," Luke said as the man climbed into a nondescript brown sedan and pulled out into traffic just behind Jeffers car. "I don't suppose you caught his license plate number?"

She closed her eyes and pictured the car. Nothing that identified its make or model. Standard Ohio plates.

"Only part of it. ESC but he pulled out too fast for me to catch the others."

He heaved a sigh as he watched both cars turn the corner. "Okay, let's head back to the hotel and I'll run his photo. But I think our detective has a tail."

"Isn't it a good thing hoodie guy isn't following us?"

"For the moment, but I've got a bad feeling your friend stumbled into something nasty."

She looked at him like he was the class dunce. "I figured that out from all the blood last night."

CHAPTER 5

If the situation wasn't so serious Luke would've laughed at Abby's quick response outside the bar earlier. He smiled to himself as he retrieved his laptop from his room's safe. Abby never cut him any slack, that was for sure.

Going through the connecting door into her room he nearly tripped over the cute shoes she'd worn earlier. He tensed, swallowing the growl that threatened. If he'd hadn't insisted she be less of her practical self, she would've been in tennis shoes—a safer choice for both of them—and they might've moved quickly enough for her to get the entire license plate number.

Stooping to pick the sandals up, he tossed them into the closet on top of the new sneakers she'd also bought and her more sensible accountant's shoes. "Why did you get two pairs of shoes?"

"Because they had two pair in my size." She answered without looking up from her work

"Do you always buy all the shoes in your size?"

She gave a shrug. "My feet fit my height. It's rare to find one pair in the store that are size ten, let alone cute sandals, too."

Her explanation sounded like she was talking to the town idiot and didn't ease his frustration. "Don't wear those again while we're here."

"Why not?" She asked from the far bed where she sat cross-legged, working on her own computer, one brow raised in question—both at his comment and the edge of anger he couldn't quite keep out of his voice.

Because seeing you in them and your painted toes peeking out at me is way too distracting.

"Because they're dangerous. You could need to move fast and being agile might be a matter of survival for you. Wear the sneakers next time." Forcing himself to relax, he kicked off his own shoes and sat on the edge of the bed bedside her. "Scoot over."

"You can sit on the other bed or at the desk." Her brows drew down in that stubborn way that made him want to grab her and either shake the expression away or kiss her. Either action would probably get him a gun muzzle in the side again.

"I could, but then I can't see what you're working on and you can't see the faces of the men on my screen."

"Oh, that makes sense," she said, the stubborn look gone so fast he almost laughed.

That was the practical Abby he knew.

She scooted over, rearranging her computer and the pillows behind her to make space for him. With his back against the headboard he stretched out his legs, one thigh pressed against hers. Not since his senior year in high school had he been so self-conscious sitting on a bed with a woman.

"I already sent hoodie guy's photo to your phone," she said, clicking away on her keyboard, reminding him they were there to work.

"Is that what we're calling him?"

"Until you can come up with his real identity." Stopping her typing, she picked up her phone and glanced at the face of it, then set it aside again.

He pulled out his phone and forwarded the image to his laptop. "Are you still working on filling in your copy of your friend's day planner?"

All movement beside him ceased at his question.

He turned to see what the problem was. She sat with her fingers frozen on the keyboard, her eyes wide as she stared at him and she'd pulled her lower lip between her teeth in a worried fashion.

How could that one little act make her look vulnerable and sexy all at the same time? It roused the need to claim her and protect her simultaneously. Problem was, who was going to protect her from him?

"What?" he asked, focusing on her worried green eyes, instead of that mouth he'd happily sampled throughout lunch.

"How did you know?"

"How did I know you've got a photographic memory?" He tapped her computer screen. "I saw that last night. You might be a novice in the field, but you wouldn't do anything to jeopardize the police finding your friend, so I knew you hadn't secreted her datebook out of the condo. That much detail on your computer, meant you had a good memory."

She continued to worry her lower lip with her teeth. He needed her to stop doing that. Pronto.

"Does it bother you that I know about your ability, Abby?"

Like clockwork the nickname drew her up straighter, more focused. "No, of course not. I just don't go around advertising it, so was surprised you'd figured it out."

"Putting two and two together is a requirement for working in the Treasury Department, sweetheart."

"You don't need to keep doing that," she said, breaking eye contact and focusing on her laptop once more.

"Doing what?"

"Using endearments. No one is here. No need to fake any intimate relationship between us."

There wasn't anything fake in the heat and sizzle simmering between them. No matter how hard she tried to avoid it. No matter how much he needed to ignore it.

"It will keep me in practice, *sweetheart*," he said just to watch her lips purse. "And as I was saying, not only am I good at addition, but I know someone who not only has a photographic memory, he has a phonographic one, too."

"Who?"

"My nephew, Nicky. Before my sister and her husband adopted him, the kid was used as a walking, talking numbers black book for Russian mobsters down in Columbus."

"Good God, how did that happen to him?"

"Like you he was orphaned after his grandmother brought him here from Russia. He was a kid hanging out for scraps in a restaurant and somehow the mob bosses figured out his ability and exploited it."

"But your sister and brother-in-law adopted him?"

"Yeah, after Jake kidnapped my sister and forced her to help stitch up Nicky, then they were on the run from the police and feds and mobsters, and from there things just got worse."

"You're making that up." She'd narrowed her eyes at him once more.

He tensed, looked deep into her eyes, lowering his voice, all traces of humor gone. "I might bullshit about a lot of things, bend rules to get a case solved, but I never, ever make things up about family. Sometimes that's all you have to cover your back. To me, family is sacred."

For a moment, she held his gaze, then her eyes grew watery and she closed them. "That's how I feel about Brianna. She's family."

Damn. He hadn't meant to make her cry.

"We'll find her, Abby." Settling his hand over hers, he squeezed it and leaned in to whisper in her ear. "Nicky's story made the local papers a few years ago.

Look it up."

With a nod, he released her hands and watched her swipe the tears from her eyes.

While she did exactly as he suggested and looked up the news feed on the case, because God forbid Abby should take his word at face value, he connected his phone to the laptop. Then he opened up the facial recognition program and uploaded hoodie guy's photo to it. "This is going to take a while. What were the license plate letters again? Might as well see if we can get a lead on the car while we're at it."

"ESC," she said, not looking up from the article on the screen about his sister's family. "Your sister and Nicky almost drowned?"

"It was the only way to save Nicky from the man trying to kill him. But my sister is a lot tougher than she looks and smart to boot." He pulled up the state license plate database. "Well, crap."

"What's wrong?"

"I was hoping we had enough to at least narrow our search to this area, but Cuyahoga county, which is where we are, and Franklin, where Columbus, the state capitol is, both have license plates that start with ESC."

"Crap."

Well, at least they agreed on something.

Abby closed out the article she'd been reading, then lifted her phone and looked at the screen a moment before setting it aside again.

"Expecting a call?"

"I know it's silly, but I was hoping Brianna would just call."

"Wasn't her cell phone at the condo last night?"

She closed her eyes and he imagined she was seeing the crime scene again.

"No. Unless it was buried under something, I don't see it anywhere in the mess." She paused, her eyes still closed. "Her purse isn't anywhere either."

Abby opened her eyes, now filled with a glimmer of hope.

Damn he wanted to bolster that look, but he had no words. Then another thought hit him and a cold chill swept over him.

"You haven't tried to call her have you?"

She gave him that "duh" look again. "Not since I arrived at the airport last night. I didn't think of it once you came into the condo and everything seemed to happen in a blur." She held the phone in her hand, staring down at the screen. "I didn't want to tip her assailants off if she had it with her. You know…in case she tried to call me."

Thank God. Practical, analytical Abby hadn't zeroed the target hanging over her any closer.

Exhaling in relief, he pulled out his phone and dialed Jeffers number.

"Got a question for you," he said in lieu of a greeting when the detective picked up his phone.

"Okay, maybe I'll have an answer."

"Did the crime scene techs find Brianna's cell phone

or her purse?"

"No. Neither, and my people are thorough. They even went through her car." Papers shuffled in the background. "We have a warrant pending to pull her phone records, then we can try to find her on the GPS."

"How long will it take you to get a warrant for the phone records?" Locking gazes with Abby again, Luke laid his free hand over hers, stilling it on the phone. With a shake of his head he mouthed the word *wait* to keep her from pushing the call button.

"If we're lucky and find a sympathetic judge who hasn't taken off for the weekend yet, a few more hours." Jeffers paused. "But then, as her *friends*, you don't need a warrant to call her. If you want to come in, we could use our system to track the phone call from here."

Yeah, Jeffers hadn't become a detective because he lived in the shallow end of the smarts gene pool.

Luke waited for the man to put more pieces to the puzzle together.

"And you don't need my program, because you have your own."

Bingo.

"If I come up with anything, we'll let you know."

"You do that. Even super feds need backup."

Luke grinned at the sarcasm in that comment. "Speaking of backs. Watch yours."

"Oh?" A sharpness filled Jeffers voice.

"Yeah. Apparently you've got a tail. Drives a dark

sedan, plate number starts with ESC."

"Numbers?"

"Couldn't quite get those. But guy wears a grey hoodie, probably like half the OSU fans in town."

"Caucasian," Abby added, leaning close to the phone.

"'Preciate the info," Jeffers said.

They disconnected and Luke released his hold on Abby's hand, waiting for the barrage of questions while he opened another program on his laptop, typing in his password to open the encrypted site.

One.

Two.

Three.

"I thought you weren't going to tell Jeffers about his tail? And why didn't you offer to send the picture of hoodie guy?"

Turning, he stared straight into those deep green eyes. "I told him because he's a good cop and needs to know to watch his back. I didn't offer to share the picture because we don't want him bringing in the guy before we discover who he is or we might not get a crack at figuring out what his connection to your friend's disappearance might be. Your friend's life might depend on that."

This made her pause and focus on their priority, finding her friend.

"You're not going to wait on a warrant to run Brianna's phone records are you?"

"Nope."

"And you don't want me to try calling her because someone could trace the call back to us?"

God, he loved how her brain worked.

"Right. But we can still try to use the phone to trace her whereabouts."

"How?"

"What kind of phone did Bethany have?"

"Brianna. She would spend thousands of dollars maintaining her looks, but high-tech upgrades? She didn't see the need in it. She had a very old cell phone."

"Damn. It would be better if she had the newest smartphone. They all have GPS installed in them." He brought up the screen. "What's her phone number?"

Abby read it off to him. "What if it's turned off? We won't be able to track it then, will we?"

"Not a problem. We can still track it as long as no one removed the battery."

* * * * *

Detective Aaron Jeffers sat staring at his cell phone and contemplating the conversation he'd just had with Agent Edgars. He didn't buy the guy's story about *just visiting his girlfriend's friend* for one second. Years of listening to criminals and people with something to hide lie to him left him with a nose to smell out a line of horseshit when he heard it, even if it was with a firm handshake and politician-slick smile.

Oh, there was something between Edgars and Ms. Whitson, he'd give the guy that. Hell, Edgars had practically marked his territory like a wolf protecting his mate. Who could blame him? When she'd walked into the pub today he'd had to do a double-take to be sure it was the same woman from last night. Who knew such a beautiful and sexy woman was hidden under all that baggy blue polyester?

A dating couple though? His instinct told him they hadn't crossed that boundary yet, but he wasn't convinced they were long-term working partners, either. Sparks seemed to fly off them when they were within ten feet of each other. Edgars was going to be a lucky man if the pair ever crossed that line.

Heaving a sigh, Aaron ran his hand over the slight stubble of his jaw.

Edgars had the capability to work on this case outside the usual channels and without the restraints that tied his hands. And didn't that just bite his ass?

With any luck, the cocky agent would get some information about the missing woman's associates or her whereabouts, or at least her phone's location, then keep him informed. No use in both of them working that angle, at least not yet.

Aaron glanced at his wall clock. Two hours until his appointment to meet with Ryan Baxter, Brianna Mathews' boss at Hollister-Klein Exporters. Maybe the company's CFO could fill him in on what the missing woman was working on for the company.

With another heavy sigh, he wiped his hand over his face.

Two hours to kill.

Since his hands were tied on this case until the warrant came through, forensics came up with something useful or Edgars called him back, he could focus on his other case. Not that he was any closer to making a crack in it, either.

Turning to his computer, he pulled up the last file he'd had open before catching the Brianna Matthews' abduction.

Five women missing over a period of three years. The case his captain had told him to drop because there was no real evidence. Only, his gut told him there was something.

At first he thought Brianna Matthews might be the sixth. Now he wasn't so sure. Pulling out a piece of paper, he made two columns, *match* and *not a match* then he began comparing the facts from both cases.

All between the ages of eighteen and thirty. Check in the match column. He read over the interviews they'd done with associates, co-workers and acquaintances of the other women.

None with family ties to the area. Flipping through the pages, he confirmed what Ms. Whitson had told him. Brianna had no blood relations in the area and her adoptive parents had both passed away in the past five years. Check.

Low-level jobs. Brianna apparently was a high-level

employee in Hollister-Klein. He marked an X in the not-a-match column.

The other five were all shy, retiring, stay-at-home types. He pulled out an 8x10 glossy he'd taken from the myriad of photos at the crime scene last night for the case file. Brianna Matthews was a blue-eyed, blonde bombshell. Nothing shy or retiring about this girl. A stay-at-home night wasn't her thing. Another X.

The other women had all used some sort of on-line dating service. Another glance at Brianna. Nope. Pretty damn sure she didn't need one. Which begged the question, why did she have a dating site open on her computer? And why were there only pictures of women on that site? Could she have been shopping for something different? Looking to play for the other team? This hottie and another woman?

Damn, that wasn't an image he needed to linger on. Not if he wanted to get any real work done today.

He lifted another of the crime scene photos to study again.

Then there was the violence of the Mathews disappearance. The in-your-face, blitzkrieg-type attack. These guys were looking for something. The chaos of the condo confirmed it. Five would get you ten that whoever had Brianna wouldn't be finished with her until she gave up the location of what they wanted.

That was nothing like the rather quiet, almost invisible disappearances of the other women. In fact, most of the leads in those cases were so cold they belonged in the Arctic Circle. Hell, no one even knew they were gone for weeks after their abduction. No one had reported anything. If his niece Stephanie hadn't called him about the fifth girl—he pulled up the picture of the mousy-blonde-haired Casey Timmons—a friend of hers from work, they probably still wouldn't have known there was a case.

Too many differences to think the situations were linked.

Six missing women. Two sets of perps. Great.

Another look through the crime scene files from last night and all the blood throughout the condo. He shook his head.

Probably at least one homicide.

* * * * *

Just a little bit farther.

Brianna slid her uninjured arm along the gritty concrete floor, then shoved with her knees to push her body forward. The metal table with her bag and its contents was only a foot away.

How long had she been at this? The fluorescent lights had been on the entire time she'd been here, disorienting her sense of time. The metal window coverings prevented her from seeing outside. Was it day or night?

It seemed it had taken forever to get free from the ropes binding her to the chair. Pretty much sure she'd dislocated her left shoulder to finally slip loose.

A little pain in exchange for your life? Is there a choice?

Who knew Abby's voice in her head could be so sarcastic. She chuckled at her own joke, then grimaced at the searing agony that ripped through her.

Damn. She didn't like pain.

Had a lover once who wanted to experiment with BDSM. She was willing to play the submissive until he decided spanking and flogging would be fun. Put the kibosh on that idea and him immediately.

This is not a game. Get a move on it or you're going to die here.

"Yes, Abby, your nagginess," she whispered and pulled her body another inch across the floor.

How had she ended up in this mess?

Curiosity, pure and simple. Sister Compassionatta had warned her more than once back in the orphanage, *a lady always minds her own business. Remember curiosity killed the cat.*

Guess what Sister C? For once you were right. Except it wasn't a cat who was going to die.

And what had she been so curious about? Like most women, where her newest man was spending his time when he wasn't with her. How stupid. Never once had she been jealous or suspicious over a man before.

A brittle laugh escaped her.

No, she'd never had those feelings over a man, because she'd never cared about them. They'd all been a means to an end for her. A way to build her ego when they fawned over her. Or get them to buy her things she wanted—cars, homes, jewelry. Some even helped her move up the corporate ladder.

Until *him*.

He'd been different. While that other lover had let her play at being a submissive, he tapped into that part of her that needed to be controlled. Instead of being at her beck and call like so many men previously had. He expected her to wait for him. To be available when he said he needed her and to stay away when he gave her that order.

Because of his position, he instigated a move for her up the corporate ladder, believing her to be an airhead that simply followed orders. The kind of woman used as a trophy girl for the company to show they met equal opportunity hiring requirements. Once again they'd underestimated her. The promotion gave her access to all kinds of corporate information and she'd taken advantage of it, starting with the audit. She'd wanted proof that he had another lover.

Ha. If only it had been that simple.

Yes. You might not be bleeding out all over this concrete floor. Get your butt in gear and move before someone comes back.

Sigh. Abby, ever the practical one, even in her own head.

Putting aside the internal dialogue, she focused on making her way to the table as if it were a life preserver floating on the dangerous sea threatening to drown her. One inch after another, she worked like a caterpillar—stretch out arm, use knees to push her ass up in the air, then slump forward.

Finally her hand connected with the metal leg.

With one more push she pulled herself forward and slumped around it. Eyes closed, the only thing still moving was her lungs as she dragged in one breath after another.

She'd made it.

Never in her life had she worked so hard for something. From the time she'd learned that opening her blue eyes wide and smiling with all her dimples any man within a two foot radius would give her whatever she wanted, she'd always taken the easy way around things. Even the sisters at the orphanage couldn't resist her. No one challenged her or expected more of her—except Abigail.

Shy, naïve, prickly Abby. From the moment they'd sat next to each other on the wooden punishment bench outside Sister Rose Thomas' office, Abigail had seen right through her sweet cute-little-girl act straight to the heart of the scared girl trying to hide her fear from the world.

They'd discovered they both loved math and puzzles. When her math grades started improving, she hid the fact that she was so good at it from the boys, by saying Abigail had tutored her all night. Abby would just roll her eyes, shake her head. But Abby had always been there for her. Always. No questions asked.

And now she'd put her dearest friend in jeopardy.

Her heartache added to the pain coursing through almost every part of her body. Maybe she should just give in, let *him* win.

You can't. Remember there are innocent people counting on you. I'm counting on you to help me find you.

"Leave me alone, Abby. I left you the clue."

Focus, Brie! Get to the phone. Help me help you.

"I can't."

Yes, you can. You've almost got it. Get up on your hand and knees. Do it. Now.

God, she hated it when Abby got that Sister Compassionatta tone in her voice. But she did as she was told. Turning, she used her uninjured hand to pull herself up onto her knees. Grasping the edge of the table, she leaned her head onto the cold metal surface, letting her eyes focus on the contents of her purse that were strewn about.

What was it she was looking for?

Your phone, Brie. Get the phone.

Oh yeah. She had to call Abby. Sweet Abby.

With all the effort she had left in her body, she stretched her arm along the table, her fingers not quite touching the new smartphone she'd gotten last year.

Almost. There.

She stretched until her shoulder ached, fingers sliding over the smooth surface then pulling it slightly closer.

"I can't." She struggled to breathe past the pain.

Yes you can. Now. You have to do it now.

A door opened somewhere. Voices in the hall.

Stretching one more time, she pulled her phone closer. Finally able to grasp it in her hand she slumped, hitting the floor hard.

"Dammit!" A familiar deep voice bellowed from behind her. *He* was here.

"How the hell did she get loose?"

"Because you didn't secure her, idiot."

He bent over, smoothing back the hair sticking to her sore, swollen face. The scent of the spicy tobacco on his breath so familiar, now nauseating. His piercing blue eyes focused on her, his face distorted with anger. Had she really thought him handsome? Had she believed she'd actually loved someone this evil?

"Well, Miss Nosy. What was so important that you'd crawl across a dirty floor to get? Hmm?"

She clenched her fingers tighter around the phone.

"Let. Me. Have. It," he said as he pried each finger loose.

Peeking up at him through the tears flooding her eyes, she let out a whimper of a cry. It was all she could manage in her defeat.

"Your phone. With the battery still in it." *He* stood and snatched one of her torturers by the throat. "Asshole, I told you to remove the battery."

The man choked a reply.

He released the man. "No. Not off. Battery gone. Those were my instructions. The GPS is still active. Anyone looking for the bitch could trace her through it."

Then *he* turned her phone over and removed the battery.

CHAPTER 6

The cursor on Luke's computer screen cycled as if it were thinking. Actually, Abigail hoped it was searching, searching for Brianna's cell phone.

"This isn't instantaneous, sweetheart," he said beside her and once more she was surprised by the tenderness in his voice. "First it has to find her cell phone signal and it has to be within the radius of a cell tower. Then the satellites have to triangulate its location."

"I know. It uses the closest cell towers to map her signal for longitude, latitude and altitude. We learned that back at FLETC."

"And you memorized every bit of the training manual, didn't you?" he asked with a small lift of the corners of his full lips. Lips she'd kissed last night and once before during their training. She remembered how warm and wonderful they'd felt.

Stop it. Luke Edgars wasn't interested in her. Hadn't he made that perfectly clear outside that bar in Georgia? She'd be a fool to think there could ever be anything more between them. His presence here was due to her request for a field agent to help her determine any fraud Brianna found at Hollister-Klein, not because he was interested in her in anyway.

"Did you hear me?"

Shaking off her inner dialogue she pulled her reading glasses off and focused on the expectant look on his face, heat flushing her cheeks to be caught inattentive. "I'm sorry, what did you say?"

His smile widened and with it her cheeks grew warmer. "I asked, how does your photographic memory work? Nicky says his is like a movie that plays in his head."

"Mine is more like still photography."

"Have you always had it?"

The last thing she wanted to do was revisit her childhood, but as her partner for this case, he had the right to know about her skills. "No. It seemed to be triggered right after my mother was murdered."

"Oh, damn, Abby, I had no idea." His tender expression and the warmth of his hand as it settled over hers once more opened up that particular drawer of memories, the images and words just spilling out. That first horrible image forever in her mind.

"When I first came to the orphanage to live. The policeman who found me told Sister Rose Thomas, the mother superior of the orphanage, that I hadn't said a word. It took a while for me to feel comfortable enough to talk to anyone, but she was very patient. One day she asked me if I remembered my mother and poof just like a crime scene photo I saw her sprawled across the bed, the covers lumped and wrinkled around her body, her skirt up around her waist, panties hanging off one leg, the pool of blood soaking into the white chenille spread, her cold, lifeless eyes staring right at the door of the closet where she told me to hide."

Suddenly she was hauled off the bed and onto Luke's lap, his arms wrapping around her and hugging her close, pressing her face right up against his heart.

"Oh, sweet Jesus, I didn't know. I had no idea. I wouldn't have asked."

He kept murmuring those words in her ear, his big hands sliding up and down her back. Slowly warmth replaced the freezing cold she always felt when she revisited that image. Closing her eyes, she listened to the steady beat of his heart in her ear, letting her mind put the photo of her mother's dead body back in the filing cabinet.

"When I described that picture to Sister Rose Thomas, she realized what a horrible thing I'd seen and that my mind had captured every detail. She called the policeman who'd brought me to the orphanage to come and talk with me."

"Dammit, she shouldn't have made you relive that again." Luke's hold on her tightened.

Warmed by his anger on her behalf, she smoothed her hand over his solid chest, imitating his soothing actions on her back.

"It was a good thing, actually." She wanted him to understand that she'd learned to think of her memory as a gift.

He leaned back and stared down into her eyes, his hazel eyes burning with anger and his jaw muscles flexing with tension. "How can you say that?"

"Because when the policeman came back, he didn't ask me about my mother. He asked me if I'd seen the man who murdered her."

"That's worse. Making you focus on the act of her murder."

"It's not like your nephew's memory, Luke." Wanting to make him understand, she pushed away from the feel of his body and the delicious scent that comforted her. She focused on his eyes. "Mine are still shots. No noise. So when the policeman asked me if I'd seen the man's face, my mind simply pulled up the image I'd glimpsed through the door when he first came into the bedroom."

"Please don't tell me he knew you were there, that you watched…" He swallowed as if he couldn't even finish the thought.

She shook her head. "No. Of course not. Mama had lots of male visitors. That's what I thought of them. I learned later that she had a bad coke habit and supplemented her income for it working as a prostitute. She usually let me stay in my room while the men were there, but sometimes she would hide me in her closet, warning me to be very quiet, and kept the men in the living room. Even in her drugged-warped mind, there were some of her customers she knew I needed to be protected from. That particular night she warned me not to make a sound, no matter what. Later there were loud noises and I peeked through the crack in the closet door."

Once again her mind pulled a snapshot out of a drawer.

"He was angry and followed her into the room. Tall, big-bodied with shaggy black hair. He had a scar on his face and a tattoo on his arm. I remember that the most, because I'd never seen one before. I described it as a black star with a circle of blue around it. Later I learned it was a pentagram for a gang that ran that part of town."

"Did you see anything else after that?" Luke sounded in more pain than she was feeling.

"No. He was mean looking and I didn't want him to find me in Mama's closet, so I curled into the corner with my teddy bear and blanket. That's where the police found me."

"How long were you in there?"

"They said just overnight. Our neighbor usually watched me for Mama when she was working at the café down the street. When we weren't at her door the next morning, she came looking and found Mama. She's the one who insisted the police search the apartment for me. I didn't really see much until the policeman carried me past Mama's body."

"And that triggered your photographic memory."

She nodded. "The man's image that I described to the police helped them find my mother's murderer. The courts set up counseling sessions for a while with a very nice lady. She helped me understand that channeling the events into snapshots helped me distance myself from the trauma of not only that night, but how I lived the early years of my life."

"And now? Do you still use it to distance yourself from events?"

Before she could answer that question, his laptop pinged beside them. Realizing she was still seated on Luke's lap, she quickly slid to the side as he reached for the computer.

"Is that Brianna's cell phone?"

"The program's picked up her signal." He typed some codes into the computer.

"That's a good thing, right?"

He stopped what he was doing to focus that intense gaze on her once more. "It means her battery is still connected to the phone. It doesn't tell us if the phone is with her or if she's okay."

"I understand that. It's just..." Unable to finish, she swallowed hard to tamp down her fears.

"She's family. Believe me, I get that. We'll just take this in baby steps, okay?" he said, reaching out to squeeze her hand.

"Okay. I can do that."

"Good." Releasing her hand, he went back to typing

away on the laptop.

Watching him so focused on the computer screen, she realized he wasn't just an arrogant flirt like she'd always believed. Except for the waitress today and the news reporter last night, he'd wielded very little of his usual annoying frat-boy charm.

Seeing the purpose-driven agent who'd shown her both understanding and tenderness just now disturbed her far more. This man was dangerous.

This Luke, she could like.

Suddenly, she needed to put some distance between them. Trying not to look like a deer bolting from a mountain lion poised to strike, she eased off the bed. She retrieved her sneakers from the closet and sat on the other bed as she slipped them on.

"Where are you going?" he asked without a pause in this fingers flying over the keys.

"Just down the hall for some ice to go with the pop we got at the store. I feel the need to walk around."

"Okay. Leave the safety latch in the door, and take your gun."

"You're not serious. No one knows we're here. It's perfectly safe in the hallway."

That got him to stop what he was working on and focus on her once more. "Sweetheart, until we find out who took your friend and why, I'm very serious about keeping you safe. Take the gun or stay put."

"Yes, sir," she said with a mock salute and a suppressed urge to roll her eyes. Following his instructions, she took her weapon out of the bedside drawer and slipped it into the back of her jeans then grabbed the ice bucket from the little wet bar in the room.

Leaving the latch in the door to keep it open for her return, she headed for the ice machine, pretty sure the most dangerous thing for her in this hotel was seated squarely back there in her bed.

* * * * *

Once the door hit the latch blocking it from closing behind Abby, Luke paused his fingers on the keyboard and slowly exhaled, trying to rein in the need to follow after her. Over the pounding of his pulse in his ears he strained to hear anything unusual in the hallway.

Nothing but the sound of her shoes on the carpet.

This was ridiculous. Why the hell was he so worried? They were five doors from the ice machine.

Because this was Abby.

Any other agent would've known not to leave the room without their weapon, but this wasn't any usual agent but Abby, who'd never been in the field. For all her training, she was still a novice and it was his job to keep her safe.

Didn't have a thing to do with how her lips or skin had tasted today when he'd been playing the part of her lover in front of Jeffers and his stalker. Damn right. He was the senior agent on a dangerous op. It was his job to think of his junior agent's safety at all time.

And all senior agents cradled their subordinates in their laps, pressed in tight to their bodies.

Fuck. And if that didn't have him all hard and straining against his pants? The last thing he needed to do was act on the desire to bury himself deep inside Abby, no matter how happy that would make him. She wasn't his usual love 'em and leave 'em kind of girl. She was the kind of woman who gave her heart only once and he damn well didn't intend to be the one to break it. Wasn't that why he'd rejected her all those years ago?

Ca-chunk, ca-chunk.

Well, she'd made it to the ice machine safe and sound.

He had about two minutes to get his hormones under control before she sashayed back into the room, still looking like the damn supermodel. With a sideways glance his gaze landed on where she'd laid her black-framed glasses.

And wasn't that a fun surprise?

Abby's brain had always challenged him and he found it very sexy. Add that to her long sensual body and most men would be done in. But who knew seeing her with those glasses on her nose, her brows crunched as she concentrated on her work, would invoke a fantasy he hadn't even known he had—Abby dressed in heels and only those glasses.

He groaned at the renewed thickness in his cock.

"What's wrong?" Abby asked as she hurried in the door, remembering to pull the latch so it locked behind her. "Did you discover something?"

Yes, that I have a thing for long, thin brunettes who are smart as hell and look sexy in glasses.

"That this program is taking a while," he said, all the while thankful that his laptop sat squarely on his lap to hide what really had him groaning. "Two satellites are in line and have picked up her phone's signal."

"That's a good thing, right?"

She set the ice bucket back on the wet bar and made herself a pop. He watched as she took a drink, the muscles of her neck working as she swallowed, then her tongue slipped out to swipe across her lips. Closing his eyes he fought the urge to moan.

"Luke?"

The concern in her voice cleared his thoughts. She wanted to know about her friend, not his perverted thoughts.

"Yes, two pings says the battery is still in the unit. What we need now is just one more to get in alignment so we can triangulate her exact location. It's just taking time to get them in place. Would be easier if I had her password. You wouldn't have any clue what it might be, would you?"

Shaking her head, she sat on the other bed. "Sorry. Brianna was just as smart about codes as she was numbers. Whatever she chose would be random words, numbers and capitalization. Drove me crazy reminding me to mix it up and change them periodically. You could say she was almost paranoid about it." She paused, nibbling on her lower lip again. "I guess with good reason, huh?"

"She definitely stumbled into something dangerous. Would she have access to any information that a competitor to Hollister-Klein might want to get a hold of?"

"I don't think so. She worked simply in the financial area of the company. Nothing with manufacturing. She mostly handled shipping or receiving data. Why?"

"Unless someone was trying a hostile takeover, I doubt they'd go to the extremes these people have just to get Brenda's codes."

"Brianna. And I can see your point. Then what could they want from her?"

"I'd say it was whatever prompted her call to you, just like we've thought all along."

With a sigh, she shook her head, stared out the window, blinking hard. "You're right. I should've gotten her tell me more, pinned her down for more information, instead of just hopping on a plane."

"Hey, don't go there" he said, trying to stop her from wallowing in guilt before it started. "This is *not* your fault in any way, Abby. She asked you to come help and like a good friend you did just that."

"I know, but—" Before she could answer his laptop pinged. She set her drink on the bedside table and leaned over his shoulder to peer at the screen. "Is that her? Did it find her?"

"It's her cell phone, Abby. Remember that. It may or may not be with her." Ignoring the warmth of her body pressed against his back and shoulder he focused on what the computer was telling him. Fingers flying over the keyboard, he typed in a request for the exact coordinates of the signal.

"Just about got it," he said, zeroing in.

Then the signal disappeared.

"Dammit!" Luke gripped the laptop, wanting to shake it.

"What happened? Where did it go?"

"I don't know. The signal just stopped." He entered codes to try and pull up the signal once more. Nothing.

"Could it be the satellites moved?"

He pulled air slowly into his lungs, calming the frustration itching at his nerves, then typed in more code to check the locations of the military satellites once more. "They're all in alignment. None of them moved. Something happened to the signal from her end."

"No. Do something. Get it back."

"I can't make something appear that is no longer there. More than likely whoever has her found the cell phone and is smart enough to remove the battery."

"You don't know that." She strode the space between the beds, turning and pointing a finger at him like he was a child. "*You* don't know that. Call DC. Get someone who's a tech on it. Someone who knows computers and satellites better than you."

There is no one better than me.

"There's no one better than you? Oh so now you're a computer expert, as well as super spy?" she snapped.

Dammit, he hadn't meant to say that out loud.

Her sharp criticism stung. He vaulted from the bed, to stand mere inches from her, pushing her finger out of the way.

"No, Abby. I'm a super spy, *because* of my computer skills." She narrowed her eyes at him, but before she could strike again with her sarcasm probably about his IQ level, he held up his hand to stop her. "Even Einstein can't make something appear that no longer exists."

"We have to go there. Now. We have to help her." She turned on her heel in a rush.

He resisted the urge to grab her arm and force her to listen to him as he watched her grab her phone, her purse and then the gun from the bedside drawer almost in desperation. The reality of his words hadn't set in, but she really wasn't going to like what he said next.

"We can't."

Something in the way he stated the fact paused her frantic movements about two feet away, focusing her gaze on him. "What do you mean we can't? You have the coordinates. We may not know where the phone is now, but we know where it was."

"I mean *we* can't go now in the daylight. I need to get you somewhere safe, then I'll go check it out."

"She could be dead by then."

Reining in his own temper, he held her gaze, willing her to understand. Slowly her anger eased, her eyes softened and tears filled them as she realized he was right and there was no miracle answer. She lowered her eyes, breaking the bond between them and ripping something inside his chest.

The connection broken, she walked past him to where his computer lay.

"She was right there," Abby stroked her hand over the laptop as if she could will the signal to return, a tremble in her voice. And with it all his anger vanished.

God, he hated seeing her pain. Only Abby could have such loyalty to someone who thought nothing of putting her in danger. Abby deserved so much better than this.

Without hesitation, he pulled her up against his chest and once more wrapped his arms around her. Holding her tight he couldn't miss the fine tremors that shook her body, pulling at the open place inside him. "Shh, sweetheart. We'll find her."

"How?" Almost eye-to-eye with him, she only had to pull back to look at him and the despair he saw in her eyes sliced him deeper.

"Somehow, I promise," he murmured a moment before lowering his lips to hers.

He'd meant to just comfort her, to reassure her, to give her some of his strength to get through this. What he hadn't counted on was the fire that ripped through his blood when she parted her lips to let him invade.

The heat of her breath, the sweet taste of her on his tongue, drove him on, making him want more. More of sweet Abby.

She slid her tongue over his, matching him thrust for thrust, making him growl with desire. He clenched his hands in her shirt, wanting to pull her into him, to give in to the need to claim her.

Then she pulled away, her hands pushing at his chest.

"Please don't," she whispered, her breath caressing his lips, which were suddenly starving for her.

"Don't what?" He held her, not yet ready to lose the feel of her in his arms, pressed against him. "Don't kiss you? Or don't hold you?"

"Don't make promises you can't keep. Don't kiss me because you feel sorry for me," she said, pushing against him again. Her words startled him into letting her go. "I'm a trained professional. I can handle this."

Watching her retreat to the other side of the room to wrap her arms around her torso and stare at the floor as she sank into herself, twisted that open spot inside his chest.

She thought he was kissing her out of pity? Couldn't she see how wrong she was?

Stalking across the room, he stood inches from her, her bent head just below his chin. "Abby."

She shook her head, her gaze locked on the floor.

"Dammit." Cupping his hands around her face, he lifted her head. "Look at me."

When she did, he read both pain and a shadow of the place she'd retreated to inside.

"You're right. You are a trained professional. Your skills and that fascinating brain of yours will help us find your friend. And you're right, you can handle this case. But you're wrong about the kiss."

When she opened her mouth to protest. He hushed her with his thumbs on her lips.

"I fought the battle to hold you and love you five years ago because we both had too much to learn, too much growing to do." Her eyes widened at his confession. "So I'm not going to let you hide from this thing between us. If you thought I kissed you out some sort of pity, you couldn't be more wrong."

Once again he lowered his mouth over hers, no hint of compassion in his. It was a conquering. Holding her head firmly in place, he plundered her soft, open mouth with all the pent up fear and desire he'd held in check since the moment he'd seen her standing in the middle of that bloodbath in her friend's condo. He tasted her sweetness and heat, stroking her tongue with his in short and long thrusts, coaxing her to follow his lead, finally eliciting a tortured moan from her.

The sound soothed the raging need to claim her, to force her to admit what he knew. Pity was the last thing he felt for her.

Slowly he eased back, willing his heart—and his now throbbing cock—to realize retreat and patience would win the battle more than brute force. Sliding his lips off hers, he leaned his forehead against hers a moment, breathing deep. "I'll let you go for now, Abigail. But this thing between us? It's not over. Not by a long shot."

He released her, grabbed his laptop and phone then headed to the other room.

CHAPTER 7

"You're still following the police and not the people he met with?"

Snake hated when the boss got all I'm-smarter-than-you over the phone at him. He wasn't some lame rookie. "Don't sweat it, man. We've got eyes on them. Knew I couldn't follow both, so Tracker picked them up outside the bar."

He knew his man wouldn't get caught tailing the pair, the guy'd been tracking since he was a kid out hunting with his old man in the boondocks. Knew a thing or two about being invisible.

The answer seemed to satisfy the bossman, since his attitude in his voice changed. "Did you get a picture of them?"

"Couldn't from the spot at the bar. Not without letting them know I was interested, you know what I mean. Ain't no way you'd miss them though, she was one hot female."

There was a pause on the other end as the bossman

considered that piece of info.

"Tell Tracker to get me a picture anyway," he finally said. "And let me know if they get on the move. The bitch still hasn't told us what she did with the package and we have product to move."

The phone went dead in his ear.

"Asshole."

The guy demanded respect, but didn't have a clue how to return it. Snake shook his head. Someday he'd be at the top and his crew would look up to him without commanding it. He hit the button to call Tracker.

"Where you hanging, Tracker?"

"West side. Burger place 'cross the street from their hotel."

"The pair still inside?"

"Beemer's still where he parked it. No one's come near it."

"Let me know if they do and the bossman wants a pic of them, if the opportunity presents itself. Once the cop settles in his crib for the night, I'll spell you."

"S'all good. Got some eats. Place to hang. Like hunting."

That was Tracker. Simply the facts. Convo not necessary. "Word. Let me know if your prey goes on the move."

"Roger that."

This time Snake ended the call. Just in time, too. The cop exited the station on his way to his car again. Snake pulled out to follow several cars behind him.

"Wonder where you're off to?"

* * * * *

Aaron Jeffers glanced in the rearview mirror as he turned onto Superior Avenue, heading to Hollister-Klein. The brown Cutlass three cars back made the turn, had been making them since he left the precinct. Edgars was right. He had a tail.

Question was—which case was he being tailed for? His guess it was the missing Mathews woman. He glanced at the picture of the beautiful blonde on top of the notebook he'd set on the passenger seat. What had she stumbled into? And who wanted her silenced? Hopefully her boss at Hollister-Klein would have some answers or a clue to help him narrow his search.

As he turned into the parking lot of the company's corporate headquarters he watched the car tailing him drive past the lot entrance and head on down the road. Once it passed he read the last three numbers of the plate—996. He parked then pulled out his phone, dialing the Department of Motor Vehicles. "Hey, Mary Jo, it's Aaron Jeffers."

"Well, hey Detective Jeffers," the lanky blonde answered in her Southern drawl that always made him think of hot sheets and sticky summer nights. "What can I do for y'all?"

How he'd love to answer that honestly, but her husband was six-foot-four, built like an offensive lineman and ran a construction company. Rumor had it he loved three things—beer, brawling and Mary Jo, and not in that order.

"Can you run a plate for me?"

"Sure thing, sweetheart. What is it?"

"Easy Sam Charlie 996."

"Take me a few minutes."

"Just text it to me when you can. I've got a meeting."

"Sure thing."

Disconnecting the call, he pocketed his phone. Mary Jo's search would probably lead to the plates of a stolen vehicle or plates stolen *from* a vehicle. He'd also bet money that when he came back out, the Cutlass would be parked on the other side of the street.

Grabbing the notebook, he slipped the photo inside and headed in to meet with the Hollister-Klein Chief Financial Officer, Ryan Baxter and Brianna Mathews' boss.

Walking into the glass-and-steel high-rise left him with the same crawling-skin feeling he experienced every time he had to meet someone at a high-end lawyer's office. Same marble floors, same dark-oak wood, same uncomfortable modernistic furniture in the lobby and same pretentious artwork on the walls. After he was shown into the Baxter's office, he wasn't disappointed when the arrogant ass waved him to a seat while he finished a phone call.

"Just get back to me as soon as you get those reports

done," the man snapped into the phone, then set it aside. "Sorry about that Detective…"

"Jeffers."

"Detective Jeffers, we're a little shorthanded today and have quarterly earnings reports to get out." Baxter leaned back in his chair and stared out over the mahogany desk at Aaron. "You said you wanted to talk with me about Brianna Mathews? I'm not sure what information I can give you. I have no idea what happened to her. All I know is what was reported on the news last night."

If the man wasn't telling the truth, he was a very good liar. Luckily, he had a knack of always finding the truth, even against liars who were experts. Aaron plastered on his I-mean-you-no-harm look and opened the notebook on his lap. "I'm really here just to get some background on Ms. Mathews."

"I'll be glad to help in any way I can, but I do have a late evening meeting in about fifteen minutes."

Too busy to talk about a missing, possibly injured, employee. The man dropped another few notches in his esteem. "Then let's get to it. How long did Ms. Mathews work for Hollister-Klein?"

"She started in the clerical division about six years ago."

"So she was a secretary?"

Baxter leaned in and opened a file on his desk, reading from Brianna's employment history. Either the man was telling the truth and didn't know the victim well, or he wanted to make sure he distanced himself well in front of the police. "An entry-level accounting clerk, I believe. She was well organized and had some ability with numbers, so she was promoted steadily over the last few years."

"And what was her latest responsibility?" He asked this even though he'd gotten the information from Abigail earlier in the day. No need to let anyone know he knew more than they might want to divulge. What people chose to leave out was almost as telling as what they thought was important to include in an interview.

"Recently, she took over payments and accounts receivable."

Jeffers made a note of that. "Exactly what does that position entail?"

"She was the head of that department with several accountants beneath her. They handled incoming payments from our clients, keeping track of what had been billed and what was still outstanding."

"Who did she report to?"

A flash of something, surprise or wariness, flashed in the older man's eyes. "All department heads in accounting report directly to me."

So he knew her better than he'd wanted to admit.

"Was she good at her job?"

"Her skills were highly appreciated."

Aaron glanced at the photo inside the notebook once more and wondered if Baxter was talking about her math skills or more personal ones. "Did she have any enemies?"

"Enemies?"

"Anyone who might want to harm her? Disgruntled employees in her department? Anyone she might've beaten out for her position who thought she didn't deserve it?"

Baxter shook his head. "Oh, no. Everyone loved Brianna. I doubt you'll find whoever did this at Hollister-Klein."

The man was quick to defend his company, almost as if trying to divert any attention from them. Interesting. Okay, Baxter wanted to go another route, he'd happily oblige him. "Hollister-Klein is an import/export company?"

The CFO sank back into his chair, happily relaxing at a question about information that anyone could easily obtain by visiting their corporate website. "Yes, we deal with exporting products from all over the country internationally, as well as bringing in products our consumers want to buy here."

"You also do some shipping of equipment and hardware for the military." It was a statement. He wanted the man to know he'd done more than cursory research on the company.

"Yes," Baxter swallowed and leaned in over his folded hands on the desktop—his jaw locking firm and his lips flattening out in a thin line. The friendly period of cooperation was over and he meant business. "But that information is classified. As I'm sure you're well aware."

"I understand. But because of that contract aren't all your employees required to pass a security clearance to work here?"

"Those that will come into contact with classified information, yes," Baxter finally said.

"And was Ms. Mathews one of those employees?"

The muscle in the other man's jaw jumped. Now he was uncomfortable. Aaron lifted the corner of his mouth while he waited for an answer.

"When she became the head of the accounts division she had to pass a clearance check, yes."

"And having done that would she have access to any sensitive government information?"

"If it had to do with payments and outstanding accounts, she could."

"I see." Jeffers made a note in his book, but mostly giving Baxter a chance to squirm. Didn't take long.

"Now, I'm not sure what you're getting at, Detective, but Brianna...er, Ms. Mathews wouldn't have been interested in or accessed anything other than the files she'd need to carry out the duties her job required. I can assure you that we follow protocols set to protect all our dealings with any highly classified information."

"I'm sure Hollister-Klein does," Aaron said, mostly to get the other man to relax again. He made a note in his book to delve into the company's government contracts, possibly with Edgars, whom he suspected knew more about the company than he had admitted. "Tell me what kind of a woman, Ms. Mathews is?"

"She's sweet. Friendly. Everyone loved her."

"Women as well as men?"

Baxter's eyes widened, caught off guard by the question. "Yes, as far as I know. Why do you ask?"

"There were a number of pictures in her condo of Ms. Mathews with different men, but none with women. Do you know if she had any close female friends?"

"Never heard her mention anyone, but I'm sure she did. Don't all women?"

"I suppose."

Baxter seemed to consider the idea, then said, "But come to think of it, I've never heard her talk about any girlfriends."

Another interesting piece of the puzzle. Either Ms. Whitson was lying about being friends, which he highly doubted, or Ms. Mathews had kept her a secret.

Baxter made a point of looking at his watch, a clue that he wanted the interview over. Luckily for him, Aaron had gotten quite a bit of information and was willing to let him off the hook—for now.

"Thank you for your time, Mr. Baxter." He closed his notebook, stood and shook hands with the businessman, whose palms were now a little damp.

* * * * *

The damn woman was driving him crazy.

Luke dropped the laptop on one of the beds in his room and stalked to the window. His own hunger for her wasn't helping the matter any. *Focus.* That's what he needed to do. Focus on the situation and keeping her safe. The tail might be following Jeffers, but it brought home the need to find a more secure place for Abby. If they were in his hometown of Columbus, he'd have several possibilities. Here in Cleveland he had few options.

Luckily, he had one source who might be able to help him.

Leaning against the window frame to watch the parking lot and street below, he hit the dial button and listened to the ringing.

"This better be good, kid," was all the gruff voice on the other end of the line said in lieu of a greeting.

"Nice to talk to you, too, Castello." Luke didn't try to hide his momentary amusement. Only a few years younger than his older brother Dave, the U.S. Marshal had been adopted into the Edgars family after he helped save the life of Katie, his other brother Matt's wife. Frank Castello was always grumpy as a bear coming out of hibernation and Luke had no end of enjoyment needling him, but today he had more important things to discuss. Sobering, he watched traffic on the street a moment. He didn't like to admit this. "I need your help."

"Tell me what you need and where you are. I can be

there as soon as I wrap up what I'm doing."

That was Castello. No questions about why he needed help. His loyalty to the Edgars family was unconditional.

"I need a safe house."

"You can use the one in German Village. You remember it, don't you?"

He remembered it. They'd hidden Katie there from the hitman stalking her until they could make plans to trap him. Of course things had taken a few left turns in their plans, but the safe house there was still a secret. Only problem was, it was in Columbus.

"I remember. But it won't work."

"Why?"

"I need one in Cleveland."

There was a pause on the other end of the phone as Castello took in and processed this information. A moment later Luke heard typing in the background.

"It's out of my district, but I've got a few options up there to keep my witnesses off the grid down here. What kind of amenities are you looking for?"

Damn, Frank sounded like a freaking travel agent. "Two bedrooms if you have it."

"Uptown or downtown?"

"Someplace we won't stick out too much. I'm trying to keep Abby way under the radar."

"Abby?"

Crap. He didn't need Castello getting curious. "A fellow agent."

"Okay, no flophouse for you two then." More typing ensued.

Luke walked over to the connecting door and peeked in at Abby. She sat in the middle of the far bed, glasses perched on her nose once more as she typed away on her laptop, looking as if nothing had happened between them. Maybe she was right to pretend they hadn't just shared a kiss that rocked both their worlds. He suspected they'd just scratched the surface of this thing and he was going to need all his attention focused on keeping them safe before it was over.

"Did you get it?" Castello was saying in his ear.

"Get what?"

"The address to the condo I just texted you."

He looked at his phone. "Yep. Got it."

"What's going on up there, Luke?"

"Just a case."

"Cut the crap. You and I both know you don't go to a safe house without good reason. Is that reason Abby?"

Shit. Castello was as sharp as his brothers and brother-in-law, and even worse, he was like a freaking bloodhound when he scented something—nose to the ground until he unearthed what he was searching for. If he thought Abby was a problem, he'd be doing a background check on her. Neither she nor he needed someone higher up looking into what they were doing before he figured out just where this all led.

"Does this have anything to do with that quiet investigation you've been doing for Dave?"

His brother had asked him to look deep into State Senator Howard Klein's background after the man's son had nearly been killed by the same gunman who'd taken Dave's wife hostage in the hospital OR where she worked. The last thing he wanted was his oldest brother barging in to take charge. Dave wasn't always patient, and until he knew exactly what he was dealing with, he needed to proceed with more discretion. *And there Frank went connecting dots*. He was going to have tell him something.

"Not sure yet. There may be a connection, but we're a long way from knowing what."

"I'm assuming you don't want the family to know anything right now."

"We've got a missing woman, so yes, until I know for sure what I'm dealing with, yeah, I'd appreciate some QT on this."

"Okay. Just texted you the entrance codes for the condo's garage and back door. Keys to the unit are inside. And Luke?"

"Yeah?"

"I don't hear from you in twenty-four hours, all bets are off with the family."

Ever since he'd been the one to discover his former partner tortured and murdered for information, Frank had done periodic check-ins with every member of the Edgars family. Usually once a week, unless he thought you might be in danger.

"Got it. I should have this wrapped up in time for the

weekly poker game," he said, trying to ease the Marshal's worry.

"Good. Still want to hear from you in twenty-four," Frank said, not buying his bullshit and hung up.

Now that he had a new, safer place to hide Abby, it was time to go on the offensive. He grabbed his laptop-tablet and sat at the desk, quickly pulling up the coordinates for the last ping they got of the victim's phone and entered it into a satellite map of Cleveland. It narrowed in on an old industrial park with old warehouses and flattop buildings. Not exactly a pinpoint location, but damn close.

"Who were you talking to?" Abby stood in the doorway watching him.

"A friend. He's setting up a place for us."

"Why?"

He closed the laptop, so she couldn't see what he was working on. No use getting her hopes up and he wanted to get her settled into the safe house before he checked the site out. "The hotel was a temporary solution last night. Now that we know someone is interested enough to tail Jeffers, we need a more secure location."

"Why don't we just go to your home?"

He gave her a half smile. "That would be a hell of a commute. Remember, my place is three hours away in Columbus."

"I thought you were the regional agent for this area." She drew her eyebrows down, causing her glasses to slip down onto the tip of her nose, and pulled her lower lip between her teeth, something she tended to do when she worried.

"It's a big region and I was en route anyways. So they diverted me here."

"Your friend is letting us stay at his home?"

"Nope. He lives in Columbus, too. He's giving us one of his safe houses."

"Safe house? He works for Homeland, too?"

"No. He's a U.S. Marshal. It's a house he uses to protect witnesses before trial." He shoved his chair back and walked over to stand in front of her. Taking a moment, he looked deep into her eyes before using one finger to push her glasses back up on her nose a bit.

"You're that sure that we're in danger?"

Damn sure you're in danger. "I'm not taking any chances. And you might as well give me your smartphone, too."

"Why?" she asked even as she went to retrieve it, a sign that she might question his motives, but was learning to trust his orders.

He took the phone from her. Flipping it over, he removed the battery, then handed them back to her. "You can keep these in your suitcase for when the case is finished, but don't use it again until then. Whoever removed Bethanne's cell phone battery may be smart enough to search her call record or contact list."

"Brianna," she corrected him again as she slipped the phone and battery into the bottom of her bag. "And they'd find my name and number."

"You need to get all your things packed. I don't want to leave even a candy wrapper behind. Okay?"

"Okay. I didn't unpack that much so I'll be ready in a few minutes." She turned to grab the things out of her closet, then looked over her shoulder at him with a you-didn't-fool-me-for-a-second look on her face. "And while you're driving to the safe house, you can tell me what it was you didn't want me to see on your laptop."

* * * * *

"You are not going with me."

"Yes, I am." Abigail resisted the urge to roll her eyes at him. They'd been having this discussion—she refused to call it an argument—since they stepped out of the hotel. Instead, she focused her attention on plugging Brianna's phone number into the new cell phone they'd picked up at a local electronics store. Luke had insisted on buying it with his credit card and using his mother's name on the account. While she understood the real possibility Brianna could compromise her, especially if her captors were using physical torture to gain information, but super-spy's paranoia was a little over the top.

"It's dangerous and no place for an amateur," he said turning left again. He'd been doubling back and forth, almost going in concentric circles, since they'd left the store, hoping to either pick up a tail or lose one. She wasn't quite sure which.

"If it's so dangerous, then that's exactly why you can't go alone with no backup. Besides, if you find Brianna, then you'll need help getting her out of the place."

"And if we find her dead body?"

His harsh words vibrated with the anger in his voice, making her lean away from the pain they caused. Damn the man. He'd always known the buttons to push to get her riled. He'd challenged her on every physical exercise during their weeks of training, almost as if he wanted to prove to her and the instructors she shouldn't be considered a field agent. Unlike some other members of their training class, however, he'd never made fun of her or tried to humiliate her. Why would he choose now to hurt her?

To make her want to stay behind.

Well, too damn bad. She was going and that was all there was to it.

"Then I'll catalogue the entire area before the local cops get there. And not just the crime scene."

He didn't say anything else, because there was no argument that trumped her special skills and they both knew it. In the dim light of the passing streetlamps, she watched him flex and grip his hands tighter over the steering wheel. He might be conceding the point and letting her accompany him to the area Brianna's last phone signal had come from, but he wasn't happy about it.

They drove a few more minutes in a snake-like pattern. Finally, assured no one had followed them, he pulled into an area of upscale apartments and condos, maneuvering the car behind one that looked like an English cottage she'd seen on the Travel Channel once. Pulling into a drive, he lowered his window at a keypad and punched in a set of numbers to open the garage door. Abigail looked around the area and no other place had this keypad feature. *What other special security devices were in the place?*

Luke drove inside, cutting the engine as the garage door closed behind them automatically.

"Impressive," she said as they climbed out of the car.

"Castello's big on keeping his people secure." Handing her his laptop-tablet, he opened the trunk and grabbed her bags with his, motioning her to the door into the house. She could argue that she was capable of carrying her own bags, but it felt nice having him haul the bag and letting her carry the lighter and more delicate electronics.

"That's your Marshal friend's name? Castello?"

"Yes. And let's get this gear inside before you start playing twenty questions."

Apparently, he was still aggravated about including her on the mission tonight. She followed him inside, fighting the urge to grin. All those weeks that he teased and challenged her during their training, she'd always been the one tense, angry and aggravated. It felt good to be the one delivering that feeling for once.

"Wow," she said as she stepped into the upscale cook's kitchen. It looked like an episode of one of the home design shows, complete with hardwood floors, granite countertops, porcelain country sink and cupboards made out of cherry wood and beveled glass. The room was part of an open-concept design, extending past a dining area and out into a great room with a leather sectional and fireplace made out of river stones from floor to ceiling. "Castello has nice taste."

"He tends to be a minimalist, focusing on the security of a building, not the comfort of it. I doubt the big guy paid much attention to the furnishings." Luke closed the door to the garage, then set the bags down on the counter.

She ran her hand over the granite countertop. "I didn't realize U.S. Marshals must made good money."

"He inherited a big chunk of money when he was in college, said he wanted to invest in property. Guess this is what he did with some of it." Luke opened the refrigerator. "Damn. He doesn't have much stocked in here."

Typical primal male. Shelter, then food. "Look in the freezer."

He glanced at her over his shoulder, lifting one eyebrow as if doubting her wisdom, but opened the bottom drawer of the fridge. It was packed with frozen food. "Ah. The jackpot. How'd you know?"

"Makes sense. You say your friend isn't interested in comfort, just keeping things secure. He's not going to have someone stock the fridge with perishable items, too risky. The more people know this safe house's location, the more likely it will lose its security feature. But he'd want to be sure he could feed his protectees a meal when they arrived. Ergo, a fully loaded freezer."

That got her one of Luke's patented grins, only this time there was a heat in his eyes she'd seen only once before—the moment before he kissed her today. "You have the sexiest brain I've ever come across."

She blinked. Then laughed. "What?"

He shut the freezer, picked up the bags and sauntered by her, adding a wink to his grin. "You heard me, sweetheart. I find the way you think very sexy."

He found her sexy. He found her brain sexy. At his words a heated flush started at her toes and spread like a summer fire. The man could change moods faster than a level four hurricane and dang if that didn't make him the most infuriating, intriguing and charming man with whom she'd ever had to work.

"Oh, hell, no," Luke said, stopping in the doorway leading off the great room.

"What's the problem?" she asked, coming up behind him and peering into the bedroom.

"Castello is such a dead man."

"Why? You can have this bedroom and I'll take the other."

"You can't." He dropped her bag inside the room, the pulled out his cell phone.

"Why not?" she asked with a sinking feeling, already

suspecting what his answer would be.

"Because my good *friend* picked the worst time to decide to pull a joke. He gave us a safe house with one bedroom and one bed."

CHAPTER 8

A knock sounded on the door.

Luke had just finished leaving a you're-a-dead-man message on Castello's phone. He palmed his gun from beneath his coat and motioned Abby to move away from the door, out of the line of fire. She nodded as she pulled her bag into the kitchen. Out of the corner of his eye he saw her pull out her service weapon and move to where she had a line of sight to the door.

Standing to one side, he peeked through the peephole. A young man in a T-shirt, denim jacket and jeans stood on the stoop.

"Can I help you?" Luke asked through the door.

"Castello sent me," the young man said, holding up a set of car keys.

Luke slipped his gun in the back of his jeans and opened the door. "And you are?"

"Kirkpatrick," he said, handing Luke the keys and slowly sizing him up from top-to-bottom.

"Thanks, Kirkpatrick."

"It's Kirk F. Patrick," he said, eyes narrowed as if he'd heard every joke about his name and wasn't in the mood for another. "Black Caddy parked two doors down. Bulletproof, with tinted windows. Return it in one piece when the case is done." The kid started to leave, then paused and gave him another head-to-toe assessment. "Fill the tank, too."

Pocketing the keys, Luke closed the door. He pulled his weapon out of the back of his jeans and slipped it into his shoulder holster once more. Ever since they'd discovered Jeffers had a tail today, he'd remained armed. He turned to see Abby putting her own gun back in her bag, her back to him, shoulders shaking. "You found that funny?"

She looked over her shoulder at him, green eyes twinkling with humor and her smile a hundred-watt stunner. "Come on. His name is Kirk Patrick. His parents had a very warped sense of humor."

He closed the space between them in three quick steps, stopping an arm's length from her. "No, his name is Kirk *F.* Patrick."

That sent her into more silent laughter. He couldn't help grinning. It was the most relaxed he'd seen her since they'd been reunited. It was sexy as hell and he had to fight hard not to reach out and pull her into his arms.

"What do you think the F stands for? Fredrick?"

"Oh, I'm pretty sure with that name, his old man probably had something more inventive."

"Fabian? Forrest?"

"I'm thinking more like Fuckyou."

A bark of laughter escaped her, followed by more silent shaking of her shoulders. Finally, she stopped and grinned at him once more. "Kirk Fuckyou Patrick. I can see that working for him. He certainly took his job for your friend seriously. How did he know to deliver the car to you so fast?"

And with that reminder of the serious situation they were in the humor drained from them both.

"Castello likes to use local talent when he wants to keep someone off the grid. I imagine Kirk F. Patrick maintains both this place and the car for a monthly fee and is at Castello's beck and call. My guess? Frank bailed the kid out of some trouble and saw potential in him. Knowing the Marshal, he's putting the kid through school, too." Moving away from the temptation of Abby's body, Luke headed for the table where he'd left his tablet. He glanced at the clock on the kitchen wall. "Nine o'clock. I'd say anyone in the vicinity of the coordinates for that cell phone have probably gone home for the night."

"We'd best change then," she said, walking towards the bedroom.

He grabbed her by the wrist as she passed him.

"What?" she asked, those eyes big with questions and her pulse throbbing hard beneath his fingers.

"You sure I can't talk you into staying safely here while I check this out?"

She shook her head. "Can't get out of it that easy, Edgars. Like it or not, I'm all the backup you have."

"This isn't a typical situation, Abby. You're personally involved in this case. Your emotions aren't particularly neutral. I may not have time to let you process them if things go bad or we find—"

"Like I said earlier," she said before he could finish. "Then you'll need me to preserve as many images of the crime scene as possible. We're wasting time arguing."

She attempted to pull her wrist free of his grip and he let her go. She was right. There was little he could do to change whatever they were about to discover. Abby wasn't a child or even an untrained civilian. Her special skills might come in handy and help them retrieve information later on. He just wished he had another choice for backup.

Swallowing the urge to growl out his frustration, he followed her into the bedroom and snagged his small duffle from the floor. "Make sure everything you wear is dark, black is preferable."

"Even my bra and underwear?" she asked, wiggling her brows.

"Jeez." He choked out a startled cough.

She took the advantage of his stunned thoughts to shove him out of the room and close the door in his face.

For a moment he stared at the door, the image of her long, lean body clad in nothing but sexy black lace filling his brain, which of course had his cock thinking happy thoughts that had nothing to do with their clandestine mission tonight. The last thing he needed was the distraction of Abby's underwear in his head.

Get a grip, Edgars. A woman's life, as well as Abby's safety, depended on him keeping focused.

Shoving the lusty thoughts into the back of his mind, he went to pull up the street map surrounding the area pinpointed as Brianna's cell phone's last signal on his tablet. With a few well-placed codes, he also brought up the traffic cams in that area. The largest building looked to be a car repair company and two one-story warehouses. Nothing seemed to be moving in the area, except for the occasional car driving down the street.

"What is that?" Abby said from right behind him.

He resisted the urge to look at her once more. "Traffic cams in the area where we're going. I'm checking to be sure we're not walking into a trap of some sort."

"Do you have clearance to access that kind of surveillance?" she asked, sliding into the chair next to him and pulling her hair up into a ponytail once more.

"Not exactly." He glanced her way. For once she'd listened to his advice, wearing the black sweater, jeans and dark grey hoodie they'd bought earlier in the day. He would *not* think about her bra and panties.

"What do you mean, not exactly?" She slipped her glasses on once more and peered over the top of them at him, like a librarian wondering why he was making too much noise in her library.

"I can gain access without going through the usual routes or gaining clearance." Without waiting to see her reaction, he focused on watching the screen, then typed in more code to run the tapes backward.

"So, you hacked in?" Abby said, no real censure in her voice. She leaned in closer, studying the images as they rolled in reverse. "What are you looking for exactly?"

To see if they've carried your friend's corpse out of the building. "Not sure really. Just thought we might notice something suspicious."

"Like someone carrying out a rolled up rug with Brianna's body inside?"

Damn. Abby had one quick mind. And he had to wonder how much compartmentalizing of this she could do before she broke down. "That would certainly be suspicious, but I was thinking more like cars coming and going repetitively or anything that stands out."

"Like a high-end sedan pulling in among the two older junkers?" she said, pointing at the computer screen.

He paused the program's reverse mode and played it forward again just as the sedan pulled into the parking lot near the car repair building. It drove around, disappearing in back. Luke pushed a timer on his computer and they continued to watch the video. Thirty minutes later the car pulled out. Nothing else entered or left for another hour. Then a large white van pulled in and disappeared behind one of the buildings. Another half hour passed and the truck left again. Finally four men exited the warehouse, climbed into the junkers and drove off in the same direction as the van.

"Can you get a close-up of the van?" Abby asked, a slight catch in her voice.

"I can try, but I doubt you can see inside it," he said, his fingers flying over the keyboard to enhance the feed and zero in on the van.

"I know. It probably has tinted windows, but maybe we can get the plate or some other detail."

Luke pulled up another video with a new angle of the van as it pulled out of the lot. "The resolution is too low. All we're getting is a grainy picture when it's enlarged."

"Crap." Abby slouched back in her chair, one hand wrapped around her middle, the other fisted just below her lips. "You know they probably moved Brianna in that van."

"No. I don't know that and neither do you."

"Logic dictates it, Luke. We waited too long."

* * * * *

As they drove through the empty streets into the old warehouse area, Abigail stared out into the near darkness, the sporadic streetlights the only things illuminating their way. Despite what she'd said to Luke earlier about being his backup and doing her job no matter what they discovered inside the warehouse, her stomach twisted at the idea of finding Brianna's body in the place.

Could she do this? Could she pull back from the horror of seeing the nearest thing she had to a sister cold and lifeless long enough to take mental snapshots of everything inside the building?

If it helps catch whoever is behind this? Yes.

Luke's hand settled on hers. The warmth of it surprised and comforted her, as if he knew she was faking the bravado she'd used earlier. But he hadn't left her behind. For that reason alone, she'd do her best, no matter what they found, to help him solve this puzzle.

"When we get there, I'll go first. You stay right behind me, okay?" he said, squeezing her hand.

She looked over to see him glancing from the road back to her, concern in his eyes and his lips set in a thin line. "Just like in training. Close enough to breathe down your neck."

The reminder of how he'd followed her into a building search once during their days in Georgia, got her a quick lift at the corners of his lips and a wink. "That's right, just like back in training."

He squeezed her hand again before releasing it to grip the steering wheel once more. The sudden loss of his touch pushed an ache into her chest and she stared at his profile for a few blocks. For the first time in her life she wanted to beg him to hold her hand, to keep telling her she wasn't alone. She wanted to clutch him like a lifeline in the coming storm, but she knew she couldn't. For so long she'd been on her own, no one to really depend on but herself. Even her friendship with Brianna had its limits. As a child she'd learned that lesson.

You can't let anyone in too close, because everyone you love dies.

Forcing herself to put away any weak urges to clutch Luke's hand once more, she looked out the window once more at the passing terrain, trying to see if anyone was moving about in the dark jungle of abandoned buildings and old cars. Nothing moved. She didn't know if that was a good or bad thing.

"We're here," Luke said, breaking the silence as he slowed to turn into the empty lot.

Abigail sat a little straighter in the leather seat and concentrated on the buildings in front of them. The car repair building sat to the left and she had to lean forward to see around Luke and get a good look, her mind snapping its picture and filing it away. Then she stared at the long flat building in front of them, cataloguing every feature and every shadow.

Luke drove around behind the flat-topped building to the third building. Before they'd left the safe house, he'd mapped out the camera angles and found a blind spot to park the caddy, saying he didn't want anyone's surveillance cameras identifying the car or them when they got out. Abigail was pretty damn sure whatever program he used to control both city surveillance and private security cameras weren't available to the average citizen or the average Treasury agent, either. Once again she had to wonder exactly how much of Luke's skills were known by their employers.

"You ready?" he asked, putting the car in park in the shadows away from the few lights on the periphery of the lot and cutting the headlights.

She couldn't see his features too clearly in the moonless night, but she heard the concern in his voice. "Yes. Let's get this over with."

They exited the car at the same time, quietly closing the doors so not to alert anyone possibly still on the premises. They headed to the back of the last building —the one they believed the sedan and the van had both parked behind. If Brianna were anywhere in the area, Luke and Abigail had determined it would be here.

At the door, Luke paused and held up his hand for her to wait. She turned her back to him to watch their perimeter while he picked the lock on the door. When he had it open, he touched her shoulder in a signal to follow him inside. Slipping into the building, literally on Luke's six, she closed the door without making even a click. They stood inside a kind of vestibule, another door leading into the main part of the warehouse. It was nearly pitch black, except for the bits of light from the lights out in the parking lot.

Luke tested the knob and the door opened with a low creak.

They froze.

Nothing moved inside the room. No sound of someone hiding or coming to check out the noise. Luke clicked on his flashlight, holding it just under his gun and Abigail did the same.

Luke went through the door and scanned to his right, motioning her to remain where she was, then headed to his right. Holding the door, she leaned through and shone her light in the same direction. Another door stood open a few feet away. A huge window beside it. Luke leaned in to see what was inside. Abigail could make out a desk that looked to be littered with pizza boxes, beer bottles and soda cans.

He shook his head to indicate no one was in there and motioned her to come out.

"Stay with me," he whispered the reminder again, leading the way inside.

Like she was going to wander off by herself in the creepy darkness?

One step behind him and to his right, she followed him into the warehouse, their flashlight beams arching slowly back and forth, top to bottom, casting eerie shadows in the cavernous space. Her skin itched, like something brushed across it and she half expected someone in a zombie costume to jump out at them like at a Halloween scare house she'd once visited. Still, nothing moved.

The building might be void of living souls except for hers and Luke's, but it wasn't empty. While Luke kept scanning the periphery, Abigail let her light focus on the center of the room where a table sat and an overturned chair lay a few feet away. Ropes were scattered about and beneath the chair, while something dark coated the floor.

"Luke?"

"Yeah, I see it, Abby," he said, not losing focus on checking the building for any danger. "Let's make sure your friend or any bad guys aren't here first, then we'll check it out."

"Right," she said, continuing to follow him into the depths of the building. She scanned her light along the back wall. "There's another door back there."

They made their way to it, where Luke once again tested the knob. This one was locked. As before, Abigail kept lookout as he picked the lock, but when she made to follow him inside, he stopped her.

"Stay out here, Abby."

"Why?" She looked beyond him to see three crates in the center of the room and nothing else. Then the stench hit her. "God, what is that?"

"My best guess is charred flesh and decomposing corpses," he said, blocking her from entering. "*You* stay out here, catalogue everything you see."

"But what if it's Brie—"

Luke laid a hand on her shoulder. "Damn it, Abby. I can eventually let this image fade, but not you. You don't need this memory permanently in your head."

He was protecting her.

The idea hit her somewhere in her chest. While she

knew she should protest that she was an agent and could handle it, the knowledge that he wanted to protect her from seeing something this horrific touched her. He was right. No matter how much she tried, if she saw what was inside those crates, it would be with her to her dying day.

She nodded. "Okay. I'll observe this room. Make my mental pictures for later. Will there be any way to know if any of them are Brianna?"

"I don't know."

She stepped out of the doorway, turning her back on what she knew must be a gruesome sight and focused her attention on the area around the furniture. Looking from the outside in, Abigail let her mind catalogue everything she saw. The dust and footprints, cigarette butts, small pieces of trash and round, red paper tabs.

Definitely a blood splatter lay beneath the overturned chair. But was it Brianna's? She slipped a cotton swab from the few she'd loaded into her purse and dabbed it over the site, then slipped it into the one of the plastic bags she'd also brought along. It might help to prove Brianna had been here.

The ropes on the floor were tied in odd spots to the chair as if someone had been restrained, probably tortured. But who and what for? Was it Brianna? Her phone had been here, so she assumed Brie had too. What information did they think her friend had? And had Brianna given in and submitted to the interrogation? Because the more she studied the scene, the more Abigail was convinced it was an interrogation.

"Abby, how tall is your friend?" Luke said from the doorway behind her.

She looked over her shoulder at him. His face was drawn tight and she'd swear he was a shade paler than his usual tan. "I'm five-eleven, Brianna is about three inches shorter. Why?"

"There were three bodies in there, burned beyond recognition, but none of them were that tall."

She sagged with relief. "Were they all women?"

"That or really small men. Let's get out of here," he said, grabbing her by the elbow and nearly dragging her back the way they'd come.

She dug in her heels, trying to pull free. "Wait, we have to let the police know. Those women have families."

"Abigail. I need to get you out of here first." His use of her real name got her attention.

"Why?"

"Whoever did this could come back at any moment. They have no fear of getting caught, or any qualms about torturing and murdering women. I don't want to risk you falling into their hands." He gripped her elbow a little tighter and she let him lead her to the exit.

Once they were safely on the road away from the crime scene, he pulled out his phone.

"Who are you calling?"

"Detective Jeffers."

CHAPTER 9

"I lost the prey, Snake. Tracked 'em a few miles, then the guy started doubling back, like a fox trying to hide his scent from the hounds. Figured I'd best back off 'fore he made me, then poof, they gone."

Fuck! Snake kicked the side of the alley dumpster with his steel-toed, shit-kicker boots. He'd followed the cop back from the Hollister-Klein building to the police station. Whoever he'd met with inside the company, the meeting hadn't lasted too long. He'd make sure to tell the bossman when he reported in again.

"Followed his Beemer from the hotel. I can try doubling back to the last place I saw the car. Works in the hills when I'm huntin', but a little trickier with cars 'steada animals."

If Tracker couldn't stay with them, the guy must have special skills to lose his tail. Special skills—as in highly trained and therefore extremely dangerous. With the detective locked down for the night and the couple off the grid, it might be time to regroup.

"Nah, leave it for now. Bossman has some merchandise he wants us to move, so head back over to the warehouse. I'll meet you there. Gonna need you to get the big truck."

"You're the boss. I'm 'bout twenty minutes out."

"Don't take any chances. The merchandise isn't going anywhere. Just be sure no cops tail you back there." He hung up, climbed in his car and eased it out of the alley. The cops were so busy coming in and out for their shift change, no one noticed him watching from the alley. Looked like the detective was planning to work all night. Time to get back and get his men busy moving the new shipment that came in last week. Should be primed and ready.

A smile split his lips.

Yeah, gonna hafta sample some of this.

* * * * *

Down the alley from the precinct, the black sedan pulled out, letting the brown Cutlass make its first right turn before speeding up and turning on his lights. It had been a while since Aaron had done surveillance work, but it was just like riding a bike. Once you learned how, the skills came back quick when you needed them.

This afternoon, when Edgars informed him he had a tail, he hadn't liked the idea that not only was someone interested in what he might be investigating, but that he hadn't a clue he was being followed. Given he hadn't noticed a tail before today, he'd suspected it had to be involved with the missing Mathews woman. However, he'd been so wrapped up in the side case of the other missing women, there was always a possibility he'd tipped his hand to the perps in that case, too. Who knows how long he'd been under surveillance?

Of course he hadn't been surprised when Mary Jo texted him that the plates and car didn't match. He'd bet if he could get the VIN number off the vehicle odds were it had been reported stolen, too.

Time to turn the tables.

He might not have a clue as to who was so curious about his cases, but he was sure going to find out where his tail was headed. Then he might just get a hold of his new best friend, Luke Edgars, and find out exactly why he and Abigail Whitson were in town. The guy's story about simply visiting a friend was just a line of fancy-dressed bullshit. Tired of the questions bouncing around in his head, he wanted answers.

As the Cutlass moved through the late-night traffic Aaron kept a good three-car distance between them, following him from one neighborhood to another. They crossed the Cuyahoga River, finally ending up in the old riverfront industrial area, west of the remodeled Flats along the river.

Tingling crawled up his spine like a poisonous centipede looking for a place to strike. Never a good feeling.

Lots of empty or abandoned warehouses dotted this

area. Good place to hide women—or bodies.

The Cutlass pulled into the parking lot of a turn-of-the-century warehouse and parked in the rear of the building next to two other equally non-descript cars. Lights were on in the lower part of the building. The driver climbed out of his car as Aaron drove down the street past the building. The guy had a grey hoodie pulled up over his head, preventing Aaron from getting a good look as he drove past. He'd go a few blocks before doubling back.

Once parked up the street from the warehouse, but close enough to see anyone coming or going, he pulled out his notebook to make notes. A lot of the other detectives, especially those just moving up the ranks from patrolman, liked to use their cell phones to take notes, but he'd always liked the feel of holding a pad and pen in his hand. It let his brain connect facts better than trying to concentrate on typing in words with his big fingers on the small keyboard, and forget texting. It was okay for someone to send him a message, but when he tried to return one, it ended up mostly gibberish full of typos. He copied down the warehouse's address and a note to look up the property owner later. Lifting the binoculars he'd brought with him, he tried to get the plates off the other vehicles, but doubted he'd get any better information than he had from the ones on the Cutlass.

Headlights up ahead caught his attention.

A large moving truck rumbled down the street

towards the warehouse. It slowed at the entrance to the parking lot and made a Y-turn, backing into the lot towards the ancient loading dock at the back of the building.

Shit.

Were they moving something in or out of the warehouse? Probably not the Mathews woman. They wouldn't need a truck that big for just one woman. However, if her case were connected to the other missing women, maybe they were moving more than one body.

Lifting the binoculars once more, he tried to get a look at the driver. Long, lanky, light-skinned. Probably some half-drugged-out Caucasian kid. Dressed in the same grungy jeans, dark hoodie sweatshirt as the first guy. This one also had a baseball hat blocking out any good description. *Dammit.* He needed to get closer.

He set the binoculars aside then pulled out his phone and opened the camera app—one of the few good uses he'd found for the thing in detective work, then slipped out of the car. Keeping to the darkest shadowed areas between his car and the warehouse, he climbed through overgrown bushes and piles of trash, dumped old car parts and worn tires until only open space remained. With a prayer that no one walked outside, he dashed to the side of the building. Taking refuge behind an old dumpster, he tried to ignore the smell emanating from behind it. Apparently the gang using the warehouse considered this the place to take a piss.

Most of the windows on the lower floor were covered in black paint, but light shone through a few with cracks in the paint. He eased his way down to one and peeked inside. Couldn't see much, but put his camera up to take some shots. Who knows what they'd find once he enlarged the images.

A huge garage door opened back where the truck sat and voices sounded. He scooted back towards the dumpster to see if he could get pictures of his tail and the truck driver.

The two walked outside and Aaron quickly took pictures of them.

"Let's get the merchandise loaded and on the road."

"Yeah, man. Gonna take mosta the night to deliver it down south," Baseball Cap Guy said, climbing back in the truck.

"Hope not, man. I got plans on samplin' me some." Grey Hoodie Guy said as he stepped back and directed his friend to maneuver the back of the truck farther into the warehouse.

Great. Now they'd blocked any hopes of him getting a look at whatever kind of merchandise they were transporting tonight. And how far south were they going? He ground his teeth and leaned back against the brick wall, mentally counting to ten and taking account of the situation.

First, he was on his own. No backup. So he couldn't go charging in. Quick death wish there.

Secondly, no warrant and no probable cause. He had

no business here, except to discover who and why someone was following him.

Third, did he follow this truck and find out what they were delivering or to where? His gut told him whatever they were doing was illegal, but with no evidence, his visceral response wouldn't hold up in a court of law.

A rumbling sounded as the driver pulled away from the loading dock.

Aaron peeked around the corner of the building just in time to see several other men exit the building, closing the garage-type door behind them. One of the other men climbed into the passenger side of the truck, while the others—including Grey Hoodie Guy—got into the other cars. Then, like a caravan, they started out of the parking lot, quickly picking up speed.

Damn, even if he sprinted back to where he'd left his vehicle, no way was he catching up to follow them. He felt like he was chasing his own tail on this case and he didn't like it. Making sure no one saw him, he returned to his car and was just reaching for his phone when the ring tone sounded.

"Jeffers," he said, not recognizing the number.

"Detective, I have some information for you."

"Edgars. Something to do with the case?"

"I think so. There's a warehouse you need to check out."

"Oh? Where?"

Edgars gave him the address and he plugged it into his phone's GPS. It was in the old industrial area several miles away. "And what am I going to find in there?"

"Three crates in the back room." The fed paused a moment. "Bring your crime scene people and the coroner. You're going to find three charred bodies, probably women, inside."

Aw, crap, his night just went to hell in a hand basket. "And you know this how?"

"Abby and I were following a lead and stumbled across this."

"You two still there?" he asked, although he already knew the answer and didn't like it.

"Not anymore. I need to ask the same favor as before."

"Keep your and Ms. Whitson's names out of the official reports, I get it. Is one of these women her friend, Ms. Mathews?" Aaron put the car in gear and headed in the direction of the other warehouse.

"According to Abby, her friend was tall for a woman. All three corpses are petite."

"Where are you staying?"

"Someplace secure."

He gripped the wheel harder as he turned the corner. He was done being jerked around by the federal agent and his girlfriend. Time to get some friggin' answers.

"Tell you what, you tell me where I can find you later and I'll keep you out of this for now. I'll call it an anonymous tip." He paused for his own effect. "Otherwise I paste your names not only all over my reports but the news, too."

Edgars cursed on the other end of the line, but eventually gave him an address. "It's a federal safe house, so guard that information with your life."

"I'll call you when I'm near," Aaron said, then disconnected. Now he had one hell of a problem. How was he going to explain this tip to his boss?

* * * * *

Luke followed Abby into the condo once more, his jaw hurting from all the clenching he'd been doing on the silent drive home. Good thing Abby wasn't overly talkative and smart enough to realize he barely had a leash on his anger. The stench that had hit him when he opened those crates nearly made him hurl and his stomach still roiled from the lingering odor in his nose.

Once inside, he checked all the doors and set the alarm, then snagged his duffle bag from the couch and a bottle of whiskey from the dry bar. Thank God Castello kept it fully loaded. "I need a shower."

"Okay. Do you want anything to eat?"

He swallowed hard, trying to keep his stomach contents in place. "No," he said, heading to the bedroom. "And don't open the door for anyone. Jeffers said he'd call before he gets here."

Before she could ask any questions, he closed the door and leaned back against it, dropping his bag on the floor with a thud. For a moment he closed his eyes, the vision of those three burned bodies floating in front of him like images from some old horror movie. The idea that anyone could do that to those women...

Damn. He couldn't decide what he wanted to do more—go to a bar and get in a fight just so he could punch out his frustration or get drunk enough to obliterate the images from his mind. He pulled his holster off and looped it over the bedpost. Walking into the bathroom, he opened the whiskey and drank a long pull, letting the liquor burn a path down his throat.

Problem was, he didn't have the luxury to really do either and the reason stood on the other side of the door.

Abby.

What if he hadn't met her at her friend's condo? What if she'd been early and walked in while they were grabbing Brianna? What if one of those bodies had been Abby?

His legs wobbled, then gave out and he sank to his knees.

Abby could've been in one of those boxes.

He took another long drink of the whiskey, waiting for his nerves to settle. Then with a reserve he pulled deep from inside, he capped the bottle. It was his responsibility to keep Abby safe. Drunk wasn't going to get the job done.

But he could wash the smell away.

For the first time he noticed the upgraded bathroom with the walk-in shower tiled from floor to ceiling in tumbled granite, with a bench to sit on and six showerheads, including the state-of-the-art rain shower one overhead. No curtain or sliding-glass door. No, this was the kind that had glass blocks on one side of the entrance and all the tiles drained toward the drain near the back.

Impressive. Whoever Castello reserved this condo for, it must've been someone very important for the amenities to be so high-end. He turned on the shower and stripped out of all the odorous clothing.

Stepping into the shower, he adjusted the side jets to hit his back hard, almost like a liquid massage.

"Ah," he said, giving into the pleasure, even enjoying the steady fall of warm water from overhead. This time, when he closed his eyes, he focused on the image that had been bothering him before they'd walked into that warehouse—Abby dressed in nothing but black lace bra and panties. The angry tension drained from his body, to be replaced by a more pleasurable one as the blood rushed to his cock, thickening it into a hard erection.

He reached for the soap and lathered it in his hands, scrubbing his face and neck first, then down his chest and abdomen until he cupped his balls to lather them with one hand, the other stroking the length of his cock, sliding slickly up and down the shaft, imagining the dark lingerie against all of Abby's wonderful creamy skin.

Abby stood outside the bathroom staring at the

closed door, popping a chocolate drop into her mouth to still her own anxiety. Chocolate usually helped, but this time she wasn't worried about herself or the case. She was worried about Luke.

All the way back from the warehouse, he'd been silent, his barely restrained anger rolling off him like earthquake aftershocks. She'd wanted to say something to help him, only imagining the horror he'd had to see inside those crates, but the hard set of his jaw and the way he'd gripped the steering wheel so tight his knuckles blanched white in the darkness warned her how bad the idea was.

Instead, she'd kept quiet, hoping he'd open up once they'd gotten home.

No such luck.

She knew he was hurting. In all the time she'd known Luke, he'd never once been this silent and she'd never once seen him intentionally get drunk. But wasn't that what he was doing? Trying to dull the images in his mind with alcohol? Images he'd seen just to save her from having them locked permanently in her head.

The urge to help him gnawed at her. But how?

Replace the image with something better. Something he'll want to remember.

Could she? Would he be willing to accept what she offered this time? The kiss they'd shared earlier certainly suggested he'd welcome more from her.

If she did this it had to be with her eyes wide open. This wasn't a fairy tale. Having sex with Luke Edgars wouldn't mean a happily-ever-after. He was only here to help her find Brianna. Once the case was closed, he was back to being super-spy and she was headed back to her desk in DC.

Could she do this? Could she be so coolly sophisticated as the other women he'd been with?

All you have to do is open the door. Don't be a coward.

Her hand landed on the knob. When she opened it the room was empty. The shower running sounded just beyond the bathroom door. Taking another deep breath, she eased it open on silent hinges. Steam rolled out of the shower turning the room into a sauna. It took her a moment to find him, but there he was.

Luke.

In the shower.

Naked.

The glass blocks blurred her vision, so she stepped around to the shower opening.

His back to her, she memorized every inch of his body.

The water sluiced down over his long, firm muscles and golden, tanned skin. His solid, strong shoulders and the muscles that bulged on the back of his arms. The angles of his shoulder blades and the V-shape of his upper torso. Between his trapezius muscles the line of his spine lead her down to the round, firm globes of his firm ass cheeks.

She swallowed hard. Her heart rate jumped, nipples

tightening as a new kind of nervousness settled over her—a sensual awareness she'd never felt before.

Few times in her life had she reached out and taken what her heart desired. Once was joining the Treasury department as an analyst, the other insisting she get extra training as a field agent. This desire was something new. It wasn't just a longing for something more. No, it was a need. A need to touch Luke, to hold him, to mate with him.

Before she could back out, she pulled her sweater over her head and wiggled out of her jeans, socks and shoes as quietly as possible. Finally, she lost her panties and bra. A shiver ran through her. Nerves or anticipation? She wasn't sure, but for once she was going to sample what she'd always dreamed of—sex with Luke.

Nothing except his total rejection would deter her.

CHAPTER 10

Letting the soap and water wash away the smell and memories of the warehouse, Luke flattened one forearm against the granite tile. Leaning over it, eyes closed, he continued stroking his cock. The image of Abby so strong in his mind, he swore he caught a whiff of the lemony scent she always seem to wear. Clean and fresh, just like her.

A warm body pressed against his back.

He froze. Recognizing the firm breasts and hard nipples pushing into his shoulder blades, he inhaled deeply to gather more of her wonderful scent and relax his body. She settled her hands on his hips, making him take in another deep breath.

"Abby?"

A short giggle escaped her. "You were expecting someone else?"

"I wasn't expecting you."

Shit. That's not what he'd meant to say.

Silence came from behind him and she started to

move away.

Snaking one hand behind him, he grabbed her ass and held her close. "Don't go," he said, his voice husky with his need and the remnants of the whiskey.

"You're sure?" she asked, whispering into his ear as her body once again pressed against his.

He turned his head to stare into those beautiful eyes of her, now a deep forest color. The hot steam from the water floated about them. Wet tendrils of her hair clung to her face and neck, the deep, dark brown looking like chocolate. As he stared at her, she darted her pink tongue out to moisten her lips.

"I'm sure, if you are." He punctuated his words by leaning in to kiss her, never breaking eye contact. He let his tongue slip in for a quick sample, then pulled back, taking her plump bottom lip in his teeth and giving it a gentle pull. His reward was her soft moan.

"Oh, yes. I'm very sure."

As if to make very certain he understood exactly what she meant, she slipped her hands around the front of him. One to caress the wet hair on his chest and slide back and forth between his taut nipples, while the other she used to replace his own along his thick cock now straining up toward his abdomen.

"Oh, fuck."

"Like that, do you?"

Her sultry chuckle in his ear sent shivers of lust coursing through his body.

"You have no idea," he groaned when her fingers

tweaked his nipple.

Bracing his free hand on the tiles in front of him, he leaned back slightly against her body as she lathered up and down the length of him. Of all the sexual fantasies he'd had about her since the day she'd bumped into him in the hallway at FLETC in Georgia, none could hold a candle to the sheer torturous pleasure she was raining down on his body at this moment.

When her lips latched onto the spot where his neck and shoulder met, he surged forward in her hand, begging for more. Her teeth grazed his skin, then her tongue lathed over his pulse.

If he didn't stop her now, he'd be coming in her hands. While his cock might like the idea, he had other plans.

"Abby." He grasped her hand, holding it around his cock while he took a few deep breaths.

"Did I do something wrong?"

The worry in her voice surprised and touched him, showing him just how inexperienced she was. He doubted in this day and age that she was still a virgin, but he'd bet she barely had more practice than that.

"No, sweetheart. You're doing everything just right." *And then some.*

"Why did you stop me?"

"Because I want this to last longer and if you keep that up, I won't."

"Oh." She gave him a little grin and the blush that crept into her cheeks was...charming. Somehow that word described her, an old-fashioned word for a very special woman.

Slowly he turned, pulling her into his arms, crushing her against his body and capturing her lips in a deep, hard kiss. Parting her lips to give him access, she wrapped her arms around his neck, sliding her fingers into his hair, pulling him closer. Her invitation snapped him into another world of need. Pulling her hips in to grind his erection against her stomach at the same time he slid his tongue in between her parted lips, tasting the uniqueness of her—the spice of her arousal and the chocolate she must've eaten before coming in to join him.

The need to be inside her, connected at the core, clawed at him and he slid one hand down to lift her thigh, moving her moist slit to settle against his aching balls. Abby clutched at him, then wiggled her hips, letting her sex slide up to the base of his cock. Stumbling backwards, he came in contact with the tile bench.

God bless the guy who designed this shower.

He sat, pulling her with him. Without hesitating, she straddled his hips, impaling him deep inside her with one full thrust.

"Yes," he groaned as they sat locked for a moment, her heat and tightness pulsing around his cock.

Then she moved, lifting her legs to wrap around behind him, driving him in deeper and tighter. The sensation was so overwhelming he dropped his head to her shoulder, clutching her to him as he sucked in air.

A whimper sounded in his ear. He lifted his head to see her biting her lip. Reality slipped through his haze of pleasure.

He knew he was big and she was little more than a novice. Had he hurt her?

"Abby? What's wrong, sweetheart?"

"I need…" She stopped talking, shaking her head.

He slid his hands up into her hair, holding her head still until her gaze met his. "Tell me. Whatever you need I'll do, even if it means stopping."

God, please don't let her say stop. Because he would. The last thing he would do was force her to go further than she wanted, even if it killed him.

"No. I need…I need to move…to…" She lifted slowly and settled back down, showing him what she wanted. "Yes."

The word literally purred out of her, sending his own pulse skyrocketing.

"You can move all you want, sweetheart." He leaned his upper back against the tiles, gripping her by her hips to pull her up and back. "Ride me, Abby. Ride me as hard as you want."

Releasing her hold on his neck, she slid her hands onto his shoulders, her fingers clenching him as she extended her slender arms to lift halfway off his shaft, then sink down completely, repeating the act. Her pussy clenched around him, her juices helping him slide in deeper each time. He focused on her, praying he'd last until she'd found her orgasm. In all his life he'd never seen a woman more beautiful or more erotic. He watched her face, her eyes closed and mouth open in pleasure as she worked her body on his.

"Oh, oh," she moaned and shifted her rhythm, staying tightly impaled on him. His gaze flew down to the spot where they were joined as she moved forward and back, rubbing the hard nub of her clit against his pelvic bone.

"That's it, baby. Right there." He gripped her hips tighter in his hands, urging her to move faster. His balls started to tingle and the need to release poured through him. He gritted his teeth, determined to last. "Come on, Abby. Do it. Come on me."

Almost as if she'd been waiting for his strangled command, she tightened around him as a spasm wracked her body, her fingers digging into his shoulders. "Oh, oh…ah."

Her half-moan, half-scream echoed around the shower's walls, sending him over the edge. Gripping her to him as he surged his hips off the granite seat and exploded inside her. "Fuck!"

She collapsed down onto him and he wrapped his arms tightly around her as their bodies rode out the storm raining through them in aftershocks. As his brain cleared and he sucked in slow deep breaths to will his heart to slow, he felt her shiver in his arms.

"Abby?" He reached up to smooth the wet strands of hair from her face.

"I didn't...know." She murmured, her face still against his neck.

"Didn't know what?" he asked, cupping her head in his hands and making her look at him.

"That I could let go like that. And..."

"And?"

A beautiful grin split her lips and lit her face. "That it could be so damn good."

He brought her head down towards his, claiming her lips once more. He took his time, pressing, releasing, stroking her tongue with his. He varied the pace. Long and slow. Quick nips until she was trying to rock on him again. His cock thickened with the need for more of her.

Another shiver ran through her. He released her face and slid his hands down her arms, noticing the goose flesh pebbling her skin.

"You're cold."

"No, I'm not," she argued, trying to capture his lips once more.

Before she could, he gripped her arms a little tighter and pulled her back.

"Not here. The water is growing cold." He let go with one hand to turn off the showerheads. Then gripping her ass to keep her legs locked around him, he stood and carried her out of the bathroom, slipping only once on the slick floor and causing her to hold him tighter even while she giggled.

At the bedside he paused, capturing her mouth once

more in a hard, hot kiss. Breaking the kiss, he knelt one knee on the bed and lowered her onto the mattress. He settled in between her thighs, his cock sliding back into the moist, hot warmth of her pussy.

"You fit me so perfectly," he murmured, before kissing her again in a long slow savoring.

She wiggled beneath him, wrapping her long legs around his hips and thighs once more. "You fill me completely."

"Aha, your former lovers were a bit lacking, huh?" he teased, leaning back to stare into her eyes, only to see the pleasure darken just before she looked away.

What the hell? Had something bad happened to her with another lover?

Cupping her face in his hands, he gently forced her to look at him. "What's wrong, Abby? You can tell me."

"It's just that…" She paused a moment. "It was only one other lover. I'd rather not talk about it."

"Why not?" Had someone hurt her? Raped her? If so, he'd find out the bastard's name and hunt him down.

"Nothing to talk about. It's in the distant past," she said, reaching down to cup his ass cheeks and pull him in tight. "Make love to me, Luke. Make me feel like flying again."

He stared into her eyes, then tucked one loose strand of hair behind her ear. Later he'd get her to tell him what happened. But for now he'd be sure to replace that old memory with another earth-rocking orgasm. Leaning in, he kissed her long and slow, letting tenderness show before the heat sparked once more.

Reaching down he pulled her hands free and brought them up to the spindles in the wrought-iron bedframe. "Hold on, sweetheart," he whispered in her ear. "It's going to be bumpy ride."

"I sure hope so," she said and the sexy, playful smile was back on her face.

Extending his arms so he rose above her, he drank in the sight of her stretched out before him. The passion in her wide, green eyes. The pert nose that balanced her glasses when she was working. The plumpness of her freshly kissed lips. His gaze traveled lower—across the long slender column of her neck, the collarbone of her strong, but delicate shoulders, finally landing on her breasts. Not huge, but big enough to fill his hands, their dusky tips taut and tempting.

Mine.

"Damn, you're beautiful," he murmured just before latching onto one tight nub and suckling on it.

His reward was her moan of pleasure and the arching of her back, making her pussy glide over his cock until just the head was in her entrance. Without breaking his hold on her nipples, he thrust forward, burying himself hilt-deep again. He repeated the motion, growing thicker inside her and his need to claim her rushing through his veins.

Releasing her nipple, he reached up to entwine his hands with hers around the spindles and rested his forehead on hers.

"Look at me, Abby," he ordered her.

She focused those magnificently intelligent eyes on him and he began the fast, hard joining of their bodies, her legs wrapped tightly around his hips as he drove deeper and deeper into her core.

As her body clenched around him, she closed her eyes, her mouth parted in her passion. He wanted to watch her release, to see her when he finished his.

"Look. At. Me," he growled as he worked harder, every muscle in both their bodies, taut and straining in the age-old rhythm of the mating ritual. Her eyes snapped open, their depths so dark he felt his soul sliding into them. Bending his knees, he pushed her thighs wider as he pumped into her with every force his body could muster.

"Luke. Oh, sweet heaven."

"That's it. Sweetheart. Come. With me."

She panted, fighting the need, until her body couldn't help itself. With one giant spasm, her body arched beneath him, gripping his cock tightly as her orgasm tore through her, bringing him over the edge as well. He sank down on her, his face pressed into her neck, shuddering as his orgasm ripped through him.

As Abby dragged in ragged breaths, her scent—lemony-citrus mixed with the heady spice of her passion—and her arms came around him, holding him close.

Then it hit him.

Twice he'd come inside her. Unprotected.

"Shit," he muttered into her shoulder. Then he lifted up to stare at her once more. Worry filled her eyes. "I'm sorry, Abby."

"What for? I don't think I could survive anything more intense than that."

He gave her half a grin. "Neither can I. No, I'm sorry I didn't protect you."

Confusion quickly replaced her worried look. "Protect me from what?"

"Abby. We didn't use a condom. Either time."

She blushed when she smiled. "It's okay. I've been on the pill for years."

"Good." He kissed her softly, slid out of her and rolled to his side, pulling her up against him. "Next time I promise to use a condom, extra protection wouldn't be a bad idea." Especially since the way his body was already warming to the idea of another go round, he doubted he could keep his hands off her.

"You're pretty sure there's going to be a next time, aren't you?" she murmured against his chest, but he could hear the humor in her voice. He waited a few minutes, listening to the rhythm of her breathing as she fell asleep.

As he drew the covers over them, he faced the truth. Five years ago he'd resisted the need for her, knew just how hot things would be between them, even if she'd had no clue. They'd both been too young, had too much to learn. He'd pushed her away and kept his distance. But now? Now that he'd tasted her, held her, claimed her body with his... *Hell, yes there'd be a next time.*

Resting his cheek against the top of her head, he wrapped his arms around her.

But first, he had to keep her safe.

* * * * *

The sound of the garage door motor grinding woke him with a start. The sun was just coming up. Grey streaks of light filtered into the room.

Luke slipped away from Abby's warm body, drawing the covers over her. He slipped on his black jeans and threw on his T-shirt then grabbed his gun from the holster by the bedside. Barefooted, he hurried quietly to the garage door and waited, willing his heart to slow as he focused, ready to take down the intruder.

The knob turned and the door opened inward. A large body with a hoodie covering his head and hiding his face entered the nearly dark kitchen, and set a bag on the table.

Luke moved in behind him and pressed a gun to the back of the man's shoulders. "Don't move."

"I hope you don't plan to use that thing. Your mama's grown to like me, kid."

"Dammit, Frank," he said, lowering the weapon and moving away from his friend. "What the hell are you doing here?"

"Nice to see you, too. I told you once I'd wrapped up what I was working on, I'd be up to help you." Castello shrugged out of his coat and hung it on the back of a barstool at the island separating the kitchen from the great room.

"I didn't say I needed help, just some place safe to stay. And what happened to the twenty-four hours you were going to give me?"

"The twenty-four hours was for notifying the family you were in trouble, not a time limit for me to come check things out. Decided you might be in over your head, what with a female witness."

"She's not a witness."

"Your female partner."

"Didn't say that either." For some reason Castello's presence made him feel like he was back in high school defending his actions to his older brothers and parents when he'd came home with a busted lip and the beginnings of a black eye. He'd done nothing wrong. Hadn't started the fight. Simply stepped in when two bullies were picking on a friend known as the school geek.

"Oh, that's right, a fellow agent." A smile lifted the corners of Castello's lips a mere millimeter. "A very sexy fellow agent."

Luke looked over his shoulder.

Shit. There stood Abby in the doorway to the bedroom. All she wore was his sweatshirt from the night before, her long, bare legs visible beneath. Hair tousled, looking very much like a woman who'd been thoroughly made love to, except for the gun in her hand, pointed at the floor. Fighting the urge to groan, Luke turned back to face his friend. The light in the other man's face triggered the need to protect his woman and Luke moved to stand in between them.

"Yes. A fellow agent."

"You must be Abby," Frank called out.

"Abigail. And you're Marshal Castello?" Abby walked over, stepped around Luke and extended her hand. "Thanks for letting us use your safe house. It was very kind of you."

Luke wanted to roll his eyes. Kind wasn't exactly a word he'd ever use for the taciturn Marshal. He sort of grew on you—like black mold.

"Please, call me Frank," Castello said, his face crinkling with a smile as he shook her hand. "Anything to keep a lovely lady like yourself safe."

Abby actually blushed.

Luke wanted to cold-cock Castello and tell him to let go of *his* woman. Which was stupid, as she wasn't his in any form or fashion, but it didn't stop him from wanting to go all caveman over her.

She stepped back, looking down at the gun in her hand. "I'll just go put this away," she said then turned and headed back to the bedroom.

"Abby," Luke said, stopping her. He handed her his gun. "Give us a minute, okay?"

She turned her head to the side as if trying to understand what he was saying, then glanced from him to Castello and back again. Finally, she nodded, her blush spreading. "Sure. I'll put on something a little more appropriate."

Any other time he'd love seeing her padding around the place in only his shirt, but not now and not with Castello eyeing her long legs. Luke watched her go until the door closed behind her. When he turned back around, Castello stood leaning back against the island counter, arms crossed over his chest, his face back to its usual granite look, except for the one eyebrow he'd lifted in Mr. Spock fashion.

"Don't say anything," Luke muttered as he stalked past him to the coffeemaker. For a few minutes the only sound was him scooping coffee from the container he'd found in the cupboard, pouring in water and hitting the on button. He stood watching the hot liquid drip into the pot, his shoulders burning from the tension building in them. "I know what you're thinking."

"Oh, you do?"

The quiet comment irritated Luke more than if his friend had yelled at him like either of his older brothers would've. It also took some of the anger out of him. Slowly, he turned, leaning his hips back against the counter and folded his arms in the same manner as Frank's and returned the stony look.

"Yes. You'd tell me it was a mistake," he said, finally breaking the silence.

Castello just stared at him.

"You'd tell me I need to be focused on the case and not Abby."

Nothing.

"That she's untried in the field and that it's my job to keep her safe, even from me."

Nada.

"That it's unprofessional to sleep with my partner, another agent, and possibly a potential target."

Still nothing.

"Aren't you going to say anything?" he growled.

"You finished?"

Luke surged off the counter behind him and moved to grip the island counter across from Castello. "Yes."

"While those are all valid points, it wasn't what I was going to say."

"It wasn't?" Luke said, then narrowed his eyes. "What were you going to say?"

"That's one fine woman and your mama's going to love her, so you'd best be prepared to protect her ass at all cost."

Luke's jaw dropped a moment, denial frozen on his lips. Then he closed his mouth and gave a nod, reading in the other man's words and face what he already knew. No matter what happened in this case, protecting Abby had just become his lifelong mission.

CHAPTER 11

Abigail secured her weapon before giving into her curiosity and pressing her ear to the door to try and hear whatever might be going on in the other room. Low male voices sounded on the other side of the bedroom door. She couldn't quite make out what they were saying, or rather, what Luke, who seemed to be doing all the talking, was saying.

She quickly dressed in her jeans, bra and Luke's sweatshirt once more, then pulled her hair into a serviceable ponytail. Taking Luke's holster off the bedpost with her, she pressed her ear to the door and listened again.

No more words sounded from the main room. Abigail wasn't sure if that was a good thing or not. The way Luke and Castello had been staring at each other—like they meant to jump into a ring and go forty rounds of face pummeling—she'd expected at least yelling, if not bloodshed. But they'd simply talked. Now there seemed to be a lull and the tempting aroma of coffee drifted into the room.

With a deep breath, she eased the door open. "Is it safe to come out now?"

Both men eased their stances.

"We're done." Luke waved her to come over.

"For now," Castello said, giving Luke another pointed look, then pulling out a barstool for her. "Have a seat, Abigail."

Luke put a mug of hot, black coffee in front of her then took the holster from her. He slipped it on and slid his gun in its place. "No cream and I haven't found sugar."

"I'm sure I'll live." She smiled, taking the warm cup in her hands.

Castello pulled out another barstool and sat next to her. Taking the coffee mug Luke offered him, he turned to study her. Abigail tried not to flinch under his hard stare as she sipped her coffee.

"So, tell me what mess Edgars dragged you into."

"Luke didn't drag me into anything. I'm afraid it's the other way around. I dragged him into this."

The Marshal arched on eyebrow at her. "How?"

"I requested the local Treasury field agent meet me at my friend's house and Luke just happened to be the nearest one." She took another fortifying sip, knowing he was going to ask her to go back to the scene at Brianna's condo.

"Why?"

"Her friend had some mysterious information she

wanted Abby to look into," Luke said, his voice tinged with anger. "Only, we didn't get to talk to her. Instead, Abby walked into a bloody crime scene—no friend, no information, and quite possibly a target on her back."

She set her mug down with a thud. Brianna was her only friend and she'd be damned if she'd listen to him disparage her, even if there was a chance he was right. "You don't know that."

"The tail on Jeffers says I'm pretty damn close."

"That tail could've been from some other case." She rose from her seat and pointed a finger at him.

Luke gripped the other side of the island counter and leaned in across from her. "Last night's crime scene pretty much says I'm right."

She opened her mouth to argue when his cell phone rang.

He snatched it up. "Jeffers?" he asked as he stalked off to the bedroom.

The man was infuriating.

Abigail inhaled and exhaled slowly, willing her heart to slow to a more moderate pace.

"He has a way of getting under your skin."

She turned to look at the Marshal. "Sometimes I just want to punch him."

"So do I, but it won't help things." Castello took another drink of coffee and patted her barstool again. "How about you bring me up to speed on the situation and your friend's disappearance?"

Taking her seat again, she forcefully blocked the

images of Brianna's home from invading her mind and looked at the situation clinically—like a trained agent should. "Luke was right. When we got to Brianna's townhouse it was a mess. Nearly everything torn, broken or overturned. A huge bloodstain on the living room floor and a bloody path to the door. All indications she'd been tortured and taken against her will. Whoever took Brie was looking for something. Quite possibly whatever it was she wanted to see me about."

Castello nodded. "And Luke thinks she probably told them about you or they were watching her place to see if anyone showed up."

Abigail inhaled and exhaled on a heavy sigh. "Yes. But despite what he thinks of my friend, she wouldn't put me in danger. Not intentionally."

"That's the point. It might not have been her intention to put you in danger, but she has. If these people aren't afraid to torture and kidnap her for whatever information she might have on them, they will have no qualms about coming after anyone they think she's passed it to."

"Like me."

"Like you." Luke's hand settled on her shoulders and he gave them a squeeze before moving back around the counter. He'd thrown on a sweater and shoes. "That was Jeffers. He's two blocks away."

"And Jeffers is…?" Castello asked.

"Police detective assigned to Britany's missing

persons case."

"Brianna," Abigail corrected automatically, then looked at Castello. "He can't get her name right ever. Detective Jeffers wanted to talk to us after he checked out the crime scene from last night."

"Last night?"

They took a few minutes to fill him on the horrific things they'd found at the warehouse and how they'd connected it to Brianna's disappearance. The Marshal didn't say much, just listened and nodded, even when Luke skimmed briefly over the charred bodies he'd found. At least this time Luke hadn't gone pale when talking about them. Abigail smiled inwardly. Maybe she'd helped a little with that.

When they finished their story, Castello pulled out his phone.

"Who are you calling?" Luke asked.

"Kirk Patrick, we're going to need some supplies. I'll be staying until this is cleared up."

* * * * *

A hard knock sounded on the front door.

Drawing his gun once more, Luke went to answer it. His peripheral vision caught Castello moving between Abby and the line of sight to the door, his gun in hand. Maybe having the big Marshal stay would be a good thing. Two people protecting Abby had to be better than one, even if he wanted to be the one at her side, not

Frank.

One quick look through the peephole showed the police detective standing on the front stoop, looking none too happy. In his hand he held a folder.

"Jeffers," he said, opening the door and stepping aside.

"Edgars, I've been up all night and not in the mood for your bullshit. I want some answers," Jeffers said as he stalked past, then froze. "And who the hell is this?"

Luke closed the door and holstered his gun once more. He slapped the policeman on the shoulder as he headed back into the kitchen. "U.S. Marshal Frank Castello. Come have some coffee, detective, and you'll get all the answers we have."

Jeffers and Castello shook hands, then the detective pulled out another barstool on the other side of Abby, setting the file folder in front of him on the counter. "Ma'am. I hope you got some sleep last night."

"I imagine we got a little more than you did," she said, giving him a brief smile.

Luke resisted the urge to reach across the counter and jerk the detective out of his chair. Abby smiling at other men really shouldn't irritate him, but it did. Instead he served the cop a hot mug of coffee. "Sorry, no sugar or cream."

"Black's fine." He took a long drink. "We just finished processing the whole scene. Probably won't get much sleep when I do get a chance. Got to tell you that's the first time I'd seen bodies in that condition.

Gonna take a while to get out of my head."

"I can imagine," she said.

Jeffers cocked his head sideways. "I thought you saw them."

"Not me. Only Luke did."

Jeffers gave him a speculative glance.

"She didn't need to have that memory in her head." That was all the explanation he intended to give on that one. "What questions do you want us to answer?"

The detective took a long drink of his coffee then nodded. "So, why don't we start with what you two were doing at the warehouse last night? I imagine it has something to do with tracing Ms. Mathews' cell phone like we discussed?"

"We'd gotten her cell to ping off three towers, but just as we triangulated the phone's general direction the signal went dead."

"And you didn't think to let me know?"

Luke shrugged. "I made a judgment call."

"You said none of those bodies we found were Ms. Mathews?"

"Brianna is only a few inches shorter than me," Abby added. "Luke said the…women…were all petite, so no, they couldn't have been her." She shot up out of her chair and headed to the bedroom, coming back with a baggie containing a cotton swab covered in dark red. She handed it to the detective. "I swabbed the blood around the overturned chair in the main room."

He handed it back to her. "Our crime scene people

did the same thing. They're already running it against the samples taken at Ms. Mathews' place."

"Oh. That's good. I swabbed it before I knew Luke intended to call you." she said, her face turning pink as she slipped the baggie into her jeans pocket.

Luke fought the desire to pull her in his arms and order the others out.

Dammit. He didn't like anyone making her feel incompetent. "Did *your* people find anything useful?"

Jeffers lifted a brow in response to the sarcasm Luke hadn't been hiding in his voice. "We're running DNA on the bodies found in the back, but you know as well as I do that's going to take weeks if not months and only if they're in a database somewhere."

"So, you have no more clue than we do who they might be," Luke said.

"Actually, I may." Jeffers opened the file on the counter and pulled out five pictures, all women all in their mid-twenties to mid-thirties. "I've been working a cold case on the side. All these women are local. All have gone missing in the past five years or so."

"Shit. Why didn't you tell us this before?" Luke demanded.

"Except for the fact they're women and missing, nothing about Ms. Mathews' case and these are similar. These women have no family, no friends, no one looking for them."

Abby sat staring at the pictures, one at a time. Luke knew what she was doing. She was taking her own mental snapshots so they'd forever be locked in her mind.

"Don't," he said, covering them with his hands.

"I have to." She looked up at him, her eyes begging him to understand. Then she laid her hand on top of his. "Someone should remember them."

Staring at her, knowing this meant something to her, tore at his heart. He clenched his jaw, breathing heavily, then moved his hand.

"What's going on?" Jeffers asked. "Do you know them?"

"No. She's never seen them before," Luke answered for her.

"Luke?" Castello looked from him to Abby then back again.

"She's like Nicky, Frank. Remembers everything she sees. Like a photograph. The images are with her forever."

"Shit." The Marshal muttered.

"That's why she didn't see the bodies last night." Jeffers sat back in his barstool. Both men looked a little stunned.

"Is that why she came to see her friend?" Jeffers asked after a moment. "Did Ms. Mathews have something for Abigail to see?"

"We don't know," Abby answered, closing the file of pictures. "She said she wanted to talk to me about some oddities she'd found at Hollister-Klein. When I asked what, she said she'd tell me when I got to her place.

Only when I got there, it was exactly as you saw the other night."

"She gave you no clue?" Jeffers pushed.

"That's what she said." Luke bit out the words. Abby might be a novice agent, but she wouldn't lie.

Laying her hand on his, Abby got him to look at her, understanding in her eyes. Then she turned back to Jeffers. "No, she didn't say any more than she wanted to talk. I assumed that since I work for the Treasury department and she is an accountant, whatever *oddities* she might've found were financial in nature."

"Did you see anything in her townhouse that might've been what she wanted to discuss?" Castello asked.

Abby closed her eyes. Luke held up his hand when Jeffers started to ask what she was doing. He knew she was pulling out each image, even the ones around the bloody stains in the carpeting. Analyzing each one. When she opened her eyes again, she shook her head.

"Nothing out of the ordinary. Her datebook, which I've already recreated, bills, old newspapers, a book of Sudoku puzzles. No files of any kind. No ledgers or spreadsheets."

"Computer?" Castello always used as few words as possible.

Again Abby shook her head. "Nothing was on the immediate screen but a dating website. I haven't recreated her search history, but I did take a look at it."

Luke searched the drawers, coming up with a piece

of paper and a pen. "Take a minute and write down what you saw. We'll look it up and see if it gives us any clues."

"Got a picture of the friend?" Castello asked.

"Abby?"

Luke looked at her, but she kept working on the list as she answered. "In my bag in the bedroom."

He retrieved the framed picture and handed it to Castello, who immediately whistled.

"She got that a lot," Abby said.

"And she took advantage of it," Luke muttered.

Abby set down the pen, narrowing her eyes at him. "How can you say that? You don't know her."

"Come on, Abby. Open your eyes. Bethanne had dozens of pictures of herself all over that townhouse. And the ones with the men? None of them had the same guy in it."

"*Brianna* liked people." She shoved her chair back and stood almost nose-to-nose with him.

"Men."

"Yes, men. And they liked her."

"Probably not as much as she liked herself. I bet if she had a psych evaluation, they'd find she was a manipulative narcissist."

"I can't believe you're judging her solely on her looks. She was my friend." Abby poked him in the chest with her finger.

"And she manipulated you like she did everyone else."

"No, she didn't. I knew her. Deep down inside we were just the same." She poked him again, her eyes snapping with indignation and her cheeks flushed.

He grabbed her finger, then wrapped his hand around her fist. "No you weren't. You might've both been orphans, but you don't use people. You never have. And you certainly wouldn't have put your friend in danger without letting them know what or who the danger was."

The fire died in her eyes, quickly replaced with the glistening of unshed tears. "And neither would she."

The conviction in her words and the despair in her voice broke his heart. He pulled her in against his chest. Castello, Jeffers and the case be damned, he wasn't going to see her hurting and not hold her.

* * * * *

What kind of place was this? Huddled on a bare mattress on the floor of what looked like a basement, Brianna tried to adjust her eyes to the dim light filtering in from the small window above her. The last clear thing she remembered before waking up here was Dylan coming into the room where they'd been torturing her, grabbing the cell phone and removing the battery.

"Who were you trying to call, Brianna? Someone at the Abbey where you left the files?"

Her mind must be muddled. He thought Abby was a

place? Like a church? He didn't know who she was? Abby was still safe. She hadn't told him. Thank God she listed Abby under her hated middle name Prudence.

"Well, they'll be too late to find you now."

And then he hit her in the jaw.

A few times she woke in the back of the van, jostled when it hit a bump or tracks, but not long enough to see who had her or where they were taking her. She had a vague memory of being carried over someone's shoulders down some steps. Must've been when they brought her to this basement.

Was it morning? Or still night? How long had she been here?

Muffled voices sounded above her. Was it Dylan? One of his men? The man with the knife who'd sliced the skin on her arms open? Or one of those thugs who'd beaten her and burned her with cigarettes?

A tremor ran through her. She didn't think she could take any more. If they came at her again, she'd probably tell them what they wanted to know.

You're stronger than you think. Abby's voice sounded in her head.

Abby.

The only person she could ever depend on. She couldn't let them know she was a person and not a church. She'd dragged her naïve friend into this. If anything happened to sweet Abby, it would be her fault. But she'd needed to tell someone what she'd found out. Someone she could count on to do something. Someone she trusted.

Had Abby found the flash drive? She'd had to hide it quickly once she realized she'd been followed. Surely Abby would've figured out where. Or the code. Abby would've found it, would've known what it was when she studied it. Then she would've use it to crack her work files, wouldn't she? Please, God, she didn't want to have suffered all this for nothing.

Heavy footsteps sounded above.

What did they plan to do with her now?

Can't take much more. Wish they'd just kill me and get it over with.

Did she really want to die? And for what? To save women she didn't even know? Damn her perpetual need to stick her nose into things.

"Your curiosity will be the death of you, Brianna," Sister Compassionatta said, staring down at her where she sat in the principal's office.

"But I only wanted to see—" She started when the ruler landed on her knuckles. She resisted pulling them back, as she knew from experience the sister would inflict more punishment if she did so.

"I do not need to know what you hoped to see in the boys' locker room, miss. It's sinful and you will not appease your sinful, willful, curious nature while you remain at the Sisters of the Sacred Heart, do I make myself clear?"

She'd agreed and made the proper promise not to tempt fate again. If only she'd heeded the warning and learned her lesson, she might not be in this predicament. Worse part, aside from the pain and eventual death? Damn Sister C was going to be right. Her curiosity was going to get her killed this time.

Voices again.

She strained to hear what they were saying. Wait. There were female voices mixed in with the rumbling sounds of men. Had they taken her to one of the houses she'd managed to map out? The houses where unusual shipments had been sent? Houses where she suspected the women from the files had gone. Did they mean to make her part of this house?

Oh, God. There was a fate worse than death.

Slavery.

CHAPTER 12

Frank watched the pair fight then Luke pull Abigail in tight.

The guy was a goner.

The moment he'd gotten Luke's call yesterday, Frank had a feeling things were more complicated than the kid let on. Serious wasn't part of Luke's usual act. Cocky, irritating, a wise-ass—he had those in spades. So when he heard that Edgars' my-woman's-in-trouble-and-I-have-to-protect-her voice coming out of the youngest brother, he'd made the decision to come find out what was really going on. And what did it have to do with the secret investigation that Luke was doing for his older brother Dave, into Senator Klein?

He hadn't expected kidnapping, torture, and charred bodies, although given the last time he helped his adopted family save one of their own there'd been bombs and hostages, so why should any of this surprise him?

Giving the couple a moment to pull it together, he

lifted the file Jeffers had brought in with him. "So tell me about these women. How do they fit into our case?"

The detective looked relieved to have something else to focus on, too. "I'm not sure how they're connected, but if any of the bodies turns out to be one of these women and Ms. Mathews' blood was at the scene, they're connected somehow."

"If no one was looking for them, who reported them missing?"

"Employers, landlords, acquaintances. But no one really pressed the issue. Until my niece came to me about her friend." Jeffers lifted the picture of a plain-looking, mousy blonde. "Her name's Casey Timmons. She and my niece worked together. When Casey didn't show up for work for a week and no one heard anything from her, the boss assumed she'd quit or left town. My niece didn't think it sounded like something her friend would do, so she went to her apartment to check on Casey. Somehow my niece convinced the landlord to let her in. All of Casey's belongings were still there. It was as if she just…vanished."

"Was the apartment trashed like Brianna's?" Abigail asked, coming back to the bar.

Frank glanced at his friend, who stood behind Abigail's chair and returned his look stonily. Yep, Luke was in Edgars-family-protect mode.

"No. It was pristine. Nothing out of place. No missing computer, laptop or iPad. I promised I'd look into her disappearance, but really couldn't find anything."

"How'd you connect the other women?"

Jeffers shrugged. "Dogged determination. I like a good mystery. Casey's disappearance was so complete, I started wondering if there were any others who had slipped through the cracks. All five disappeared over a period of three years. When I started looking closer, there were similarities in backgrounds—no families, few friends, low-level positions at work."

Frank laid out all the pictures. "All rather ordinary looking. Not ugly, but not stand-out pretty, either."

"No, they would've been called spinsters a hundred years ago," Abigail said. "Wallflowers."

The detective nodded. "I thought the same thing, which lead me to thinking what else they might have in common. None of them had memberships to the same gym, if they had one at all. None frequented the same bars or restaurants on a regular basis. Those with church ties were on the fringe and none of the same denomination."

"But you found something," Luke said over Abigail's shoulder.

"I did." Jeffers pulled out one of the papers in the file behind the pictures. "What if they wanted to meet someone, but didn't feel comfortable doing it out in public because they'd blend in with the surroundings?"

"That can be very depressing. Nothing worse than going out to try to meet someone and ending up by yourself."

Abigail stared at the pictures. Frank blinked at her comment then exchanged puzzled looks with the detective and Luke. How could she have such empathy for the women? No way would she ever fade into the background. Or had she—before Luke and this case drew her out of the shadows?

When no one spoke, she lifted her gaze to them. "What? You don't think being taller than most boys in school, smarter than most of the class and pretty much a math geek didn't have me sitting on the bleachers during dances or in the corner at parties? Working for the Treasury department hasn't exactly helped the reputation, either. I've spent many a night alone in a bar or restaurant, simply because I didn't want to stay home, but had no date."

Frank swallowed hard, his mouth suddenly dry from her confession. Luke settled his hands on her shoulders and squeezed, he, too, unsettled.

"Well, yeah, anyway," Jeffers stammered as he laid the paper out for the others to see. "That got me to thinking. What if they tried to do a little shopping at home?"

"Shopping at home?" What the hell was the cop talking about?

"An on-line dating service." Luke said. "That's why you asked us yesterday about whether Babette had been a subscriber to one."

"Brianna," Abigail automatically corrected him. Frank wanted to comment on the name errors, but it seemed to be some odd game the two were playing. "And no, she wouldn't need to use one."

Frank pulled up the list of URLs Abigail had written down earlier, reading down the list. A number of the sites were dating services. "Well, she certainly was looking at them."

Jeffers pointed to the eleventh line of the list. "That's one of the sites all my missing women frequented."

"Do you think your friend learned something about these sites? Would that be why she was searching them?" Frank asked.

Abigail shrugged. "She could've been, but why call me? And what would it have to do with her job or whatever it was she wanted to tell me? I wish she'd left me some clue as to where the information was."

"Maybe she tried to send it some other way. If she's as smart as you say she is, wouldn't she have made a separate file from Hollister-Klein's financials and posted them email?" Frank said.

"No. More than likely it was on a flash drive. Easily copied too, small enough to hide somewhere to get it out of the building," Luke said. He looked at Abigail in question.

She shook her head. "I didn't see a flash drive anywhere."

They both looked to Jeffers.

"Nope," he said, holding his hands out. "No flash drive was listed on the evidence list from the townhouse."

"Emails can be traced by the company. Many corporations have spyware for employees' emails just so they can track them." Luke pulled up his laptop and started clicking away. "But she might've set up a dummy file buried in some other files with a personal code on it."

Screens flew by as they watched. Abigail had to admit he knew his way around the internet and computer security systems.

"There. That's the one," he finally said, pointing to a folder inside a folder marked hairstyles.

"How do you know that's it?" she asked.

"Because it doesn't belong and when I try to enter it this happens," he pressed the enter key and a yellow triangle with an exclamation mark popped up. "Problem is, I'll bet your girl has it rigged so that if anyone enters the wrong code the whole thing deletes."

"That doesn't do us much good, if we don't know the code then," Jeffers said.

"Sudoku," Abigail said, her mind already pulling up the image she'd discarded as useless.

"Sudoku?" Frank looked at her.

"There was one on top of her day planner. I just assumed it was one she'd finished. She was addicted to any games involving numbers." She stared off into space and studied the picture of the puzzle closer. Then she noticed the odd pattern. "There's numbers in all the boxes, but the numbers don't solve the puzzle. No two numbers are supposed to repeat in the boxes or the same vertical or horizontal lines."

"What are you seeing, Abby?"

"Double numbers, one in each box." She looked at Luke, his fingers poised to type. "Six, four, seven, three, nine, eight, two, six again."

He typed them in, his finger hovering over the enter button. "You're sure?"

"Yes. I told you she's brilliant when it comes to numbers."

Without questioning her further, he gave her a nod and hit enter.

The screen flickered, the file disappearing and Abigail sucked in her breath. What if she'd been wrong? What if she'd just erased all the information to find Brianna?

The screen flashed again and up popped up pages and pages of spread sheets.

"Whoa!" Frank leaned in closer.

"Oh my God," she whispered.

"Damn, she must've copied the company's entire financials," Jeffers said.

"Yep, and it's going to take a while to decipher it all and figure out what she found." He looked up at her. He was right. It would take both of them to wade through this mess.

A knock sounded on the front door and the group stilled. Luke took up position between Abigail and the door while Frank pulled his weapon from his shoulder holster and headed for the door, Jeffers to the other side.

Frank looked through the peephole and shook his head at the others. He resisted the urge to grin as he opened the door. "It's just Kirk Patrick."

Kirk stopped just inside the door, seeing guns in both Edgars and Jeffers' hands still trained on him. "Hey, don't be shootin' the delivery man."

Frank nodded and the others lowered their weapons as he holstered his own. "'Bout damn time, kid. I should shoot you myself. I'm starving."

"Well, you could've eaten the frozen stuff in the freezer like most normal peeps, old man," the kid said, sauntering past with his arms full of groceries. He looked Abigail up and down as he sat the bags on the counter. "Hello, pretty lady."

"Keep your eyes to yourself, unless you want to lose them," Luke growled out, stepping between them.

Kirk tilted his head and eyed the gun Luke had replaced in his shoulder holster, moving back and hands out in submission. "Hey, man. No disrespect meant."

The kid had major street smarts and common sense enough not to mess with a man armed like Luke. He also read people well and knew an alpha protecting his turf when he saw it. Those skills were the reasons Castello had plucked Kirk off the streets and set him up as his caretaker on this unit. He'd set the kid and his grandma up in a unit two doors down, with a few rules for Kirk. He maintained the Caddy and made it available when Frank called. He kept watch over this unit, kept it clean and the freezer stocked. He stayed out of the gangs, kept his grades up and had a part-time job working for a caterer. In return, Frank paid the rent and utilities on both places and had helped secure a scholarship for Kirk to go to college. Hadn't surprised him in the least when Kirk decided to major in criminal justice.

"What do I owe you?" Frank said as he started unloading the food into the fridge, setting the creamer to the side.

"That's right. It's all about the green stuff." Kirk pulled out the sales receipt and handed it over. "Total came to forty-five-sixty-two, but I think you owe me an extra twenty for making me get this sissy stuff for your coffee." Kirk held up the French vanilla creamer.

"Kid's got a point, Castello," Luke chimed in. "What kind of cop drinks frou-frou crap like this?"

"The kind that can shoot your ass before you can make it down the street." Frank took out his wallet and paid Kirk, adding in the twenty anyways for a tip. "How's your grandmother?"

"Nana is good. She's been making me help her and the other church ladies take soup and sandwiches to the homeless, which is way better than having to drive her to the beauty parlor, you know?" He glanced down at the pictures of the missing women on the table, stopping to stare at them. "This the case you're working?"

Luke started turning the pages over. "Not for your

eyes, Kirk F." But the kid stopped him before he could turn the last one.

"I'm just askin' coz she looks familiar." Kirk picked up the photo and studied it.

"You know her?" Abby asked.

"She looks like this girl I saw over at a party my boss catered last month. You know, real swanky party for some rich dude."

Jeffers leaned in and tapped the photo of Casey. "You saw *this* girl at a party?"

"Well, she looks like the girl, only a plain version of her. The girl I saw looked like a supermodel—short but blinged out to get attention. Like a working girl, you know what I mean? In fact a lot of the women at that party looked like high-paid…" he glanced at Abigail a moment, "…escorts."

"Who was the party for?" Luke asked and Frank recognized the speculative look in his eye.

"I didn't get the name and it was held at a private club, but there was some serious dudes in that room."

"Senator Klein one of them?"

"White-haired dude, tall and skinny? Stands like he's a general or something?" Kirk said.

"That would be him."

"Yeah, he was there. Along with his son."

"Greg?"

"Nah, I heard someone call him Dylan. He's the one the girl in the picture was with."

"Son of a bitch," Jeffers growled and before anyone

knew it, he had Luke by the shirtfront, pushed up against the refrigerator. "You knew about this senator's involvement with missing girls and you've kept it to yourself?"

Frank held a hand out to stop Kirk from interfering. Might do the hacker-genius some good to get a little sense knocked into him.

Stunned, Abigail watched the fury etched on Jeffers' face.

"How many more women were you going to let them take before you passed the information on?" He shoved Luke harder against the fridge. Despite the anger in Luke's face, he wasn't resisting the detective's attack.

"I. Didn't. Know," was all he said.

"Bastard! Don't you lie to me. Three women are dead and you could've stopped it."

Jeffers shoved him again and this time, Luke moved —so quick you would've missed it if you'd looked away. He held the detective in a choke hold.

"Luke," Frank said, finally moving to stand in front of the pair. "Take it easy, kid."

"Back off, Castello. He started it." Luke looked around at Jeffers. "I said, I didn't know. Not 'til just this minute, when all the pieces started coming together." He paused and seemed to squeeze the other man's neck a little tighter. "Now, do you want to listen or am I going to have to take you down?"

"Listen," Jeffers managed to choke out.

"Good." Luke released his hold and the pair stepped apart.

Abigail looked from one to the other, both breathing heavy and enough tension between them that one wrong word and she was sure they'd be at each other's throats again. Her own heart pounded in her chest. She'd never seen that kind of male aggression except on television or at the movies, and certainly not in a confined space of the kitchen. It was way scary up close and personal.

"Wow, dudes, that was...intense," Kirk said in awe beside her.

"You. Sit." Luke pointed at the teen, the intensity in his eyes suggested Kirk obey. "I'm going to need details."

Kirk sat as Luke went into the bedroom, returning with his tablet-laptop.

"Jeffers," he said, opening the computer and running his fingers quickly over the keyboard. "When you started investigating these missing women, what was your gut instinct?"

"That I had a serial killer on my hands."

"What made you think that? There were no dead bodies."

The policeman leaned his hands on the counter, his head down a moment and he took a deep breath. "I had women of about the same age and body type, loners, no one really missed them when they went missing."

"You had an MO and a gut suspicion the cases were all connected. Classic signs of a serial perpetrator."

Luke kept typing as they talked.

"Right. But if this kid," Jeffers pointed at Kirk, "saw Casey alive, then it's not a serial killer I'm looking for."

"No. What I think we're looking at is something just as sinister. Maybe more so." Luke flipped his computer around. If you take your MO for the missing women, plug them into all the missing-women reports from major cities in the Midwest alone, this is what pops up."

Everyone stared at the page as Luke scrolled down, showing name after name.

"Dear God, there are hundreds of names!" Abigail whispered. "How can that be?"

"A few here, a few there, none too close in any one area for a pattern to really occur."

"How did you get these?" Jeffers asked. "I couldn't find any national database."

"There isn't one," Castello said. "Edgars is the black sheep in his law-abiding family. He's a hacker."

"Dude's a fed and a hacker?" Kirk said, awe written all over his face.

Luke took a moment to focus on Kirk. "When it looked like I was headed down the wrong path, my brother Dave set me straight. Said I could spend my life in jail, because I *would* get caught, and no more computers ever, or I could take my skills and use them to help people."

"So, if it's not a serial killer, what are we looking at here?" Jeffers said, redirecting them back to the case.

Luke looked at Abigail, sympathy and compassion in

his hazel eyes. "Human trafficking."

She shook her head, not breaking the connection in their gaze despite the pain in her chest. "Not just that. We've found a sexual slavery ring."

Luke hated to see the pain in Abby's eyes and the pallor of her skin, but she was too smart not to put the pieces together just as he had. "It doesn't mean she's part of it yet."

"If she's not dead yet, it's only a matter of time."

He reached across the island and took her hand in his, willing her some of his strength. "No, it's not. They don't know we're looking for her. This bunch has been doing this so long, they've grown cocky, as evidenced by them leaving three bodies almost out in the open. They think of her as just another woman with no one to care about what happens to her. But Billie Jo is different."

"Brianna." She smiled, a shaky one, but a smile nonetheless. "She's different because she's got me."

"And us." He gripped her hand tighter and looked around the room at the others. Each man, including Kirk F. Patrick, nodded their heads, a look of pure determination in their eyes. "But I do think we need to move fast. After the police raid on that car repair warehouse last night, our criminals may get a little nervous. You good now?" he asked Abby.

She squeezed his hand and nodded to let him know she was okay. "Where do we start?"

"You pull up each missing girl case on this list, study

each file and memorize the face." He held up his hand when she opened her mouth. "It's a lot, but if a State senator is mixed up in this, we have to assume some police officials may be, too. I'd rather not use official channels to get the files right now. Also look for patterns of any kind."

"So, I'm the filing system," she said, but there was less tension in her voice this time.

"A very sexy filing system," he said, ignoring the groan and cough coming out of Kirk and Castello. "While you're doing that, I'm going to see what Kirk F. here can remember from that party."

"Not sure what else I can tell you, spy dude." The kid held up his hands, palms out. Despite the submissive action and Castello's faith in him, Luke wasn't buying Kirk's innocent act. He'd learned to read people from years of hanging out with his older brothers. Both cops said you could tell a person's true nature in their eyes. Kirk's pale-blue ones were sharp and intelligent. Innocent? Not buying it.

"You might know more than you think and the name's Luke Edgars," he said, then nodded to Abby. "That's Abby, but she prefers you call her Abigail." Abby was just for his use. "You know Castello and this is Detective Jeffers."

The kid nodded at each person, offering a smile to Abby that Luke had the bizarre urge to wipe off his face, especially when she returned it. "Focus, kid," he all but barked at Kirk, but he had the kid's attention.

"Let's start before you went to the party. Did your boss say where the party was?"

"Some new private club down on Shoreline Drive, built into one of those old estates. The driveway from the gate to the house was like two miles long."

"Well hidden from any prying eyes."

Kirk nodded. "From the street. But there was a great view of the lake. Saw it a couple of times when I had to circulate the canapés out on the patio and balcony."

Castello lifted one brow. "Canapés?"

Kirk gave a nonchalant shrug. "Hey, I have to tell guests what they are when I carry the trays out and about. Boss sort of insists on it."

"So like fancy cheese on crackers?"

"Nah, man. Paolo, my boss, has more style than that. He has these bruschetta that are like one-bite steak sandwiches, and then there's the lime shrimp wrapped in bacon. Great leftovers."

"There was an upper balcony, so at least two stories?" Luke asked, drawing him back into the more important facts and away from fancy food.

"Three. Like I said, mansion, dude. The serving staff wasn't allowed up to the third floor and only on the second floor balcony. Nowhere else. Even Paolo couldn't go into the basement where the wine cellar was. One of the house staff guys went. Lucky Paolo got what he wanted, since those guys looked like they drank the cheap stuff and wouldn't know a Merlot from a Chablis." An odd look crossed over Kirk's face. He'd remembered something.

"What?" Luke asked, his eyes meeting Castello's.

"You know, it was a little weird. I was making my third pass through the main room. All the guests had gathered there. Must've been a hundred or so."

"What's so odd about that?"

"Been doin' this about a year now, so I've been to a butt load of those auctions for charities and when the peeps gather together, that's when the bidding starts takin' place. Only, you usually see what they're auctioning off. The guy running the thing, some old, skinny, bald geezer would just call out a number. Then the men would raise a hand. No amounts was called out or nothing. Then after a few minutes, he'd say sold, then move on to another number."

"Fuck." Luke ran his hand over his face and stared at Abby, seeing her brain taking it all in.

"Dear God," she said, growing pale. "They were auctioning them off right there in the room."

"Son of a bitch," Castello said, shaking his head and his jaw clenching tight.

"But that's just it, Abby—I mean Abigail—I'm telling you there wasn't nothing there to auction off," Kirk said.

"Oh, they had something to auction off," Jeffers said, his voice deadly calm.

Kirk looked at the others, his brows drawn down and his head tilted slightly. "What?"

"The girls. They were on display the whole evening

and those bastards were selling them right in front of everyone." Abby gripped the side of the counter and tensed her shoulders. Eyes narrowed, she stared straight into Luke's eyes. "Treating those women like cattle. How dare they?"

Damn, she was pissed, like an avenging angel or an Amazon warrior. And wasn't he a bastard for thinking she looked sexier than ever? "We'll find them, sweetheart."

She jumped out of her seat, nearly toppling the barstool if Jeffers hadn't caught it. "I want them dead, Luke. Every one of them. Dead."

He held up his hands. "Whoa. You know our job is to take them in alive, unless of course, we can't help it."

"You try to take them alive. Any of them that get in between me and freeing those women I'm planning to shoot in the crotch." She stormed into the bedroom, slamming the door behind her.

Luke and the others stared in uncomfortable silence at the closed door, still reeling from the passionate threat she'd just made.

"She didn't mean—" Kirk started to say.

"Oh, she meant every word," Luke said.

"She's a trained agent for real?" Jeffers asked.

"Yep, same class as me."

"How accurate?" Castello asked.

"Only person to beat my scores."

Frank let out a low whistle and Luke couldn't agree more.

Abigail stalked the confines of the bedroom from the window to the door and back again, hands clenched in fists at her sides. Stopping at the bedside table she drew out her gun. She checked the clip and chamber then slid the clip back in place, finally placing her gun back in the drawer. As angry as she was, she didn't trust herself to have the weapon at easy access if one of those arrogant males in the other room dared to bother her right now.

"Men," she muttered pacing again. "Whoever put them in charge? Mucked things up since the beginning of time. Politics. Wars. Famines. Making slaves out of women."

She stopped at the window, crossing her arms across her torso and leaning her shoulder against the frame, she shivered and stared out onto the street.

Where was Brianna? Was she alive still? There was so much blood at the Brianna's home and then at the warehouse. Could she have survived all that torture only to be turned into a toy for some man's pleasure? Was fate getting even with her friend for all her years of using men?

"Men are so easy to manipulate, Abby." Brianna slipped on the stilettos and looked at her outfit in the full-length mirror.

"You're going to get hurt, Brie."

"You worry too much," she said, grabbing her bag and heading for the door.

"Dating two guys at once is bad enough, but now you're seeing the computer lab teaching assistant on top of it?"

"It's just a friendly dinner."

She looked at her friend's slinky black dress that revealed too much cleavage and leg to be anything less than a seduction waiting to happen. The guy wasn't going to know what hit him. "Yeah, right. Just a friendly dinner."

Brianna laughed. "If he decides to raise my grade above the two-point-eight it is now, I can't help it."

Strong arms wrapped around Abigail and pulled her back against Luke's solid frame, the heat from his body soothing the chill that had replaced her anger. She leaned her head against his neck, feeling the steady thrum of his pulse against her cheek. "After what I just said out there, I'm surprised you want to come within ten feet of me."

He chuckled. "The others think I've got brass balls for coming in here."

For a moment she allowed herself a smile, then set it aside. "I wasn't making an idle threat, Luke. When we find this scum—and I have every faith we will find them—I plan to make them pay for treating women like this, especially my friend."

"I'm not planning to stop you, unless it means you go to prison, sweetheart. I'm not into conjugal visits." He continued holding her and looking out the window. "You know, Brenda might be more important to these guys than just for what information she has."

"Brianna, and exactly what would that be?" she said turning her head to look at him.

"If they are selling women, she'd bring big bucks. Probably more than the other women."

"Because she's so beautiful. You know, she's more than a pretty face and sexy body. Inside she's smart and she does care about people." Abigail took a deep breath and tried to pull away, but he held her still.

"You're right, she is much more, but in this case her outer shell may be what's keeping her alive."

"And you're telling me this why?"

Releasing her, he stepped back as she turned, setting his hands on her shoulders. "Because I believe she's still alive and you should too. Planning to sell her as one of their sex slaves explains why they haven't killed her, but given what we've just found out, how big this slavery ring is, we need to focus and move fast—"

"—before they move her out of the area and we never find her," she finished his thought.

He nodded.

"What do you need me to do?"

"What you do best." He grinned that charming grin that used to irritate her in their training days. "Follow the money."

His words struck another sensitive spot with her, his belief that she was better suited behind a safe desk somewhere and not out in the field. Almost from the day they first met he'd voiced his opinion on that.

Apparently it hadn't changed.

As he turned to leave she grabbed his arm to stop him. "I need to know something."

"What?" He drew his brows down slightly, fixing his hazel eyes and all his attention on her. She ignored the way her body warmed at his intensity.

"When we were training in Georgia, why did you try so hard to make me fail?"

With a deep breath he looked around the room before settling his gaze on her once more, as if he were looking for the right words to say. "We don't have time to go into this now."

"I need to know why. You and I both know I ended up chained to a desk in Washington because of how you pointed out my analytical skills over my physical abilities to the trainers at every turn." She released his arm and bit the inside of her mouth to stem the burning of tears in her eyes. Dammit, she thought she'd gotten past this, but even five years later it still hurt.

"You know your analytical skills were miles ahead of the rest of the class, Abby. You have the kind of brain the agents in the field depend on to feed them accurate intel. I didn't think it should be wasted out in the field."

"Bullshit."

He blinked.

She'd shocked him. Heck, she'd shocked herself. She rarely cursed, but Luke seemed to bring out the worst in her.

"It's the truth."

"No, Mr. Hacker, you have great analytical skills, too, yet no one questioned you being a field agent." She poked him in the chest. "You targeted me from the moment we met. At first I thought it was because I was a woman."

"That's crap. I have no problem with women being field agents."

"I know." When she'd had time to think about it after their training ended, she'd acknowledged he treated all the recruits the same, male or female, everyone but her.

"You know? Then what is this paranoia of yours about?" His brows had drawn down as he studied her in puzzlement.

"I realized it wasn't female agents you had a problem with. Just me. What I want to know is, why?"

Silence filled the space between them and she was sure he wasn't going to answer. Then he said, "Because of the dream."

"What dream?" Now it was her turn to be confused.

"The night after we met I had a dream about you."

"About me? What kind of dream?"

"The kind of dream that wakes you up shaking and in a cold sweat." Suddenly he plopped down on the bed, his coloring pale as he stared out the window. He spoke as if he no longer saw her. "It was dark and we were on a mission together. We'd entered this run-down office complex and I lost sight of you. I kept calling your name, but you didn't answer. I kept turning corners, like in a maze. Then I saw you, lying face down on the floor. When I turned you over, you were dead."

She sat down beside him, slipping her hand in his. "It was just a dream, Luke."

"You don't understand," he said, and the tightness of his voice sent a chill through her.

"Help me to understand it, then." She grasped one of his hands in hers. Its coldness frightening her.

"I don't remember dreams. I'm sure I have them, I just *never* remember the details. They don't stick with me. No names, place, images, certainly not action or color. But every time I have this dream it's as if I'm there and it's real."

His words stole her breath for a moment.

"You've had this dream more than once?"

He nodded, lifting his hazel eyes to hers, fear deepening them until the flecks of gold were almost gone.

"How many times?" she whispered.

"Almost nightly when we were in training. It went away once you were in Washington and I was out in the field."

"You haven't had it since?" Some of the anxiety left her body.

"I had it the night before last in the hotel. Only…"

"Only?" The tension in his hands and face slammed her own fear back full force.

"It was different."

"How?"

Once more he stared off into space as if reliving the dream. "You were covered in blood. Your eyes cold and lifeless. And you talked to me."

"What did I say?"

"Why didn't you help me?"

CHAPTER 13

A knock sounded on his office door.

Senator Howard Klein looked up from the files he was studying for the next interstate highway bill to see his eldest son standing in the doorway. "Did you get our merchandise moving and our little problem taken care of?"

"Delivery of the trained merchandise to the supply houses down south is on its way with Snake and his men." Dylan shrugged, then sauntered in to slide into the leather chair across the mahogany desk. "Our other little problem still won't confess where she's hidden the flash drive, but I've got her secured in the big training house."

"You should've gotten rid of her permanently."

"You've seen what she looks like, sir. Once she's healed and trained properly, she'll bring a very hefty price. Well worth more than the trouble she's causing right now."

His son was right. The bottom line was finding

quality merchandise and the Mathews woman was a natural beauty—what they'd called a stunner when he was younger. That kind of high-end female flesh was hard to come by. "See that she doesn't cause any more trouble. The last thing we need is for anyone to get their hands on that information. Hollister says she copied locations of the houses throughout the Midwest area."

"She'll be docile and ready to please by the time I get done with her."

He fixed his gaze on Dylan and arched one brow. "How can you be sure when you haven't gotten her to give you the location of that drive yet?"

"I think it's time to change tactics. Like any good mare, the first thing is to break down her spirit. The torture by our men has been quite...brutal." His son smiled like a cobra watching its prey. A well-practiced look the boy learned from him at a young age. "All I have to do now is show her how to please me to stop any further beatings. Part of that will be to tell me where she hid the drive."

The senator felt his cock growing hard at just how his son would bring the woman under his control. He'd used the same tactic on more than one of his slaves over the years. "Too bad she won't be healed up and trained by Friday. There are big spenders coming to trade merchandise at the next auction. Many from overseas."

Dylan rose from the leather chair and headed to the bar in the corner of the office. He poured two glasses of imported whisky. He brought them back to the desk, handing him one before taking his seat once more and taking a healthy drink of the amber liquid. "Is Master Lee going to be there this time?"

"Yes, he is. Why do you ask?" He watched the idea form in the ice-cold blue eyes that mirrored his own.

"If I can get the information from the slut before tomorrow night, perhaps he'd like to take her off our hands. He'd pay a large sum to do so. The condition she's in is something he treasures."

"With the added benefit that he'd move her out of the jurisdiction of our courts and make her virtually disappear." He opened his laptop and logged into the account only his special clients could access. "We'll send him a live feed of her now and see if he's interested."

Dylan set aside his glass and stood to leave. "Then I'd better go visit our little traitor. I'd say by now she'd do just about anything for a kind word or gentle hand, wouldn't you?"

He watched his son stride from the room like a man in control of everything about him. His eldest was everything he'd wanted him to be. One day he'd be sitting in the White House, he was sure of it. But for now—the senator turned on the camera to the training stable at the big house where the bitch giving them all the trouble had been deposited—for now he'd enjoy watching his son get the little whore to service him.

* * * * *

Hours of reading files about more than a hundred missing women had Abby happy to open the financial data Luke sent to her laptop. The women's files had angered and depressed her in equal measure. So many lonely women, desperate to find love only to end up in a hell a group of over privileged men had created for their own amusement.

After her little tirade and talk with Luke, the group decided on different areas to investigate and Luke had assigned them each information to gather. Castello had driven Kirk to work so he could talk with the caterer about the party last month, but hadn't returned yet. Jeffers had headed back to his precinct office for a few hours to see if there was any information about the three dead women, even though they all knew that unlike what most people saw on TV it would be days, if not weeks, before the forensics people came up with anything. Since his return this evening he'd been working another database Luke had hacked. This one seemed to be a shipping firm owned by a company that was owned by another company that ultimately was owned by Hollister-Klein.

"You okay, Ms. Whitson?" Detective Jeffers asked from across the table.

She sighed, but nodded. "Yes. At least with the financials there aren't any faces staring back at me. And please call me Abigail. After today, I think formality is a bit overrated, don't you?"

"Yes it would. And I'm Aaron." He gave her a

tentative smile and the corners around his deep-blue eyes crinkled a bit, though a sadness still remained.

What had made him so unhappy? His job? Or something more personal?

"Is that what you do back in Washington?"

His question caught her still wondering about his story and it took a moment for her to realize he was talking about the information on her computer. "I'm an analyst for the Treasury Department."

"Isn't that a branch of Homeland Security now?"

"Only part of it. The Customs Department, Secret Service and FLETC moved under the umbrella of Homeland. The rest remains still as the Treasury Department."

"You don't usually handle missing persons cases then, I bet."

A laugh escaped her. "Not really. I mostly look into international money laundering and fraud."

The humor left Aaron's face. "So if your friend hadn't stumbled onto something odd and contacted you, we wouldn't have a clue this was going on right under our noses, would we?"

"You would've caught on to the problem at some point." Luke looked up from his laptop where he sat on the couch. "No one stays hidden forever. This group is getting sloppy and cocky. Otherwise Abby's friend wouldn't have found out whatever information it was that has them running scared."

"You're assuming anyone could've found what she

did," Abigail said, fixing him with a stare that dared him to say her friend was stupid.

Luke set aside what he was working on, stood and stretched, pulling the dark sweater tightly over his chest and flat abdomen. Heat surged through Abigail remembering all that warm skin and firm muscles beneath that she'd run her hands over last night. When he stopped and their eyes met, she knew he was thinking about the same thing. Her face grew more flushed but she wouldn't break the contact between them as he slowly sauntered over. Field agents weren't cowards and neither was she.

"No. I'm saying they left a trail that only she was smart enough to find—at this time." He stopped right beside her, forcing her to look up at him. "What I'm also saying is that was probably the first mistake they've made. Had your friend not found it, they would've gotten more arrogant and started making more blatant and obvious mistakes."

"Like the burned, murdered women," Aaron said, drawing Luke's attention.

Luke nodded. "Right. You would've eventually seen a pattern in the investigation you started before we arrived."

"But how many women have already been enslaved? And how many more would've been taken or murdered before then?" The edge in the detective's voice spoke of the controlled anger and frustration they were all feeling.

Luke pulled out a chair, turned it and straddled it. "Let's not go there. Luckily, we're here now and on their trail."

"And hopefully that means no more innocent women will fall prey to their vile plans." Abigail laid her hand on Aaron's arm, squeezing it then releasing it when Luke made a pointed stare at her. She tried to shove down the little feminine imp inside her that wanted to fist pump like a quarterback hitting his man in the end zone at Luke's jealous reaction to her act of sympathy. Never in her life had a man reacted to anything she did, much less in such a possessive manner. The feeling was...*exhilarating*. Now she understood why Brianna had spent so many years getting men to act like idiots over her.

"Which brings up something we've not done yet," Luke said as if nothing had just passed between them.

"What's that?" she asked, willing her mind to focus on the case and not just Luke.

"We need to profile our victims."

"Why? You know everything I know about them," Aaron said.

Luke nodded at him. "True. We know their statistics, but I want to know their psyche—what made them take the plunge into on-line dating, risk the chance of meeting someone in person."

"You're going to make up a fake profile," Abigail said, almost reading the scheme rolling around in his head.

He grinned at her and for the first time ever it didn't irritate her. "You got it, sweetheart. Let's see if we can draw these guys out."

"So where do we start? The only victim we really know is Ms. Mathews," Aaron said, "and she'd not our typical target."

"True. But I think we have an untapped source to reveal some of the thought processes these women might've been going through to put themselves in such jeopardy."

"Who?" Aaron said and Abigail could've kissed him because she knew who Luke meant.

"Me," she said.

"You? You wouldn't need a dating service any more than your friend did." The detective looked so incredulous, she couldn't help but laugh a little.

"Thank you, but Luke's right. I do know exactly how they'd feel. I've been there." She sobered. She'd been so lonely on more than one occasion she'd browsed the different sites, some of them on the very list she'd made from Brianna's URL history. But her own prudent nature kept her from ever filing her information.

"You're right, Jeffers. She doesn't need them now or *ever* again," Luke said and the heat in his gaze warmed her clear to her core "But I suspect you can tell us how the missing women might have been thinking. Am I right?"

Damn him. He knew how desperate she'd been. Then she looked into his eyes and saw something warm and understanding there. He knew and he didn't judge her.

Something flipped in her chest—like an on switch—and warmth spread throughout her.

Her height had always intimidated men, but not Luke. Her photographic memory she'd kept hidden, but Luke discovered it and accepted it. Loneliness had been with her all her life, Luke not only understood it, but knew they could use the experience to save Brianna and other women. How could she not love him?

"Abby?" Luke laid his hand on hers and the concern in his voice brought her out of her reverie.

"Yes. I've been in that mindset before. What do you want to know?"

Luke turned her hand beneath his so they were palm-to-palm. "What would our girl, let's call her Mary, what would make her join one of these sites to begin with?"

He was asking her to bare her darkest moments. Taking a deep breath, she let her fingers curl around his hand. She could do this.

"Mary would've always been a loner, the geeky girl no one invited to parties, never dated in high school and maybe only a few times since then. Even other girls didn't include her into their group."

"Except her best friend," Luke said squeezing her hand.

"Yes, though if she had a best friend she probably wouldn't be so desperate for companionship or love as to try these services." She stared into his hazel eyes, wanting him to realize she wasn't just looking for Brianna because she was missing, but because she owed her so much.

"So loneliness is motivating them to put their lives at risk?" Aaron said.

She broke the mental contact with Luke and nodded at the detective. "That and hope."

"Hope?" Aaron truly sounded perplexed.

God bless the man. He was so clueless.

"Hope that out there in the great unknown is someone meant for them. Someone who will love them for what's inside them. Someone who will want to spend time with them, talk with them, ease the loneliness." She inhaled slowly and blinked to keep any tears from forming. "They're also curious."

"Curious?" Luke turned his head at a tilt. "What are they curious about?"

"How the process works. Who might respond. *Will* anyone respond? What will they talk about? Just the possibilities of that kind of interaction is enough to push some women into putting all their personal information on the internet."

"Okay, I can buy that," Aaron said. "But what makes them decide to meet a stranger in real life. They have to be smart enough to read all the reports of stalkers using the internet to rob, rape or murder people."

"I imagine whoever answers their posts taps into their need and desperation," Luke said, releasing her hand. "They'd lay on the charm, probably working on them slowly, maybe even acting as shy as they are to gain their trust."

"Like a con man who reads the faces of their marks, convincing them it's their idea for the meeting." Aaron said, understanding in his eyes.

"And because the women think they've suggested the meeting, they think they're in control and nothing bad could happen to them, only the men trick them into meeting them at a place where they can get them alone..." Abby looked from Luke to Aaron and back again.

"Then poof, they're gone."

Luke stood and paced the length of the front room, letting his mind see the puzzle pieces. With Abby's help they'd figured out how the men were preying on the women, but which site would be the best on which to post his fake Mary's profile.

"We don't have time to look at all the sites the women might've frequented. We need our Mary to be quickly hit upon."

"There were three sites that the five girls missing from this area used," Abby said, pulling up the list. "In about half the cases I read I saw at least one of those sites listed."

"But which one is the one they're using?" He ran his hand through his hair. The need to do something ate at him.

"What if they're using more than one site?" she asked.

He stopped pacing and shook his head. "I don't know. That might be too variable for them. This group is powerful. They'd want to be in control of every detail. My bet is they're running whichever site they're using to troll for the women."

"I think Abigail might have a point," Jeffers said, standing to pace, too. "It's like being a fisherman."

"Fisherman?" What the hell was the detective talking about? He eyed the man with the look he'd learned from his brother Dave, the one that said, *are you crazy?*

Jeffers stopped and held out his hands like a professor teaching a class. "They'd cast a wider net. A good fisherman realizes he can't catch all the fish in one place without it playing out and depleting the source. He studies the stream and the fish, learning their feeding habits, their breeding habits, what spots attracts the fish more frequently and at what times of the day."

Of course. "They know the kind of women they want, so they troll those sites they would visit. Probably in the early evenings or late at night just before bed."

"Times when the women would feel loneliest or want some sort of human contact," Abby said. Then a delicate blush filled her cheeks and she looked away.

"What is it?" he asked, wondering what had her turning so rosy.

She shook her head, suddenly concentrating on her computer screen again. "Nothing. Just a stupid thought."

"Sweetheart," he said, walking over and slipping his hand under her chin. He lifted until she was meeting his gaze once more before he released her. "I've learned the hard way that nothing you think could be termed as stupid."

"I was just thinking maybe they might even convince the women to participate in cybersex." She rolled her eyes and shook her head. "See, I told you it was stupid."

He stared at her a moment, realizing she'd cut right to the reason the women were so willing to go meet their mystery men. Slowly he smiled at her, then, cupping her face in his hands, he kissed her, slow and deep. When he lifted his lips from hers, he was rewarded by the wide-open gleam of her emerald eyes and her pink lips still slightly parted. "No, it wasn't stupid. It's brilliant. You're brilliant."

"The women participating in cybersex is brilliant?" Her brows drew down and all the soft glow of her passion dissolved into confusion.

Jeffers plopped back down in his chair. "You're right. Why didn't I see that all along?"

"Because you were looking for a serial killer not mass kidnapping," Luke said.

"What are we talking about?" Abby asked.

Luke straddled the chair once more. "You figured out why the women were so willing to go put themselves in harm's way with a total stranger, sweetheart. They'd been chatting with the men on line, slowly letting their guard down. Until—"

"Until they'd had cybersex." Abby, pale, finished the sentence. "The women were seduced into believing they'd found that someone special and trusted the men. They weren't meeting strangers. They thought they were meeting their lovers."

CHAPTER 14

Castello parked his car off the road almost a mile past the entrance of the address he'd gotten from Paolo. After talking with the caterer about who had hired him he'd learned two things. The group was hiding behind the name The Titan Club, and all the details, including payment, were handled through a corporation, which he suspected led to layers of more corporations.

He'd also decided that before he met with Luke and the others it might be a good idea to get a lay of the enemy's territory.

A hedgerow hid him from anyone passing by this late at night. He studied the map of the area on his smartphone. When the department first issued it, the new technology drove him crazy, but he learned some of the features like maps and GPS made his job easier at times, like tonight.

Luke's phone call yesterday made him mildly curious about what the kid had gotten himself into, and he'd headed up from Columbus to check out the situation. Like he'd suspected, if an Edgars male got intense about something, a woman in distress was usually at the root of the problem—but neither he nor Luke had expected this pile of shit the pair had stepped into.

Before Frank had left the condo to take Kirk F to work, Luke had pulled them and Jeffers aside to explain why he was trying to keep Abigail's name out of any official reports. The kid suspected her missing friend had information sensitive to the case but before she could hand it over to Abigail she'd been taken by the slavery ring. If she gave up the information or who she might've spoken to, Abigail was in serious trouble.

Now that he'd seen Luke with his woman, he planned to do everything to help keep her safe. Reconnaissance on the possible auction house, gather intel, even call in the other brothers if necessary. So, first things first, time to scope out the security in this place.

He set the phone on silent and slipped it into his pants pocket, then grabbed the PVS-14 night vision scope he kept in the trunk. It seemed every time he was on a fugitive hunt lately it was at night. Might as well have the scope close by. Tonight it would come in handy for scoping out the grounds of The Titan Club.

The Titan Club.

Figures they'd named themselves after Gods. Nothing subtle or timid about this group. It also meant they weren't afraid to not only kidnap women, but sell them as cattle, which made the group dangerous.

The idea of women being abused and used as sex slaves ate at his gut. To think someone thought they were above the law and could blatantly get away with the crime set his blood to boiling.

Lips pressed tightly together, he inhaled and exhaled.

Once he was calm and focused again, he climbed out of the car, locking the door manually. No need for an electronic beep to announce his presence. He just hoped the place didn't have guard dogs. Man, he hated guard dogs—had since a shepherd tried to take out his leg while he closed in on a fugitive meth cook.

He checked to be sure no traffic was headed his way before stepping out from the cover of the bushes. With a quick jog back towards the estate, he watched for the spot where the wrought-iron-topped stone wall gave way to chain-link behind the hedgerow. When he came to it, he scanned the area with the night scope to be sure no cameras were in the vicinity. Seeing none, he slipped the scope into his jacket pocket and wiggled his body in behind the hedge, cursing when a loose branch scratched his face. He reached up, broke off the offending stick and pocketed it. No need to leave behind his blood for DNA testing should someone suspect he'd infiltrated the estate.

The chain-link fence was at least eight feet tall and wedged in tight to the stone wall. Reinforced with rebar.

Shit. No way was he scaling that then dropping

down the other side. Last thing he needed was to break a leg on private property without a warrant.

He studied the stone wall. Then a grin slowly spread on his face. The top of the wall was only about five feet with wrought-iron spikes extending upward another three feet. Very impressive. Except someone forgot to add the last spike before the fence started, leaving about eighteen inches of space. Just enough for him to squeeze through.

Using the scope again he scanned the space between the fencing and the trees about twenty yards off for any movement.

Nothing moved.

He scanned higher. No electronic equipment such as cameras or motion detectors. That could be a good sign or not. Either they only expected trouble to come up the main drive and ignored this area of infiltration, or they were so cocky they didn't think anyone would find their compound, much less try to gain entrance covertly.

The scope back safe in his pocket, he scaled the stone wall, using the chain link on the right side for grip. He hauled himself over the top and dropped to the other side, then squatted in the shadows to listen around him. No hum of electronics. No alarms. Most importantly, no barking of guard dogs.

Inhaling, he dashed to the copse of trees, then paused and exhaled. His pulse pounded in his ears. He strained to listen over it.

No unusual sounds. The wind rustled the new leaves

on the trees. Crickets chirped. The occasional hooting of an owl.

He moved farther into the trees before pausing to pull out his smartphone to study the map again. Increasing the scale of the estate on the screen, he tried to determine how far the trees ran before he'd reach the mansion itself.

Best he could tell about the length of six football fields, or a third of a mile. His old partner Pete always thought in terms of football fields since he'd been a star running back in college. The habit had transferred to him when they started working together. He still used it as a good measure and to honor his friend after Pete retired then died at the hands of a thug who worked for a maniacal cult leader.

Steadily he worked his way through the trees and closer to the mansion, pausing every so often to use the scope to scan the area for movement and listen to the sounds. Nothing moved. And the only sound seemed to be his own breathing. Thankfully it wasn't autumn or he'd be crunching dry leaves as he went. As it was, the ground beneath him was wet from the last spring rain and nearly silent to walk on—slippery as hell, too.

Finally, he reached the edge of the tree line.

He let out a silent whistle.

Before him was a three-story brick mansion worthy of any European royalty. A few lights were on at the front of the building. He took out his camera and took some photos, zooming in on the cameras at the entrance. Two guards armed with semi-automatics paced near the entrance. Satisfied he couldn't learn anything more there, he worked his way toward the back of the building, using the trees for cover. This area of the mansion was dark. No floodlights, no guards. He took some more pictures.

Dammit. Had he been wrong? Was this only the staging area for their flesh auctions? He'd been so sure this secluded spot might be where they also housed the women.

Suddenly a rumbling noise came from the back of the house.

What the hell was that? He glanced down at the map again.

Fuck. He'd missed that the estate butted up against Lake Erie. The sound was some sort of boat motor.

Quick as possible without alerting anyone to his presence, he wove his way to where the property met the lake. And here was where all the security focused.

Floodlights illuminated the path from the patio to the wharf out onto the lake where a large boat sat, engines running. Guards armed with the same automatic weapons as up front stood nearby. Several bodybuilder-type men dressed in suits and coats, stood out on the dock as several hands tied the boat securely. Words were exchanged between the suits and deckhands.

Damn, he wished he had some listening devices.

Hunkering down behind a huge fir tree, he pulled out his phone and set the camera feature to record. He zoomed in to try to catch faces. They'd need them to identify the players later on.

One of the men went below decks. When he reemerged he had a young Asian woman by the elbow. She was unsteady on her feet and the man seemed to be helping her across the boat and onto the dock.

Castello focused his camera on the woman, zooming in as close as he could. There were cuffs on her hands with a chain leading up to a collar around her neck. He bit down on the sudden rage that shot through him.

Focus on the details. Know their MO. Focus. Think logically. Emotions can get not only your witness killed, but you, too.

His old partner Pete's words from his training days, in that smoke-clogged, gruff voice of his, sounded in his head. He let them smooth out his anger and shove it on the back burner. Inching a little closer, he concentrated on the woman's face as she stumbled along beside the men leading her up the dock. She looked like she'd just come off a four-day drunk. Which meant they were keeping the women drugged to keep them docile and easy to control.

Had they done the same to Abigail's friend? Or had the torture been enough to gain her cooperation?

The deck hand disappeared below decks once more, returning with another woman in the same condition as the first. This continued until a total of six chained women, all of apparently Asian descent, stood on the dock, each clad in miniskirts, tank tops and sandals.

Given the cool spring breeze coming in off the lake the women had to be freezing, but not one of the men made an effort to give them a coat.

Bastards.

He clenched his hand at his side. With the element of surprise on his side he could probably take out the guards. But then what would he do with six drugged women and no escape route? Besides, it would tip the masterminds of this group they were under surveillance. Brianna Mathews would be dead before sunrise.

One of the guards stepped forward, handing a briefcase to one of the crew on the boat. Hands were shaken and finally the boat pulled away from the dock. As the guards led the women up the boardwalk to the mansion, he slipped back into the cover of the trees.

Time to get back to the condo. They needed a plan and the stakes just got higher.

* * * * *

Through her non-swollen eye, Brianna watched the new girls being led through what she was now thinking of as *the dungeon*. Minutes before, she'd managed to drag herself over to the door that had a barred window in it and held onto the bars to peek out. Across what looked like a hallway—but was more a path—was another door that looked just like this one. She'd called out to whoever might be held there but no one answered. Leaning first to one side then the other, she'd determined there were more of the cage-rooms farther down the walkway.

How many girls were they keeping imprisoned here?

Was this what she'd stumbled onto? Not corporate fraud, but human trafficking? Had her boss known? Surely not. But Dylan had. He'd been with the men who'd attacked and tortured her. She laid her hand on her swollen jaw. He'd hit her, too.

What was going to happen to her next?

"Get her cleaned up and brought to my room."

That was Dylan's voice coming from the top of the stairs. Who was he talking about? Her? What did he want? She couldn't tell him anything more. She'd told them over and over the information was with Abby, but they didn't believe her.

Footsteps sounded on the stairs.

She stumbled back from the door to land on the cot in the corner once more. What would they do if they knew she'd been watching them bring in the women? She couldn't take any more punishment.

The footsteps stopped outside her door. Keys jangled. She held her breath trying to cower into the thin blanket on the cot.

The door swung open and in stepped her two tormentors.

"C'mon slut. The boss wants us to bring you to his private room," the smaller of the two said with a sneer in his voice.

The bigger man grabbed her by the arm, wrenching

it as he hauled her to her feet. Pain shot through her. He'd done the same thing earlier and something had pulled—a muscle, tendon, ligament? Or maybe a bone had broken? No. She was pretty sure if he'd broken her arm she wouldn't still be able to use it.

"Please…don't hurt…me…any…more," she managed to squeak past her dry, busted lips.

"Oh, the boss has somethin' different planned for ya now. Ain't that right, Johnson?" He laughed and Johnson joined in, sending shivers of dread down her spine.

"Sure is, Hal."

Something different? Every part of her body was bruised, battered or broken. What more could they possibly do to her?

They half led, half hauled her through the path between the cage rooms, up two flights of stairs and finally into a luxurious bathroom. Johnson turned on the water in the shower, while Hal just started ripping what was left of her clothes off her body.

"Please, no," she whimpered as she tried to fight his hands.

Hal caught her by the hair and wrenched her head backwards. "Boss said to clean you up. Those rags ain't clean and you're not going anywhere you need clothes anyways. Hold still or we'll get rough with ya."

Like they'd been gentle?

She swallowed the small spark of defiance. Survival was everything. Being a smartass wouldn't do anything but get her killed. *See Abby? I can learn.* Blinking back the tears brimming in her eyes, she nodded and held still while the brute finished stripping off her clothes.

"Man, look at them tits," muttered Johnson, squeezing them hard with his beefy paws.

"Don't leave no bruises there. The boss won't like it. He always has to be first." Hal tweaked her nipples hard and leaned in to bite her ear. "But we can have lots of fun with her once he's done."

Bile rose in her throat and she swallowed hard trying to keep it inside. Throwing up on her captors probably would get her more punishment, of that she was sure.

Hal released her nipple. "Get in the shower and wash up. Be quick or I'll be doing it for ya."

She walked into the enclosed glass shower, then realized neither of them was leaving. The last time she'd washed naked in front of others, she'd been in gym class back in school. That had been with friends and they'd all giggled at seeing each other naked. Having these two men watch her made her skin crawl, but she had no choice.

"Use the soap and shampoo. Need to wash the stink off ya."

The hot water stung when it hit her cuts, making her hiss at the new pain, but after a few moments, her muscles almost moaned with the relief the heat brought. She took the shampoo and lathered her hair with it, letting it sit piled on her head while she worked a soapy washcloth gently over her cuts and cigarette burn marks. Trying not to remove any scabs and start the blood oozing from them again, she cleaned the caked-on blood from her body. Each spot brought back a memory of the past few days, each torture session, every question, every shot of pain. By the time she leaned her head back to let the shower spray wash the blood, grime and shampoo from her hair, she'd finished crying and was ready to meet whatever fate Dylan had planned for her today.

"Time to get out." Hal reached in and shut off the water and handed her a towel.

Once she dried off, she started to wrap the towel around her, only to have him rip it from her fingers.

"Boss said to clean you up. Didn't say nothin' about coverin' ya up."

Heat of a blush coursed through her, but she tried not to let them see how disturbing it was to be led naked from the bathroom down the upstairs hall to the room at the end.

Hal paused before opening the door. He looked her over from head to toe with a leering grin, his yellowed teeth making her cringe again. "Just remember, we always get to play with Boss' toys when he's finished with 'em."

The door opened and she stepped into a room right out of Decorator Monthly. Opulence was almost too cheap a word to describe it. Marble covered the floors, but two beautiful cream-and-blue Aubusson rugs covered the marble. One under the four-poster bed in the center of the room, the other in front of the marble fireplace where someone had set a roaring fire. An overstuffed couch stretched in front of the fire.

In one of the leather chairs flanking it sat Dylan Klein.

The man she'd thought she loved.

* * * * *

"We'll start again in the morning," Luke said as stood at the door with Detective Jeffers.

"I'll monitor the profile on the sites tonight, just in case our girl Mary gets any activity," Aaron said. "Although I doubt much will happen the first night it's up."

Luke nodded. "It's a long shot, but maybe we can shut down their mode of luring these women in."

The two men shook hands before Jeffers left and Luke set the condo alarms after him.

"Aren't you expecting Frank back soon?" Abigail asked, looking up from the spreadsheets on her laptop. Her eyes were crossing from all the information stored there.

"It's Castello's condo. He knows the code." Luke sauntered over, his gun still in the holster around his shoulders. "I think you and I need to talk."

Quickly, she looked back at the spreadsheets. "I'm not done here."

"It can wait until morning," he said, reaching over

her shoulder and gently closing the computer, then turning her head to stare into her eyes. "I want you to tell me what happened back there."

"Back where?" she asked, even though she knew he was talking about her reaction to the conversation about cybersex. She didn't want to have this conversation with anyone and certainly not Luke, ever.

He took her hand and pulled her up, capturing her lips with his in a soft, pleasurable kiss—no heat, just a man kissing a woman. "Come with me," he said when he broke the kiss.

Dreading the embarrassment to come, she let him lead her over to the leather sofa. He sank down beside her, leaning so he was nearly stretched out on the sofa and she was snuggled on top of him. Pulling her in close to his body, he took the scarlet-and-grey afghan and draped it around her. The cocoon of warmth relaxed her as he held her close and stroked her hair.

"You went completely pale when you realized the women had been having cybersex with their captors before being taken. Why?"

She kept the side of her face pressed against his chest, listening to the steady beat of his heart. "Who wouldn't be? The men used something so intimate to gain their trust and lure them into danger."

"But that wasn't the only reason you were so upset, is it?"

Damn. The man was the definition of persistence.

A moment or two passed before she answered. "No."

He cupped her face in his hands, gently turning her until their gazes met. "Abby, you can tell me. I promise it's not as bad as you've imagined."

Yeah, right. When he heard her story, he'd see just how pathetic she was.

"Abby, have you had cybersex with someone?"

Heat burst into her face and she lowered her eyes, breaking the connection. "Yes. Well, almost."

A deep rumble sounded in his chest. He was laughing at her? Her eyes shot back up to see the smile on his face and the corners of his eyes crinkled with mirth. She swatted him on the shoulder. "Don't laugh at me. I know it's pathetic."

He captured her hand in his and brought it up to kiss her knuckles. "I'm not laughing at the fact that you had cybersex."

She pursed her lips together and arched one brow. "Really?"

"No. It's the *almost* that's funny." She tried to pull away, but he held her firm. "You know lots of people have cybersex these days."

"They do?"

"Sure. Couples who live long distance do it. Couples who are bicoastal or travel extensively for their work."

She gave a halfhearted nod, admitting he did have a point. "But they're couples. I doubt that people do it with complete strangers, like our girls did." *Or I almost did.*

"More than you think. Some people have cybersex

just for the fun of it or the fantasy of being with a stranger. Some like it because there's no strings attached."

For someone whom women threw themselves at, he seemed to know a lot about the whys of people having cybersex. She narrowed her eyes and turned her head slightly. "Oh my God, you've done it."

"Yes." The answer was straightforward and honest. She stared into his eyes, the humor almost gone.

"How many times? Once?"

"A few times. Mostly when I've been on long assignments."

"With girlfriends?" The question was out of her mouth before she could stop it.

"No," he said, smoothing a lock of her hair behind one ear. "I preferred anonymity. At the time, I thought it served the purpose. I needed a release, someone was on-line to provide the temporary sensation. But now I'm thinking it was a very hollow effort."

"Why?" Other than when he told her about his dreams of her, she'd never seen him this open about anything—certainly nothing this intimate.

He leaned in and captured her lips in a warm kiss for a moment. "Because of you. Because of last night."

"Me? Last night?" She knew she sounded like a parrot mimicking him, but her heart was pounding so hard it was making it difficult to comprehend what he meant.

The humor returned to the corners of his eyes. She

was beginning to like that look.

"Last night was beyond incredible, sweetheart." He caught her lips again for a quick kiss. "It also showed me what I've been missing. Sex, physical or cyber, is just a body function unless it's with someone you care about."

The words slammed into her heart.

"You care about me?"

He cupped her face again with his warm hands, his thumbs brushing against her cheeks as their gazes locked. "I suspect I did from the moment we first met, although I didn't want to admit it."

She laughed. "Admit it? You did your best to make me think you thought I was incompetent and not anyone you'd ever be interested in. Even the night of graduation when I threw myself at you."

"Oh, I was interested, all right."

She stared at him open-mouthed for a moment. "I know I was drunk, but I was kissing you and before I knew it you were pushing me away, telling me to stop."

"Hold it right there. I think you missed a whole lot of what happened that night."

"I did?" She narrowed her eyes. "We went out as a group to the bar and billiards room down off campus from the FLETC facility. Right?"

"Right."

"The bunch of us drank, played pool and danced. Right?"

Yeah, she'd been dancing with half the guys from

their class, getting drunker by the minute. He'd stayed sober just to keep an eye on her. After the hell he'd put her through it seemed only fair that she get to cut loose before learning she'd be back in Washington at a desk.

"Then you took me home. I threw myself at you and you left me standing there like an idiot."

"What you didn't see was the bet the guys in the class had going on over who could get you naked first." His jaw clenched at the memory. He'd wanted to take them all outside and beat them senseless.

"So you wanted to win the bet?" Her eyes were wide with shock and anger.

"Dammit, no. I wanted to be sure you got home safe. I also realized how drunk you were. Despite what you and the others might think, I do not take advantage of women in that state. No matter how much I wanted to follow up on that kiss that night."

"So you were saving me from my own stupid—"

He stopped her with another kiss, long, slow, hot. Tongues tangling, lips devouring. She couldn't get enough of his taste—hot, spicy, masculine. A whimper sounded in her throat and she wiggled up to get even with him, her lower stomach grazing against the hard erection just behind his jeans. He groaned against her lips, the rumble in his chest teasing her aching nipples as he slid his hands up under her sweater, their warmth sliding over her back sending heat straight to her core.

The garage door motor rumbled on the other side of the kitchen.

They froze.

"That's going to be Castello," Luke murmured against her lips as he eased his hands out of her sweater. "We'll continue this conversation later."

"Just the conversation?" she whispered.

"More, if there's time." He winked at her then eased them both up to a sitting position. "Depends on what Frank has to say."

CHAPTER 15

Frank strode into the room and dropped down into the leather chair across from them, more than the usual tension lined his face.

Luke draped his arm around Abby's shoulders and pulled her a little closer. Frank hadn't said a word and already Luke didn't like whatever news he had. "What took you so long?"

"Paolo gave me the address with a little verbal arm-twisting and I went to check it out."

"What did you find?" The little hairs on his neck started twitching.

"Not much security protocol beyond the main entrance gate, from what I can tell."

Luke nodded. "Good."

"That is, until you get to the house and out back where they have a dock onto the lake." Frank looked over at Abby then back at him, twisting his mouth a moment before continuing, apparently deciding what to tell them. "They brought in a shipment by boat while I was there."

"A shipment?" Abby asked, her body tensing beside Luke's.

Frank ran his hand over his face. "Our boys aren't just dealing in just kidnapping women here in the states. They've gone international. At least six Asian women were brought in by boat. Each of them chained from the neck to cuffs on their wrists. Drugged, too."

"Oh, God," Abby whispered.

"Shit," was all Luke could say to the sudden sense of rage that hit him even as he drew her in tighter.

Frank stared straight at him, no compromise in his face. "Yeah. If they're bringing women into the States, they're just as likely to be sending them overseas, too."

"Brianna." Abby turned to look up at Luke, fear widening her eyes. "What if they plan to sell her and move her out of the country? We'll never find her then."

"We'll do everything possible to find her before that happens." He knew he shouldn't make her that promise, but he meant every word. He *would* do everything in his power to find her friend.

"Shipments!" Abby nearly vaulted off the couch and dashed to her laptop.

Luke and Castello exchange curious looks, but followed her.

"Why didn't I see it?" Abby asked, more to herself than to them, her fingers quickly flying over the keyboard.

Luke leaned in to see the spreadsheets fly past once more. She'd been working through them before he'd decided they needed to discuss cybersex. "What are you looking for?"

"Shipments. Boats. Canada." Abby slowed her fingers on the keyboard, then ran her index finger down the columns of one. "Brianna took over as Hollister-Klein's Controller just a few months ago. First thing she would've done was her own audit of the company's records. She would work backwards, the newest accounts more pressing, but she was thorough. She would've checked every account the previous department head okayed, ever."

"What would she be looking for?" Castello asked, standing on the other side of Abby, one brow lifted in curiosity.

"Any discrepancies that might come back to bite her in the...butt," she said, a light blush coming to her cheeks as she edited her words for Castello.

Luke bit back a laugh. The Marshal had no problem swearing when the mood hit him.

"She would've wanted to know if the person she replaced had done their job," Abby continued, "or if there might be questions of fraud she'd have to deal with."

Luke nodded. "Easiest time to find it is when there's a shakeup in management. But if they were using the company to hide their slave trade, why would they hire someone as diligent as your friend? Surely they'd know the first thing she would do is hire someone to do a back audit."

Abby grinned at him, her eyes sparkling. "You forget, Brianna was good at manipulating men. She let them *think* she was helpless and not nearly as intelligent as she was. I'd bet they advanced her to be a trophy girl. Pretty, but not too smart."

"Eye candy," Frank said.

Abby nodded. "Right. And she wouldn't have wanted to let them know any different until she'd made sure everything was on the up-and-up, and that her job was secure."

"So she did the audit herself." Luke saw where she was going with this. "Quietly and on the side."

"And she found this." She enlarged the section of the spreadsheet and pointed to a column.

"What is that?" Frank asked, leaning in and staring at a screen full of numbers.

"That is a bill of lading out of Toronto and Vancouver."

"They're international importers and exporters, Abby." Luke loved watching how her brain worked and she'd found something.

"I know. And everything matches except for once a month this year, when cargo was received, but no payable amount was dispersed and cargo sent was not billed for." Using her finger to follow the lines, she led them over to the other columns with the missing holes. "It only happened for one year, then there are no further monthly shipments noted to that port with missing bills."

Damn, she was right. "Someone got wise and started keeping a second set of books for these shipments. How far back did she have to go to find this?"

"Five years."

Castello let out a low whistle. "That's determination."

"Brianna used to say, *men will lie, the numbers shouldn't.*" She tapped the screen with her finger. "*This* is what she wanted to talk to me about. And I'll bet she was smart enough to put whatever she stumbled upon on the dating sites with these shipments."

"Do you think she approached anyone at the company about it?" Luke asked.

She gave a little shrug. "The logical thing would be to take the information to her boss, Ryan Baxter, Hollister-Klein's CFO." Suddenly she lifted her head, her eyes dancing as if she were searching through images again. "What was the name of the Senator's son again? The one that was at the auction."

"Dylan. Dylan Klein," Luke answered. "Why? Do you think she might've known him? Might've gone to him with the information?"

Without answering, she pulled up the official site for Hollister-Klein. "What if she didn't go to Baxter? This is Dylan Klein, the CEO of the company. What if she went to him instead?"

"Gutsy move, leapfrogging her superior," Castello

said.

Luke nodded his agreement. "What makes you think she did that?"

A slow smile spread over Abby's lips and he so wanted to kiss her even before he heard what brilliant thing she'd figured out. She typed in another few words and up popped the pages she'd recreated from her friend's day planner and pointed at the name Dylan several times over the pages. "Because she was dating him."

* * * * *

"Come here, Brie," Dylan said in a quiet command, holding his hand out to Brianna.

Dread slithered up her spine. She should turn and run, but she'd heard the key in the lock after the pair of henchmen had closed the door behind her. There was no escape. And he knew it.

Slowly, she made her way across the room. The shivers she tried to control came only partially from her nude state, which made her feel even more vulnerable than when the men had attacked her in her condo. Fear danced a merry tune across her body, but she needed to brave this out somehow. She'd known he'd asked her out because he wanted her as a trophy to show off to other men, and she'd allowed him to think she was nothing more than an airhead with a great body and beautiful face. As skilled as she'd been at reading men,

Dylan had been equally talented at hiding his true nature behind a suave and sophisticated mask. All their times together, he'd never shown his temper. Never, until he'd hit her earlier.

So what game was he playing now?

Slipping her uninjured hand into his, she didn't fight the tremble that started in her fingers and ran up her arm. He led her forward until she stood between his spread thighs, the warm fire at her back.

"Oh, little Bri, what have they done to you?" he said, his eyes looking her over from her toes up to her face. Too bad his sympathetic words didn't reflect in his eyes. Instead, there was a heat she'd never seen before.

Dear God, the cuts and bruises turned him on.

"I hurt all over, Dylan," she whispered just to see his reaction. There it was. Fire in his eyes.

He traced a finger up her cheek. "Have you seen your face?"

Tears welled up and she let them slide down. "No." And she didn't need to. She could hardly breathe through her nose from where they'd smashed it in the first day, blood caked inside and clogging it. One eye was nearly swollen shut. Her lips felt inches thick and the cuts along them stung every time she talked.

"Such a shame my men damaged so rare a beauty as yours. But it's your own fault, sweetheart," he said, letting his hands trails down her arms. She tried not to wince when he squeezed the left one just above the elbow where dark bruises covered it.

"It is?" He was crazy if he thought she'd take the blame for this torture.

He slid his hands down her sides, past the ribs she was certain were broken on both sides, because it hurt too damn much to inhale.

"You shouldn't have gone snooping into things that weren't your business," he said, letting his hands glide over the knife cuts on her thighs. "I see Bertram decided to practice his knife skills on you. He has quite the talent, wouldn't you say? Able to inflict enough pain and bloodshed without really risking your death too soon."

He was crazy. And crazy was tricky to manipulate.

Not waiting for her answer, he moved his hands between her thighs, making her open them wider with a nudge.

She obeyed. Her survival might very well depend on which one of them played this game of seduction and lies better.

* * * * *

"You're going to need to move up the timetable," Frank said, drawing their attention again.

"Why?" Luke asked, already dreading the answer. "We've started a profile on the dating sites to see if we can make contact with whoever is drawing the women into their scheme. It's only been up tonight. Will take a little more time than that."

Frank shook his head. "Won't work. Paolo, the caterer, also told me he'd been hired for another event this Friday night."

Two days.

"If they're planning to ship Bonnie out of there, it will be during or right after that party," he said, his mind already trying to find a way to get into the mansion. "We could go in with the caterers."

Frank nodded. "I didn't give Paolo details about why we wanted to know the group's location. Got the idea he didn't want to know details. But with some more arm-twisting we can get a few people inside with Kirk."

"We'd need to do an assault from outside, too. I wonder how many people Jeffers can get us?"

"You and he don't know who can be trusted. You're going to have to call Columbus," Castello said, giving him a meaningful look.

Call the family.

"We need to find *Brianna* before anyone storms from outside. I'll need to go inside, too." Abby said beside him.

"No."

Both Abby and Castello looked at him.

"No to calling the cavalry?" Frank asked.

"Or to me going in to find Brianna?" Abby asked, that stubborn glint in her eyes.

"Both." He ran his hands through his hair while they both stood there watching him. He focused on Castello, because he couldn't deal with the idea of Abby even remotely close to this operation. "I'm trying to keep this off official records for as long as possible. You know they'll storm in here, take over and Abby'll be in danger before the group's leaders are caught."

"It's your case. They'll move on it how you want. Besides the Fed has resources we're going to need to bring down a Senator," Frank said.

They both knew Luke's brother-in-law would have to be called into the situation.

"I won't be in danger with you by my side," Abby said, crossing her arms beneath her breasts, her brows drawn down in that stubborn set he'd learned meant she was digging in her heels.

He couldn't deal with her right now, so he turned to Frank. "Okay, I'll call them. But if any of them get hurt, you get to explain it to Mom."

That caught Abby's attention "Exactly who are you calling?"

"Three of the biggest pains in my ass," Luke said, taking out his phone and punching numbers. He pointed to Castello. "He makes it a quartet."

The dial tone sounded in his ear as he watched Abby. She'd turned her head to one side, her glasses resting on the tip of her nose. Gently, she nibbled on her bottom lip, reminding him how it had tasted earlier when she'd been snuggled on top of him.

"This better be good, Luke. Judy's about to put dinner on the table."

"Dinner can wait, Dave, it's about Senator Klein."

Luke had walked out onto the patio in back, leaving Abigail with a ton of questions. That left Frank to answer her questions.

"Who is Dave?"

"His oldest brother," Frank answered, apparently not wanting to give more information.

"And why would Luke be calling him?"

"He's a cop. Other brother Matt is a highway patrolman and their brother-in-law, Jake, is FBI."

"Oh. I thought he'd be calling people in his own agency."

"Neither one will have the jurisdiction Jake will. Other than the possible fraud that you and your friend may have found, this doesn't fall under Treasury. Besides, this is personal. Luke's been looking into Senator Klein for some time now."

"Why?"

Frank patted the barstool beside him and she sat down, waiting for the explanation.

"Because a crazed gunman took Dave's wife hostage along with the senator's son last winter. Something in the way the senator's people handled it tipped Dave and Luke's radar that something might not be on the up-and-up. They've been thinking it was illegal arms sales."

"But since it's not, Homeland won't be too interested in what we've found," she said.

"Kidnapping and transportation of illegal aliens, sex-slave trade? This is all going to be under the Federal umbrella, but Luke wants to keep your name out of anything official." Frank winked at her. "So we call family."

She couldn't help but grin at him. "You're part of their family, aren't you?"

He lifted his eyebrows and nodded. "Matt's wife, Katie, was once in my WITSEC program. When her cover was blown and Matt came into her life, I sort of got attached to the crazy Edgars clan."

Before she could tell him how envious she was, Luke sauntered back in the room to stand on the kitchen side of the island. "Jake, Dave, Matt and Katie are on their way."

"Your sister-in-law is law enforcement, too?" she asked.

Luke shot Frank a narrowed-eyed look. "See you've been filling her in on the family dynamics."

Frank shrugged, looking none too concerned that he'd been sharing family secrets. "Just a little background information I thought she might need to know before the gang gets here."

"Katie's a neonatal nurse," Luke said, turning his attention back to her, "but she grew up in a paramilitary cult and handles herself well with guns, as well as disarming security systems and bombs."

"Bet she volunteered and Matt wasn't happy," Frank said, a bit of humor in his voice.

"Actually, once he heard what these guys were doing

to women, Matt just said she'd be coming, too. Guess he wasn't going to even start the fight over her staying home."

"And the Fed?" Frank asked.

"Jake said he'd get the details once he was here and decide how to proceed. He wanted to know about the local cop situation and I let him know we had them involved, but Jeffers hasn't contacted his boss, yet. The rest we'll deal with in the morning." Luke yawned and stretched, then walked around the counter. He took her by the hand and pulled her off her seat. "You get the couch, old man. We've got something to discuss in private."

Without looking back he led her into the bedroom and closed the door behind him.

"You might've just announced to him that we're sleeping together," Abigail said as she stalked across the room, her cheeks still warm from his highhandedness.

"Sweetheart, he figured that out this morning when you came out dressed in my shirt," Luke said, slowly advancing on her.

She held up her hand and took a step backward. "Don't touch me."

"Why?" he asked, even though he stopped more than an arm's length away.

"Because we need to talk and I can't think straight when you touch me."

He smiled that little-boy grin of his and her heart did

a flip. She forced the charm from her mind and subdued the urge to walk into his arms.

What she had to say was important.

"You *know* I have to go in to the mansion." She hurried on when he opened his mouth to speak. "I'm the one Brianna called. If they've got her imprisoned there I'm the only one she'll know and trust. She saved me once and I now it's my turn to save her."

"How did she save you?" he asked, all humor gone.

"When we lived at the orphanage I was bullied quite a bit, especially by the boys." She folded her arms around her middle. "One day, a gang of them had me cornered behind the gym. They'd broken my glasses and were calling me names, like ostrich and freak. Just when I thought they were going to do more, Brie comes running out of nowhere right into the middle of them with her back to me and both hands up in fists, threatening them."

"She was going to take them all on for you."

Abigail nodded through the tears welled in her eyes. Dashing at them with one hand, she fought to gain control of her emotions. She needed Luke to understand why she had to do this.

"It wasn't just that. For the first time since my mother died, someone had shown that I was worth caring about. Someone showed me that I mattered to them. And I learned I could trust people—or at least Brianna."

"She's not the only one you can trust, Abby," he

said, understanding and a promise in his eyes.

"I need to do this."

"I know."

"You know?" she asked, trying to determine if he truly meant what he said. He wasn't going to fight her? Or was he just placating her?

He inhaled slowly and exhaled even slower, a big decision coming with the action. "I knew it in the other room as soon as the words were out of your mouth."

She blinked hard, some of the tension that had filled her since they came in the room easing.

He frowned. "Just because I agree that yes, you do have to go in to identify Brianna and you've earned the right to be there when we rescue her, it doesn't mean I like putting you in danger any better."

Then it hit her.

The big super-spy, Luke Edgars, cared about her. It wasn't her lack of field experience that had him concerned. It was his feelings for her. And it was fear. Fear for her. Fear that his dream would come true.

Slowly she approached him like a wounded lion. "I won't do anything rash."

"Damn right you won't."

She stopped inches away. "I'll follow your every command."

"Damn right you will."

She slid her hand up his arm, over his shoulder and along his jaw. "I'll stay right by your side."

He jerked her into his body, lowering his lips to

hover just above hers. "Damn straight."

Then he claimed her mouth with all the tension she felt strumming through his body pressed so tightly to hers. She wound both arms around his shoulders, letting her fingers play in his thick, dusky-blond hair. He slid his hands down her back to grip her by her ass and lifted until she was pressed tightly against the ridge of his erection. A moan escaped her as he rocked them both in the rhythm of mating. When she parted her lips for him and he slipped his tongue inside, he growled inside her mouth and the feeling sent thrills down her. She'd caused this need inside him. Her. No one else.

God, she wasn't going to last. She gripped him by the hair and pulled back until their lips parted and he stared down at her with passion-filled eyes. "I need you," she said.

"I know, sweetheart," he murmured, trying to capture her mouth once more.

"No, Luke. Now!"

He laughed. *The damn man laughed.*

Then he lifted her, forcing her to release her hold on his hair and grip his shoulders, at the same time wrapping her legs around his hips. And wasn't that the best thing? The thick ridge behind his pants rubbed even harder against her. She forgave him the laugh.

He walked backwards until he landed hard on the bed, which creaked with the new weight.

Abigail froze. "Oh, my God. What about Frank?"

"He can get his own woman," he said with a grin

just before catching her mouth with his again.

Then it was a sudden flurry of hands and fingers until their clothes landed into piles on the floor. Straddling his lap, she looked into Luke's eyes as he handed her the condom, the powerful connection in his gaze speaking of trust and need. Her fingers shook as she covered him—the first time she'd ever done such a thing with any lover.

Another first with Luke.

Then he lifted her until she slid down onto his shaft, impaling her and sealing them as one. A deep moan escaped him.

"You fit me so well," he murmured as he gripped her hips and helped her ride them both to completion.

* * * * *

In the near dark Aaron hunched over his kitchen table, the overhead pot light letting him study the files again. The faint light from his laptop flickered as he clicked it to update. Still no activity for their fake girl, Mary's profile. It was after midnight. Doubt they'd get a hit tonight. Might as well shut it down.

He signed out and closed the lid. Then he reached for the glass of rum and coke he'd been sipping on since coming home.

The information he'd learned at Edgars' safe house had stunned him. He'd been so sure he was looking for a serial killer. How had this sex slavery ring been working right under their noses all this time? Could someone in the local political scene, besides Senator Klein, be helping to keep the group's activities off the radar? If so, did their tentacles reach into his own department?

"Don't go looking for cases when there aren't any, Jeffers," his boss, Captain Davis, told him when he'd brought his suspicions to him about the possibility of a serial killer. *"Our job is to try and locate those people we know are missing, not those that might be."*

"There's an unusual amount of similarities in their backgrounds, sir."

"Doesn't matter. You stick to the cases assigned or I'll have you back in uniform. Is that clear?"

Yeah, the message had been loud and clear. Drop it or else.

Was the warning for a different reason than wasted man hours? Had his captain or someone higher up been involved with the slavery ring? If so, who did he trust with this?

If he went to the wrong people, the women could all disappear—permanently.

In the end he'd acquiesced, but only so far as not pursuing his investigation openly. After that conversation, he'd kept all his inquires on the down low and watched for any other women who might fit the similarities of his victims—and he'd been sure they were all connected somehow.

Only, he'd been way off base.

Lifting the pictures of the suspected victims, he looked at each of them slowly until their images burned in his brain, finishing with Brianna Mathews. He turned off the kitchen light, took her picture and stretched out on his sofa.

He studied Brianna's face.

Something about her fascinated him. Sure, she was drop-dead gorgeous. He'd noticed that the night she went missing. Hell, how couldn't he? Her home had been littered with pictures of her.

Normally a woman that narcissistic wouldn't interest him. The more he learned about her, the more intriguing she became. Abigail was loyal to the woman, so there was something more to her than vanity. According to Abigail, Brianna was quite good with numbers, so she was intelligent, but smart enough to hide the fact when it suited her. They hadn't discovered what she had planned to share with Abigail before her abduction, but he'd bet money that she'd somehow stumbled onto the slavery ring herself.

All the blood at both crime scenes—her condo and the warehouse—bothered him. Could she have survived that much blood loss? From what he knew about her, if there was one woman who could've lasted that torture, Brianna Mathews fit the bill. But to what cost?

The ringtone of his cell phone broke the silence in his apartment. He pulled it out of his pocket and looked at the caller ID.

"Haven't gotten any activity on the profile, Edgars,"

he said without preamble.

"Didn't expect you too. We're going to have to put that on the back burner for now."

The back of his neck tingled. Something had changed since he left the condo. "Something new come up?"

"Can you be at the safe house before noon tomorrow?"

Aaron checked the calendar on his phone. "Got to check in at the precinct, but then I can be there. Why? What's up?"

"There's another auction scheduled for Friday."

"Damn." He looked at the photo in his other hand again, a sinking feeling in his stomach. "You think they're going to move Ms. Mathews then."

"That's our guess. It's time to go on the offensive."

That idea suited him just fine.

CHAPTER 16

"Why the hell did you call the Marshal instead of one of us?" Luke's oldest brother, Dave, stood almost nose-to-nose with Luke, his voice and accusation rising over the conversations taking place all over the condo's great room and kitchen.

Abigail, sitting on one of the barstools, swiveled around to watch the pair. Ever since the invasion of Luke's family she'd been overwhelmed with the amount of people and noise surrounding her. She'd expected his brothers, but was surprised that not only had Luke's sister-in-law Katie come along, but his sister Samantha had, too. Both were nurses and thought they might be able to help.

"I needed a safe place here. Frank had one." Luke had his arms crossed over his chest. "What good would it have done me to call you?"

"Might've kept you from getting up to your ass in trouble." Dave poked him in the chest.

"You do know this is my job, right?" Luke took a

step closer, indignation written all over his face.

Were they seriously going to start hitting each other?

"They might shove a little, but they haven't hit each other since Dave left for college, except during kickboxing matches." Their sister, Sami, scooted onto the stool beside her. "Now, if it were Matt and Luke, yeah, it might come to blows."

"Or any of them and me," Sami's husband Jake said from the other side of the island. He was making another pot of coffee.

"They only attacked you once," Sami said, with a grin. "And that was only because you'd kidnapped me."

"He did?" Abigail turned to study the couple.

"Sure did," Jake said with a wink. Then leaned across the counter to kiss his wife. "Best damn thing I ever did in my life."

"Even if it meant Matt and Luke beat you up?" Sami teased.

"I gave as good as I got, and there were two of them and only one of me." Then his lips lifted in a mischievous grin. "Besides, I had to take it easy on them, I was already wounded."

"You've been using that excuse since the day we met," Luke said, his attention diverted from his older brother.

"That's because you attacked me the moment you walked into the cabin."

Matt wandered over from the sofa where he'd been seated next to his wife, watching his brothers. "In case you don't remember, you held our sister captive in the woods."

"He did?" Abigail asked Sami.

She leaned in to talk softly. "Yes. But it was only because he'd been wounded and needed my help."

"Doesn't matter, a man doesn't take a woman by force," Dave said.

The smile on Jake's face eased a little and a predatory gleam entered his eyes. "Trust me when I tell you I never *took* your sister by force, ever."

"Jake!" Sami stared at her husband with an open mouth and her face flushed bright pink.

And with that the two older brothers cornered their brother-in-law in the small kitchen.

"Want to take us all on now?" Matt said, shoving Jake in the shoulder.

Abigail looked over her shoulder at Luke who'd come to watch right behind her. "Aren't you going to stop them?" she said in a hushed voice.

He shook his head, resting his hands on her shoulders. "Nope. Figure let them take out their pissy attitudes on Jake, then they'll be more receptive of a plan from their little brother."

Dave muscled past his brothers. "Just you and me, Carlisle."

Jake stood nose-to-nose with the eldest Edgars. "You'd like that since you didn't get your chance last time, huh, Dave?"

"You need to learn to treat our sister with more

respect."

This statement froze the FBI agent. He looked at his wife, his face softening. "There's no one in the world I respect more than your sister. Even if I think she should've stayed home with our kids."

"And I told you, as a forensic and ER nurse I'm the most qualified to triage the injuries to Abigail's friend, as well as any other women we find tonight," Sami said.

A somber quiet filled the room. Abigail studied all the men in the house. Determination set along the thin lines of their mouths. Katie had come to stand by Matt, her hand slipping into his. Castello leaned against the door to the garage, part of the group, but still on the edges.

"Which brings me to the plan," Luke said as he squeezed her shoulders, the warmth of his hands easing some of her own tension. He filled his family in on as many details as possible, not even skimming over the charred female bodies they'd found. Finally, they talked about the mansion and scheduled party auction they suspected was happening the next night. "If they're going to move Abby's friend they might use the auction as a way to transport her out of the States." He squeezed Abgail's shoulders again. "Dead or alive."

"Make sense," Dave said. He looked at Jake. "Can your people cover the perimeter?"

"I'm meeting with them as soon as we're done here. We've called in the National Guard as part of a special task force. How about the local cops? Any help there?"

"We've been working quietly with a Detective Jeffers," Luke said. "He's bringing a few officers he trusts over around noon. We'll work them into the perimeter. Frank did some reconnaissance the other night so we know they have a dock on the backend onto Lake Erie." He moved to Abigail's side and punched a few keys on his laptop, bringing up the estate's ground schematics. He pointed to the lake side of the estate. "We'll need people here to prevent anyone escaping that direction."

"I can get Coast Guard backup," Jake said. "Dave you want to ride along with them?"

Dave nodded. "Always love a good boat ride."

"Good." Luke looked over at Castello. "We'll need to get eyes on the inside. We'll get Paolo to add me and Abby to the catering crew list. We'll use that as a way to search areas not in use for the party."

"That's not going to work," Abigail said, bracing for the argument about to happen.

Everyone stopped talking and turned to look at her.

"Not like we can knock on the door and ask to search. Without the evidence BettyJo was trying to get to you, we don't have a warrant," Luke said, pointing out the obvious. "To make any of this stick and shut them down, we're going to have to go in as staff and catch them in the act."

"It's *Brianna* and I know we have to go in undercover." When he gave her that I'm-so-glad-you-see-things-my-way-smile she continued, "Going in as staff won't work because Kirk F. Patrick told us the staff was limited to only certain areas of the house last time. They weren't allowed near anything that even hinted at the Senator and his son's involvement in human trafficking. Only guests of a certain type would have that access."

The smile died on his face and his eyes hardened. "No."

"She has a point," Dave said.

"Stay out of this, Dave," Luke growled without breaking eye contact with her.

"We could have two sets of people inside," Matt said.

"Matt and I could go in with the caterers," Katie said.

"And you could be a guest with his girl," Castello finished.

"No." Luke never took his eyes off Abigail.

"You know it's the only way," she said.

"We'll find another way."

"If we're going to find these women, we have to be able to play the game, for just one night."

"She's right, wonder genius," Castello said. "Someone's going to have to walk in there like they belong or we'll never find Brianna and the other women."

She laid her hand on Luke's, knowing he was thinking about the dream again. "I'll be safe, right beside you. You won't let anything happen to me."

"Damn straight." He stared at her hard, then at every other person in the room, slowly making his decision. "We'll have two pairs of operatives in the house. Katie and Matt, you can go in with Paolo's catering team." He looked at Castello. "We'll have Kirk F. Patrick get them uniforms."

"Who's this Kirk F. Patrick?" Jake asked.

"And what's the F stand for?" Matt asked.

"He's one of Castello's minions. And you can ask him about the F tonight." Luke winked at Abigail then went back to the estate's layout. "A lot of the party seemed to take place out on the balcony area in back last time, so we'll need a team there. Jake, you coordinate your people at these exits and Sami, you're going to need to be close enough to come in once we have the women. Let's have you just outside the estate and down the road. We'll need a van to carry the injured. You think you can handle that?"

His younger sister's face lit up. "If it's got wheels and a gear shift I can handle it."

"No stunt driving, Samantha," her husband said, his voice full of warning.

"Who, me?" She batted her eyes at Jake and all her brothers laughed.

Certain it was a family joke, Abigail was just glad to have the tension in the room eased a bit.

"There's still one problem," Dave said. "How are you going to get onto this exclusive list?"

Abigail looked at Luke then grinned at his oldest brother. "Not a problem at all. He'll hack us in."

* * * * *

What was taking her so long?

Luke looked at the bedroom door for the second time in five minutes and tugged at the collar of his silk dress shirt.

While he'd been busy hacking into Dylan Klein's private email accounts and files—a very sordid place that left him feeling slimy, but nothing to connect him directly to the women or the dating websites—and setting up two extra attendees among the hundred-plus on the guest list, Sami and Katie had taken Abby on a shopping trip. They'd managed him this getup of gray silk shirt, skinny black tie, and charcoal suit, as well as medical supplies the girls thought they might need. Once he'd gotten cleaned up and dressed, they'd shoved him out of the bedroom to get Katie in her catering uniform and Abby into her undercover clothes.

An hour and a half ago.

He checked the guest list on line once more. Their names were still on there. Or rather, his was. Deciding to go with the master and submissive idea, he'd posted his real name—easier to keep track of the truth than try to remember a lie—and kept Abby as "a guest". If anyone asked, he planned to introduce her as *my girl* or Ms. Whitson.

He'd made sure to attach his cover ID as a computer software engineer and CEO of a Fortune 500 company, along with a contact to his fictitious company's website in case anyone got curious and wanted to check it out. Hopefully, it would withstand any scrutiny at least for tonight. He just hoped that if Senator Klein was at the auction party, he wouldn't remember their brief meeting back in December.

Dave, Jake and Sami had headed out to meet with the Jeffers' police team, Jake's people and the National Guard. They wanted to be in place and deep in cover before guests arrived. He and Abby needed to find her friend before Jake's team closed the dragnet. Jake also wanted to be sure the Coast Guard was far enough out that no guests arriving by boat would get spooked.

That was forty-five minutes ago.

Matt had already collected Katie, both of them dressed in black pants, white shirts and black bowties—the server uniforms to help them blend in—and the pair headed out to meet up with Kirk and join Paolo's catering crew. They'd double checked their weapons before leaving and thanks to Jake's team of FBI agents all of the family was wired with ear buds to hear the team's actions. They also had the new fancy phone watches that allowed them to communicate if needed. They'd coordinated numbers and how to conference call to their ear buds before they left.

That was thirty minutes ago.

The front door opened and in walked Castello,

looking very chauffer-bodyguard-ish. "Don't say it."

He couldn't help it. "Is the car ready, Jeeves?"

Frank narrowed his eyes at him. "Screw you, Edgars. If it weren't for Abigail going in there with you, you'd be driving yourself. Speaking of which, where is your date for this shindig?"

"Still getting ready." He looked at his watch and strode over to the bedroom door, knocking a little harder than usual. "Abby, we need to leave. We want to be going in with the rest of the crowd, not standing out by showing up last."

The door opened and there stood every man's teenage wet dream.

He started at her toes and worked his way up past her long legs encased in black leather boots up to her mid thighs. A small patch of her creamy white skin peek out between the tops of her boots and the hem of the black-lace mini dress with a V so deep it nearly went to her belly button, beneath which he could make out her black panties and more acres of pale flesh. Her dark hair was sleeked back into a shiny ponytail. Around her neck was a metal necklace that looked like a series of bent half-moons strung on a gold chain that dipped down to cover the exposed top of her cleavage, which only drew your eyes to the swells of her braless breasts. Large round hoop earrings dangled from her ears. Makeup had been applied with the brush of an artist, the final pop of color being her crimson lips.

As if she knew he couldn't take his eyes off her lips,

she parted them and slipped her tongue out to lick across them.

"Whoa," Castello murmured behind them, snapping Luke out of the seductive haze swirling through his mind and body.

"You have to change." It wasn't a request. No way was he taking her into that den of jackals looking like the tastiest morsel for them to consume.

"I can't," she said with determination in her eyes.

"She can't."

He looked at Castello.

His soon-to-be-ex-friend shrugged and pointed at his watch. "If we're doing this we need to leave *now*."

With a growl he reached for the long trench coat slung over her arm and held it for her. "Where's your weapon hidden?"

"I'm not wearing one," she replied as she slipped her arms into the coat and headed out the door to the car.

"You're going to an operation completely unarmed?" Fury swept through him. Even as untried in the field as she was, she was smarter than this.

"I'm not unarmed," she said, smiling sweetly at Castello as he held the backseat door of the sedan open for her, making Luke want to tear the grin off his friend's face.

He settled into the seat beside her. "You aren't unarmed? With no weapon?"

"I have a weapon." Opening the long purse dangling off her shoulder by a thin chain, she showed him its contents—an ear bud, a gold compact and a tube of lipstick.

"Unless that lipstick's some sort of James Bond gadget gun, that's not funny, sweetheart," he practically growled at her.

"This is a special bag your sister-in-law gave me in case they're searching the women guests' bags," she said, pulling back a flap and there, below the other items was a small gun. She took the ear bud and fixed it deep in her ear, then smiled at him. "Katie gave me this one because it's so lightweight. The beads of the bag and the heavy compact will explain the weight if anyone holds it besides me. See? I have a weapon, I just don't have it on me, besides, I have you by my side. What more protection do I need?"

As they headed out for the mansion, the sense of dread he'd had since the evening he found Abby standing in that bloody chaotic crime scene intensified. He grasped her hand in his, staring down into her eyes. "No matter what happens, don't leave my side tonight."

* * * * *

"We're in position," Aaron Jeffers spoke into his headpiece.

He and a handful of cops he trusted were mixed in among the federal agents Edgars' brother-in-law had supplied for the operation. Right now he and a rookie cop, Jackson, were settled in the bushes directly across from a small door several feet from the kitchen entrance on the west side of the mansion. The area sloped downward from the front and back of the house into what he assumed was the basement level.

The caterer's trucks and crew arrived, along with Edgars' older brother and sister-in-law. He had to admit the guy's family was impressive with not only their skills and connections, but their loyalty to each other. When Luke had called, the only issue any of them had wasn't with him needing their help, but him waiting too long to call.

Dave, the oldest brother, had been particularly pissed off that Luke had called Marshal Castello instead of him. A small, humorous thought hit him. He might envy Luke his big family, but as an only child he'd never had to answer to an older brother or two.

Light at the kitchen caught his attention as someone came out to the van then went back inside. The area on this side of the house was dark as most of the party activity seemed to be on the north side where the main patio and balconies were and to the east where the patio extended into the garden.

Since he knew the files of the five women he'd been tracking, the team thought he should be one of the ones inside searching. The idea was to get him into the mansion to help locate and secure the women, in particular Ms. Mathews, since she could bear witness to how the women were bought and sold.

Once the party was underway he was to gain access

to that door and wait for instructions from Edgars. If Edgars' schematics of the place were correct, that entrance was near the stairwell that led to the basement—the place the women were most likely being held.

Images of all the blood at both the condo and garage crime scenes filled his mind. He just hoped Ms. Mathews was alive inside this place. Such a beautiful and courageous woman deserved to get justice.

* * * * *

"Sami?"

"Yes, Jake?" She smiled in the dark. It was the third time he'd checked her position in the past thirty minutes.

"You know to stay hidden until we've secured the women and all the gang, right?"

"Yes. We haven't moved since you left us." She resisted the urge to roll her eyes. Really the man was such a worrywart about her. She was in the safest place of everyone.

"Special Agent Malcom is there with you?"

She glanced at the young agent seated beside her. "Yes, he's videoing every car and license plate that passes us on the way into the mansion. Just like you instructed him."

Jake had left Malcom with her. Another team, including some highway patrolmen Matt had called in, were just a few yards farther back down the road, ready to shut off access in or out of the estate once the action started inside the mansion.

"Good," Jake said. "Luke and Abigail should be passing you soon. Stay safe."

Shaking her head at his overprotective side, she glanced at her watch as another SUV passed their hiding spot. They'd agreed on the time for Luke and Abigail's arrival, so the teams would be on alert that their operatives were in the building. Once inside the mansion, the GPS on Luke's watch would ping off the similar one Matt wore and on the watches of the other main team members, Dave, Jake, Castello and the police detective Jeffers. That would be the signal for the detective to get inside the building.

Her job was to be ready to drive onto the estate once the women had been found and the perpetrators rounded up. She clenched her hand around the steering wheel.

How many women were there? Was Abigail's friend still there? Was she alive? According to Abigail and Luke, they believed she'd been tortured and had lost quite a bit of blood. The physical injuries would be her first priority, but how much mental torture had she and the other women suffered?

Another car passed them. Special Agent Malcolm snapped the license plate with his infrared camera, then checked the letters and numbers against the one for Luke's sedan.

"It's a match, ma'am," he said.

She talked into the watch phone on her wrist. "Jake, they're here."

Time for the party to begin.

* * * * *

While the undercover operation might be Luke and Abigail's to run, it was Jake's responsibility to see that everything went off without a hitch. Especially keeping Sami out of the mix until all the danger was complete. She wasn't happy about it, but she was part of the mop-up detail.

Hunkered down beneath a copse of huge Michigan pines, he studied the map of the estate on his phone with Captain Davis of the National Guard. As a Supervisory Special Agent, Jake had let the Special Agent in charge of his area know the bones of the case and the suspected kidnapping and enslavement of women. They'd quickly formed a makeshift task force for tonight's operation and called in the National Guard, Coast Guard and highway patrol to pad their numbers, as well as make a tight net for capturing anyone involved.

"Jeffers' team is on the west side of the building. Dave's team from the Coast Guard will cover the lakefront. That leaves us with the east side where the patio extends and the main entrance." He pointed to the two spots on the map. "You take half your men, Captain, and scatter them on both sides of the main entrance. The highway patrol are securing the road on both sides to prevent anyone else from entering now that my people are inside. I'll spread the rest of your men on the east side. No one moves until the word Omaha comes from me, understand?"

"Yes, sir. Omaha is the go word."

Silently, Davis and half his detail moved out using the trees as cover on their way to surround the main entrance.

Jake turned to the young sergeant left with him. Using hand signals, he instructed them to move out in pairs, spreading through the trees and slowly making a net to prevent anyone escaping.

"Erie One come in," he said into his watch phone.

"This is Erie One, Eagle's Nest. We're in position," Dave replied.

"The net is in place. Close the water exit."

"Roger that."

Jake inhaled and slowly blew out the air. Everything was in position. It was up to Luke and Abigail now.

* * * * *

Standing on the bridge of the Coast Guard boat about a football field's length down the shore from the estate's pier, Dave heard Sami's announcement that Luke and Abigail had arrived. A final boat steered into the dock. He contacted the second Coast Guard boat to move closer. No one was to enter or leave the area now that their people were inside the mansion.

He wished he was inside. It ate at him that both his younger brothers and their women were inside where all the potential danger lay and he was working the perimeter. Matt and Katie didn't worry him too much. The pair worked well together. He'd seen that when they'd helped rescue his wife last winter. They'd watch each other's back.

It was Luke that had him concerned. Usually, he was the smart ass who would take unnecessary risks. Hell, that's how he'd gotten into hacking and nearly jailed as a teenager. It had taken a few rounds in the kick boxing ring and a serious conversation to convince the kid his skills could be put to better use. In the past, he'd always been a good team member, but this was a different case. This time he was in the epicenter and his life was on the line, not to mention the lives of his partner, Abigail, and their witness, Ms. Mathews.

For the first time his youngest brother seemed to be taking the situation very seriously. It was as if finding these women and stopping the slave traders had become personal.

A smile tugged at his lips.

Okay, it was Abigail that had made it personal to Luke. That was evident from the moment he'd introduced her to them. Sometimes it just took the right woman to make a man step up.

As the boat neared the shoreline and the mansion came into view, he lifted his binoculars to watch the last group of guests exit the small yacht.

A large bodyguard exited first, securing the gangplank. Behind him came an Asian businessman and a young, barely dressed woman. He shook his head. In all his years in law enforcement, it never ceased to amaze him what kinds of kinks people would get into.

The trio walked down the gangplank and to the entrance to the patio where dozens of people mingled. He adjusted his scopes to study the crowd. Although there were definitely guards walking discreetly around the perimeter—big, bulky guys in suits—none seemed to be openly carrying weapons. What they had under the suits was a whole other question.

After a few minutes, Luke stepped out on the patio, a scowl on his face and on his arm—

Holy shit!

Abigail looked like a supermodel dressed to catch the eye of every male in the place.

* * * * *

"We're glad you could join us tonight, Mr. Edgars," Peter Hollister said, shaking Luke's hand.

As they'd driven to the mansion Abigail had studied pictures of all the guests expected to be at the auction party tonight, as well as the management staff of Hollister-Klein, on her laptop. Peter Hollister, the Chief Marketing Officer for the company, was just as movie-star handsome in person as he was on the website. A number of their guests tonight were corporate managers for their clients. Was being part of the sex slave ring a perk for doing business with Hollister-Klein and part of Peter's marketing plan?

"I'm most happy to be included in tonight's gathering. Such a nice change of pace from the usual country-club fare most companies offer," Luke said, using his charming I'm-harmless smile on one of their hosts. He turned to nod at her. "This is *my girl*, Ms. Whitson."

"Welcome, Ms. Whitson." Not offering to shake her hand which would suggest she was his equal, Hollister slid his gaze over her from head to toe and back, stopping at her chest where the black lace dress hinted at everything beneath. She tried not to shiver in disgust at the leering interest the man didn't even bother to hide.

Despite Luke's displeasure at her outfit, compared to the other women in the room, she was almost dressed conservatively. Other than a lingerie fashion show she'd once attended with Brianna, she'd never seen so many corsets and thongs on display in one place. While she maintained an exterior calm and subdued image—a submissive woman on the arm of the man responsible for her every need—her inner self wanted to gawk open-mouthed like a kid at a circus sideshow at the other women on display.

To keep from smacking the arrogant prick Hollister, she gripped Luke's elbow tighter, lowered her eyes and gave what she hoped was a demure smile.

It must've worked because he shifted his attention back to Luke. "I see she's quite well trained."

Luke gave a scoffing laugh. "She is now, but it's taken quite a bit of effort to convince her who was ultimately in charge. But the training has had its benefits. She meets my needs on every level."

Grinding her teeth, she subtly pinched the inside of Luke's arm as they discussed her as if she were no more than a pet or piece of property. She knew it was all part of the act to fit into their environment, but he didn't have to enjoy her humiliation quite so much.

"I can see how she would." Hollister gave her another creepy onceover, then turned away, dismissing her as unimportant. "I wonder why, then, you've chosen to attend our little party tonight?"

"As delightful as it is to have my girl so well trained," Luke said, glancing at her, then turning back to Hollister, "I find I'm in the mood to acquire new property that might need a firmer hand, if you will. Nothing like taking raw material and forging it into a rare gem. And no cost would be too high."

At least on paper. The cover he'd given himself and the backstory of his bank account she'd set up was one of the reasons Hollister singled them out right after they arrived. Other people's greed was such a useful tool.

It was Hollister's turn to laugh. "I think you may be quite interested in what we have available tonight. Perhaps you'd even consider making a trade or offering your girl as part of a discount on new merchandise?"

Luke's arm tensed under Abigail's hand. As much as she didn't want to blow their cover, she was glad the other man's suggestion made Luke angry. It made her feel secure, something she hadn't felt since she stepped foot inside the mansion.

"Oh, I'm not done with Ms. Whitson yet," Luke said, then nodded to the right corner of the patio. "Isn't that Judge Pardell?"

Hollister's attention pivoted to the far corner and a smile of pure greed parted his lips. "Yes, it is and I must have a word with him. Do feel free to sample any delights you might find, won't you? The main art gallery is open tonight."

And with that he wove his way through the crowd like a shark searching for fresh blood.

"Damn, I need a shower," Luke muttered as he reached for a champagne flute on the tray nearing them.

"Don't say that too loud," Katie said, holding the tray as steady as any experienced waitress and offering a smile. "They may offer to take you up on it."

Abigail bit back her grin. She liked Luke's sister-in-law. She didn't hide her disdain for the people circulating around them.

"Be careful not to get too close to these guys," Luke said quietly to Katie as he handed the glass to Abigail and reached for a second. "Don't want you disappearing tonight or Matt will have my head."

"Don't worry, I can handle myself." Katie smiled at

them and moved back a bit. "Yes, sir, we're circulating canapés, too."

Luke clinked his glass with Abigail's then took a slow sip, turning to scan the crowd on the patio. She followed suit, not making eye contact with anyone, but cataloging each face with those from the guest list. Besides Judge Pardell there were two county judges from the southern portion of the state, an assistant district attorney, corporate heads of several technology and financial companies, as well as foreign businessmen.

"I don't see either Senator Klein or his son Dylan," she leaned in to whisper in Luke's ear.

He nodded, then turned and stroked a finger down her cheek, gazing into her eyes so deeply she almost forgot they were on a case. "They're here somewhere and they'll be the ones to lead us to your friend. But we can't make a move until we've located her, so perhaps it's time to peruse the mansion's artwork?"

Oh, great. She'd seen glimpses of some of the art around the main ballroom. Little more than black-and-white porn, in her opinion. Given the sliminess of Peter Hollister, she could only imagine that the club's gallery held more of the same.

"Smile, darling," Luke said as he steered her towards the French doors leading back into the ballroom. "The women in the photos might just be some we're looking for."

Even though she knew she'd never forget anything

she saw, she put on a smile and walked beside him. She'd look at the photos for the evidence, but planned to make a deep, dark file in her brain and never bring the images out once she put them there. Please God, don't let any of them be Brianna.

CHAPTER 17

Dylan stood at the foot of the bed, tying his black bow tie and studying the woman stretched out before him. Her hands firmly bound the railing of the headboard, she would be a tempting vision to several of their guests. He let his gaze wander over her alabaster skin from her toes to her face, the cuts and bruises inflicted upon her by his men in various stages of healing—a sensual palette of black, blue, purple, green and darkly dried blood against all her white skin.

Yes, in this condition Master Lee would pay quite a price for her tonight.

He retrieved his black onyx cufflinks from the dresser and worked them into his cuffs as he watched the gentle rise and fall of the slut's breasts as she slept, exhausted and drugged on the bed. Despite his mastering of her body and commanding her to tell him where she'd hidden the flash drive with the company's secret accounts, she'd held firm to her story of leaving it with an Abbey. Even when he'd resorted to sodium pentothal, she'd never wavered from the same statement.

It was a shame, really.

Had he known she possessed such strength of will, endurance to pain and stubbornness, he would've taken great pleasure in taming her to meet his needs. The combination of those traits in a female was rare. He would have to search long and hard to find another such specimen. But there was too much at risk in keeping her around. Even if he never found the flash drive, getting rid of her as a witness was the best option. Obtaining a substantial financial boon to his coffers was an added bonus.

Given Master Lee's proclivities, he doubted even Brianna could withstand his special brand of torture for long. Then he wouldn't have to worry about anyone from whatever Abbey she'd left the flash drive with finding her or proceeding with exposing the company's most lucrative investments.

Shrugging into his tuxedo jacket, he slowly pulled the sheet up over her body. It would be a special delight to reveal to Master Lee what was beneath.

* * * * *

Aaron moved into the bushes near the side entrance of the mansion. He paused and listened for anyone raising an alarm at his movements.

None came.

He flashed his laser pointer three times at where he'd left Jackson to signal he was in position. The kid was to stay put unless he got the SOS signal to come running.

Slipping between the bushes and the wall, he studied the door to his left.

Simple dead latch lock. Should be easy enough to pick.

With deft fingers, he used his two picks on the lock, opened the door and slid inside. Pressing his body against the wall, he waited for his eyes to adjust to the dim light inside the basement hallway.

Again, he listened for the sounds of an alarm or the pounding of feet as guards ran to answer a silent alarm.

Nothing.

No noise but the sound of the catering team farther to his left.

Apparently the club suspended any alarms on a gala night such as this. Made sense. No one wanted the intrusion of the local authorities while they sold humans to the highest bidder, just because a caterer or guest opened the wrong door.

He eased his way down the hall, staying against the wall. Coming to a doorway, he tested the knob and breathed a sigh of relief when it opened.

The scent of chlorine hit him.

Great, he'd found the cleaning closet.

He slipped inside. It was actually a good spot to study the map Edgars had sent his phone without worrying about getting caught.

"Carlisle, I'm inside just south of the kitchen in the lower level. No alarms. No guards," he said over his watch phone on the frequency the FBI agent was monitoring.

"Do you have a clear sight to the area?"

"The hallway from the door is free of personnel. I can start working my way inward." He was itching to get moving and find the women.

"Hold your position for now. Luke and Abigail just moved farther into the house."

"I'm a go when you give the word."

He hunkered down near the door, keeping it cracked to watch any activity in the hallway. He just prayed no one came looking for a mop.

* * * * *

Matt moved in tandem with his wife staying within a few feet of her as they worked the rooms with glasses of expensive champagne, wines and delicate hors d'oeuvres. He'd snuck a sample of a few back in the kitchen and had to admit that Paolo was quite a talented chef. Too bad his highest-paying customer was a pervert whose sex slave ring they planned to shut down tonight.

Katie moved to a group of older gentleman with her tray of drinks. Something one of them said made her smile, but not her friendly, happy smile. No, this was the slightly tight one she gave whenever she was uncomfortable, but didn't want the other person to know it.

Damn, what had the gray-haired bastard said to her?

He slipped around two couples just in time to see another of the men reach out and grasp her ass.

A growl sounded low in his throat, but he swallowed it and moved closer as Katie moved out of the man's reach with a forced laugh and headed out of the ballroom.

"Easy, Matt," she said into the ear bud in his ear. "You can pummel them later once we have what we came for."

"Stay clear of them when you go back in," he muttered, heading in the same path she'd just gone towards the kitchen. "The bastard touches you again and I'm breaking his hand. Accidentally, of course."

Turning the corner, he slammed right into her, clutching her to him with one arm and balancing the nearly empty food tray in the other.

"What the hell—?" he whispered.

"Shh." Putting her fingers to his lips she pointed to the stairs leading up from the outside door to the lobby area they'd just left.

Walking through the lobby was an older oriental man with a bodyguard proceeding him, but what caught Katie and Matt's attention was the slim woman walking behind him. Eyes downcast, she had a bracelet on one hand which was attached to a diamond chain, the other end clutched firmly in the man's hand.

Matt pushed Katie farther down the hallway, away from the group and out of sight. Just as they stepped into a shadow to continue watching, the group bypassed the main ballroom to a room off to the left. A quick rap on the door and it opened. A face very familiar to the Edgars family appeared.

"Ah, Master Lee, it's good to see you've arrived," Senator Howard Klein shook the Asian man's free hand and ushered them into the bookshelf lined room.

Matt hit the button to communicate with all the team. "Senator Klein is on the premises."

"Any sign of Dylan?" Luke asked.

"None yet. He may be in what looks like a library with his father. Another player was escorted there."

"Who?" Jake asked.

"A Master Lee."

There was a pause, then Luke came on. "Abby says he has a major international import-export firm like Hollister-Klein with ties all over Southeast Asia."

"You any closer to finding Ms. Mathews?" Jake asked.

As the team talked, Matt moved Katie farther down the corridor so as not to attract attention, but still able to keep an eye on the door still guarded by Master Lee's bodyguard.

"Not yet, although Hollister hinted there might be something special available this evening. He directed Abby and me to the art gallery hall. There are a few couples milling about in here as if they're waiting for something."

"Perhaps Dylan Klein?" Katie asked.

"Could be," Jake said. "But now we have a bigger problem. If Lee has international ties and gets Brianna out of there we'll never see her again."

They could all hear a soft gasp from Abigail. Katie looked at Matt with wide, worried eyes.

"We'll start closing the perimeter. Matt, can you and Katie meet Jeffers on the lower level and start checking the rooms down there?"

"We're on it."

He grabbed Katie's hand and headed back to the kitchen. They deposited their nearly empty trays on the counter, then went into a hidden area by one of the hot boxes. Katie pulled out her over-the-shoulder bag and was handing Matt his weapon when Kirk F. Patrick stepped into the kitchen.

"Where you two headed?"

Matt slipped his weapon into the small holster in the back waistband of his pants. "It's time to start searching the place. You know what you're supposed to do?"

Kirk nodded. "Herd Paolo and the other wait staff into this room when you give the signal and don't let anyone in or out until the all clear."

Matt looked the kid straight in the eyes. "And stay low. Especially if there's any shooting. No heroics."

"Learned that in grade school, man. Duck, cover and roll out of danger." Kirk went to secure the kitchen exit to the drive. "You just find those ladies."

"We'll see you when it's over." He turned to Katie and gave her a quick kiss. "You ready?"

She gave him a sassy grin. "Oh, yeah. Let's go kick some ass."

* * * * *

"Do you think Hollister steered us this way on purpose?" Abigail leaned in to whisper in Luke's ear.

With a lusty look he slid his hand down and squeezed her bottom. "I'd bet on it. Look who's around us."

Eight other couples milled about the long gallery. Abigail focused on cataloguing the men. Each of them could afford to buy an island nation if they wished, so purchasing slaves wasn't out of their financial realm. Each of the men exuded confidence and an arrogance that they had every right to buy another human being. As disturbing as knowing such men existed, keeping her attention on them was more palatable to her than actually looking at the photos of women in bondage—each more graphic than the next.

The whole situation turned her stomach.

"Easy, Ms. Whitson," Luke whispered in her ear. "Any sign of temper in your character would require me to show you discipline or risk blowing our cover. Remember why we're here."

Quickly, she dropped her gaze and masked the rage boiling through her.

I can shoot the bastards later. I can shoot the bastards later.

The words repeating in her head and the heat of Luke's body pressed along the length of hers took the edge off her rage. Brianna and the other women were depending on them. No matter what, she couldn't let her feelings show until they were safe.

Just as she'd gathered her composure, the door at the far end of the gallery opened. In walked Peter Hollister with the judge on his heels.

"Those of you who were invited to view the gallery are a very select group with special tastes. I do hope these images have whetted your appetite for what we have for sale today."

Murmurs from the group confirmed they were indeed excited to be included in this private auction. Luke nodded his head and gave a look that indicated he was quite interested in seeing what was offered.

"Good, good," Hollister said, opening the door behind him once more. "Then please follow me to the library where viewing of our specimens can begin."

The small crowd moved into the library. Luke maneuvered her so they stayed almost on the periphery of the group. Interested, but not attention seeking. Very deftly he pressed the buttons on his wrist phone. They'd planned to have an open channel to the small team and record the evening's activities now that the real show had started.

Inside the library the Asian gentleman, Master Lee,

his bodyguard and female slave were already seated. To Master Lee's left sat Senator Howard Klein—with the cool, calm poise of a seasoned politician and the posture of the privileged.

Many large wingback chairs faced several flat screen TVs, and the other men settled themselves in the chairs, their female companions standing next to or just behind each chair. Luke followed suit, but pulled on Abigail's hand to have her sit on the arm of his chair, draping his arm around the curve of her bottom. Despite the comfort of him keeping her close, she suspected he wanted to keep her from lashing out once the videos started.

Good thing. She was itching to do something, anything to stop this.

Hollister stood in the front of the room between the two largest screens. "Gentlemen, welcome to The Titan Club's Pygmalion auction. Tonight you can purchase a raw, plain woman and with discipline and training turn her into one of the rare submissive beauties that already grace our room tonight."

Abby tensed beside Luke.

He squeezed her outer thigh to remind her to stay in character. As she relaxed again a surge of pride in her rushed through him. The old Abby wouldn't have made it into the mansion without losing her temper and shooting someone, much less be ogled by strangers, act like his property and obey a silent command to behave.

This undercover Abby was very impressive.

"First up is a brunette."

The two main screens flashed on and there, bound to a wooden chair in what looked like a room made of a gray concrete blocks, sat a young woman dressed only in a thin-strapped dress—her long hair was pulled up into a ponytail and no makeup on her face. Her eyes were downcast, but appeared dull.

Drugs?

No evidence of recent abuse such as scars or bruises were evident on the video.

"As you can see she is a very ripe specimen for a Master with a strong hand to mold her. We can start the bidding at fifty thousand."

"How long ago was this film made?" A white haired man seated near the front asked.

Hollister smiled. "This isn't a video, sir. It's a live feed from our holding rooms on the premises."

At that the arm of a man reached in and lifted the girl's chin so her face was center on the camera.

"They've got cameras on them, Jeffers," Jake said over the ear bud in Luke's ear.

"Got that. The caterers are here and we're headed down another back stairs."

"Ah, a fresh specimen, indeed," the white-haired man said. "I'll bid with fifty thousand."

And with that the auction began in earnest. For the next thirty minutes, one woman after another appeared on the screen, each being sold as if little more than cattle. Luke's stomach turned each time a new captive appeared. He was surprised that there were no young teens in the mix. Apparently the group didn't want to run afoul of pedophile laws, too.

Just to confirm his interest, Luke made an initial bid a time or two, but never fully engage anyone. An antsy anticipation itched along his spine as Jake and Jeffers' chatter played in his ear.

"There's a long hallway down here. Every door has a barred window in the top."

"Guards?"

"Only two who are moving from cell to cell."

"Any sign of Ms. Mathews?"

"None, yet."

Then something changed.

A plain-looking woman with dark hair and eyes almost hidden by her glasses came on the scene. There was a small mole near the left corner of her upper lip.

Abby tensed beside him again, this time her attention fixated on the screen nearest them. She recognized the woman. It wasn't her friend, as Brianna was a blonde and very tall, like Abby. No, this woman appeared to be petite.

He pulled Abby's hand to his lips and she looked at him, nodding slightly.

It was one of Jeffers' missing women. Now they had evidence to connect them to the case. Probable cause to be here.

The bidding was fast and furious once more. When it

ended a huge, bald man with gold studs up the entire side of one ear owned her—for the moment.

The screens went dark and Hollister stepped forward again. "Gentlemen, that concludes our auction of untrained specimens for tonight. However, we do have one more item up for sale, but because this is such special merchandise, the bidding will begin at one million dollars. If you are unable to cover that bid, we'd ask that you go ahead and return to the main ballroom. All deposits must be made and confirmed to the account number you were given on your email before merchandise can be claimed tonight."

A wave of male murmuring rolled through the room as all but three of the buyers left the room.

Luke studied the remaining men in the room. Besides himself, Hollister, Senator Klein and the distinguished looking Master Lee, the other man looked to be an Arab prince of some sort. Abby could probably quote him the man's complete dossier if he had the time and privacy to ask her.

The thought stopped him short.

From the moment they'd reconnected in that crime scene, he'd come to depend on Abby for so many things. It wasn't just that she had a unique brain and was a smart agent. Her heart and caring for her friend, as well as all the other women, wove around him. He respected her abilities and found himself wanting to talk about everything with her. What would it be to just sit and talk about ordinary things with her over a quiet dinner?

He lifted her hand once more, kissing her fingertips as she turned to look questioningly at him. With his other hand, he gave her a gently reassuring squeeze to her hip. The only item left for the club to auction off had to be her friend and they both knew it.

"The guards have finished and are out of commission."

"Any alarms?"

"The caterers found it and Katie is dismantling it now."

"Let us know when you're ready to go in. Castello, you in position?"

"Just down the hall with eyes on the library."

"Luke, you need to give us some sort of clue as to where she is."

"Now, gentlemen, I have a very rare item for you tonight. This is the kind of specimen that can take quite a bit of discipline without breaking her spirit."

The screens came alive again.

There stood Dylan Klein, complete in tux, in the center of a well-decorated room. "Welcome to each of you, gentlemen. I have behind me something quite unique, as you are about to see. A specimen with great stamina. Imagine, if you will, a woman so strong willed who can not only survive the punishment that can cause these types of markings, but still maintain her silence on a sensitive subject."

He moved to the side and the camera focused in on a

large four poster bed. Dylan moved up the side of the bed on which the form of a woman's body lay beneath a white sheet, the only part visible were her arms bound with black rope to the wooden slats of the headboard. The camera focused in on the bed as Klein moved the sheet from over the woman's face.

Abby clutched his hand tight, her fingernails digging into the flesh of his thumb, but damn, she didn't make a sound.

Luke sat forward, swallowing both the bile and rage that threatened to spill out at the site.

Brianna's face was in different shades of black, blue and green. Her lips were cracked in several places and one eye appeared to be swollen shut. Given what her pictures had looked like, he'd guess her nose was broken in at least one, if not more, places.

"As you can see," Klein's voice narrated as the camera shifted up her arms. "We've tested her stamina at great lengths and yet she's kept her spirit."

Dark bruises and large, scabbed-over gashes extended from her fingers back down to her shoulders. Klein moved the sheet further down to show her naked body. Bruises again covered her torso below her breasts, which moved with easy motions to indicate she still breathed, and down to her hips.

No doubt about it. The bastards had systematically beaten and tortured her.

* * * * *

"One million dollars," Luke said, signaling to the team he'd found Brianna Mathews.

Jake listened intently as more bids could be heard in the background from Luke's wrist phone. Time to close the net.

He accessed the main team's wrist phones. "Erie One, secure the dock. Jeffers, how's it coming down there?"

"Alarms are off and we have half the women free, moving them cell to cell to keep safe, over."

He pressed the button for Kirk F. Patrick's phone. "Kid start getting the catering crew out of harm's way."

"Roger that, G-man."

Jake switched over to the walkie-talkies for the National Guard and local police teams. "Close the perimeter by fifty feet, then hold your positions."

"Fifty feet closure and maintain." Captain Davis said and Jake watched as the men flanking him inched toward the mansion then dropped to the grass and froze.

"We're in position, Luke. Just give us her location or use the call word."

* * * * *

Of the twenty women they'd rescued only two of them were in the case files Aaron had been working before this all started. Likely the other three were either among the bodies they'd found charred in the garage warehouse or had already disappeared into the slave ring's system—never to be seen again.

Katie, a nurse by trade, walked among them, reassuring them they were safe, checking pulses and eyes. She looked up at her husband and Aaron and shook her head. The women were all drugged to various stages of lethargy.

Matt motioned with his head to move to the door. "We've got this. Luke, Abigail and Castello may need more man power."

"You're sure?" He looked over at the women huddled in a group on the cot and floor.

"Katie isn't leaving them, and I'm not leaving her," Matt said, determination lacing his words. No one was getting between him and his woman.

The picture of the beautiful blonde woman that had been smart enough to decipher what was going on filled Aaron's mind. A surge of protectiveness hit him. Brianna Mathews deserved to make it out of this alive. And he damn well wanted to make sure of it.

"Then I'm going." He lifted his wrist and spoke into the phone. "Castello, I'm on my way to you."

"Roger. Watch your six."

With a nod to Katie and Matt, he opened the cell door and slid into the hallway.

* * * * *

Fighting the tears that burned her eyes, Abigail studied the room in which Brianna was held. And it *was* a room, not a concrete dungeon cell like the other women. Despite her wounds, she looked almost posed for a pornographic photo or film.

As if she were a willing participant.

The Brianna she knew might indulge herself with dating numerous men, but she'd never sell herself so short as to be part of some kinky photo op. Would she if she'd been tortured? No. She'd worked too hard for her own self-respect. But if she were drugged?

She leaned a little forward, studying her friend's unusually still form. Her chest moved with the slight effort of natural breathing, otherwise she remained completely motionless.

They'd drugged her.

As Dylan exposed her friend, the camera panned to show her body. To the left of the bed was a window. And in it shone the moon.

"Four million," Luke said firmly beside her, still participating in the auction. In the car on the way to the mansion, he'd explained he wanted to try to buy Brianna if she was one of the women for sale. It would be the easiest way to get her out of the place before they took down the ring. Option two was take her by force.

Her hand still in the grasp of Luke's with the watch phone on it, she slowly leaned in to his side, a forced smile on her face, as if she was saying something suggestive about the bound victim.

"She's not in the basement. She's upstairs somewhere," she whispered near the phone for the others to hear.

Master Lee cast a narrow gaze at Luke, then spoke to Senator Klein.

"We have a bid of ten million dollars," the Senator said, then stood. "I do believe that will close this auction. Thank you, gentlemen for coming."

Neither the Arab nor Luke argued. They simply rose and shook both Hollister and the senator's hands.

No!

Abigail wanted to scream. She wanted to pull her weapon, hold it to their heads and demand they take her to Brianna. But she didn't know how many men were in the room with her friend. Dylan for sure, and quite possibly the cameraman. If she caused a scene before they located Brianna, someone could warn them and they could kill her.

Instead, she gripped Luke's hand tightly as he led her from the room.

They had to do something. Somehow they had to gain access to the upper portion of the mansion.

Suddenly, she stopped and turned into Luke's body, draping herself over him like a cat in heat. Luke didn't miss a beat, but caught her tight up against him.

"What is it Ms. Whitson?"

"Master, I *need* you," she said as seductively as she could and just loud enough for Hollister to hear her from the doorway.

"You need me?" Luke leaned back to stare into her eyes.

Desire coursed through her at the heat in the depths of his intense gaze. She parted her lips and licked them slowly, rubbing against him slightly, her nipples hardening in the thin material covering them. "Yes, Master. Seeing that…that woman. It was so alluring."

"Sounds like your girl needs a little extra training on self-control, Mr. Edgars," Hollister said, approaching them.

Luke let out a sigh worthy of a long-suffering parent. "Unfortunately, Ms. Whitson does need training reinforcement upon occasion. The sooner the better, or she regresses. I don't suppose I can ask you for the use of a private room. I don't think she'll wait until I've gotten her out of here."

"Of course, we have some secure rooms above." Hollister led them over to a bank of elevators, slipping a pass key similar to an electronic hotel key into a slot, then handing the key to Luke with another leering look over Abigail, who was busy nibbling on Luke's ear as they entered the elevator. "Pick any room on the second floor. The key will work on them except my private corner suite. Return the key to me when you're finished."

Once inside the elevator, Abigail opened her mouth to explain to Luke why she'd acted that way.

He grasped her head between his big, warm hands and claimed her lips like a Viking warrior plundering a defenseless village.

* * * * *

Erie One cut its engines and drifted close to the shore about fifty yards from the estate's dock and the five yachts moored there.

Dave and his team of National Guardsmen slipped over the edge of the boat and quietly waded onto the shore. They split into three teams and slowly approached the dock. Two armed guards stood on one side, talking quietly in the shadows, their backs to the lake. Two more paced the pier from the dock up to the house and back.

Using hand signals, Dave instructed one team of his men to take out the two stagnant guards first and another to ambush the other two guards as they neared the more shadowed end of the pier.

His men were good. One by one the slave ring's guards went down with no more than an *umph* of expired air and not one discharged weapon or alarm sounded. A couple of minutes later two of his men assumed the position of the downed guards in the shadows to prevent anyone coming to see what was wrong.

"Dock secure," one of them said in the walkie-talkies.

Dave took the remaining men and headed towards the first yacht. Time to prevent the loss of a victim or any chance of an escape by water for these slimeballs.

* * * * *

As the elevator rose Luke didn't release his hold on Abby's head or relinquish the near brutal pressure of the kiss. He let the anger over all those brutalized women, especially Abby's friend and the frustration at losing her in the obviously fixed auction, drive his barely leashed passion. The fact that it was Abby and that they were on a case with hidden cameras probably on them, kept him from making the elevator ride a more sensual one.

The discreet ding of the elevator door let him know they'd arrived. He released Abby and taking her hand led her into the hall. Pulling her close as they walked, he whispered a warning in her ear. "No talking. Cameras and mics."

Stopping a few feet from the elevator, he surveyed the hall. Six rooms, three on each side. "Look, Ms. Whitson. We have our choice of six rooms," he said loud enough for both any hidden mics to pick up and his own team to be aware of the situation. "Which would you like?"

Abby giggled. "Master Luke, you always know the right one to choose."

Damn, she was way too into her character.

Slipping his arm around her waist, he pulled her with him to the nearest door. "Then we'll take the first one. I wouldn't want you cooling down while we checked them all out."

He slid the key card into the slot. The green light to signal it unlocked flashed and he quickly ushered Abby inside, slipping a shoe off to prop the door open slightly. Before she could ask any questions, he laid one finger against her lips.

"As tantalizing as the bit of voyeurism was to you downstairs, Ms. Whitson, this is going to be an exercise in self-control," he said, slowly moving around the room. "So I hope our hosts don't mind, but I'd like to not have this filmed."

He studied the dresser across from the four-poster bed identical to the one Brianna had been strapped to. There it was. A tiny camera discreetly hidden among the silk flower arrangement. And yes, a second stationed just under the base of the lamp. Standing tall, he pulled off his suit coat and draped it over the entire desk, being sure nothing could record through the black material.

"And since this is all about my control over you, we'll have to gag you to keep you from making any noise," he said, hoping whoever was listening on the other side of the cameras would believe the scenario he'd just set up.

Sitting on the bed he motioned Abby to come sit beside him, letting their listeners hear the bed creak a few times. He leaned in to whisper in her ear. "We have to get out of here to check the other rooms. But not just yet. I have a feeling Master Lee will come up and collect his property himself which may save us some effort, so let's give it a few minutes. Get your weapon out and have it ready, okay?"

She nodded, slipping the purse from her shoulders. Taking her weapon out, she laid it on the bed beside her. Her eyes slightly wide as she anticipated the coming actions, her lips still puffy from the elevator kiss, she was a tempting vision. One he couldn't resist. He cupped the far side of her face, rubbing his thumb over her cheek and leaned in for a gentler kiss. One to warm and reassure her.

"We'll find her, sweetheart," he whispered, staring deep into her green eyes. Her gaze one of trust. A trust he'd do everything to keep.

Something shifted hard in his heart.

Mine.

For this woman, *his* woman, he'd do anything.

"*Okay, Luke,*" Jake said in his ear. "*We've got the perimeter set, the women are safely tucked in with Katie and Matt. Castello's coming up the stairs. He said the senator and Master Lee's group are in the elevator.*"

Luke walked to the door, pulling his shoe out, but keeping the door slightly open. With his finger on his lips he reminded Abby not to speak. She wiggled on the bed to keep the pretense of someone on the bed for the microphones he was sure still listened.

The elevator ding barely sounded across the hall. As the doors opened, he eased the room door together until the smallest crack possible remained when they passed it.

"You will be able to take her out of the country as soon as possible?" Senator Klein said as the group passed the door.

"My yacht will be more than capable of having her in Canada and then we'll board a plane for my island before morning," Master Lee said in a clipped Asian accent.

After the group passed their door, he opened it enough to watch their progress all the way to the end of the hall and the door on the opposite side from their room. He motioned for Abby to join him. She jumped on the bed for a few more creaks, letting out a moan, then hurried over, her gun in hand and pointed at the floor. Easing the door open as the one down the hall closed behind the group, he pointed to the room where Abby's friend was more than likely being held. She nodded that she understood. Silently, he slipped his shoe back on, then opened the door.

Time to save Brianna.

CHAPTER 18

"Time to wake up, slut." Dylan's voice sounded just before someone slapped her face hard.

Brianna tried to move away, but her arms were chained or something above her head. She opened her uninjured eye to peek at him. He looked so handsome in his tuxedo with the neatly tied bowtie.

Why was he hitting her again? He'd been so nice to her before.

Before what?

They'd been in the bed. He'd been loving, putting salve on her cuts, kissing her, making love to her, even as he asked her questions. Questions about the flash drive. About the Abbey. He thought it was a church. She hadn't corrected him. When she'd refused to talk about it, he'd gotten mad and smacked her.

Then there was a pinch. Things had gone dark, like she'd been drifting down into a deep cavern. Now he'd bound her hands, trapped her, and was hitting her again.

"Why?" she whispered over her sore, cut lips.

"Why do you need to wake up?" He slapped her again. "Because I told you to. You're leaving now."

Tears burned in her good eye and an ache started in her chest—hope that this ordeal was finally ending. That she'd been right and somewhere inside Dylan Klein was a sliver of love for her, enough that he would take sympathy on her plight. "I'm going home?"

He laughed harshly as he leaned in close. "Wrong, whore. You're going with your new Master."

Grabbing her by the hair on the top of her head, he forced her to look to the far side of the bed. There stood an Asian man in a tuxedo similar to Dylan's. He had salt-and-pepper hair and finely manicured fingers, with gold rings on them and a gold watch on his wrist. Sophisticated and rich. The kind of man who'd always attracted her attention. Only when she looked into his eyes, cold dread snaked up her spine.

Lust.

Not the kind she'd seen in other men's eyes for her beauty. No, he was focused on her injuries. She didn't know how she knew that, but she did. The desire in his eyes promised pain, even more than she'd already suffered. He'd break her, then throw her away, like yesterday's trash.

Swallowing hard, she tried to look back at Dylan. "Please..." she whispered over her parched mouth and lips.

"What did you say, bitch? Speak louder." He pulled her head back, arching her neck, but finally letting her see him again.

In his hand he held a knife.

He wanted her to beg. Okay, she'd beg. Anything to keep from going with the dangerous man at the bedside.

"Please…" She swallowed again, forcing her voice to gain strength. "Please don't," she begged as loudly as she could.

* * * * *

Footsteps sounded on the steps near the elevator. Abigail turned so her back was to Luke as they progressed toward the door where they suspected Brianna was being held. She raised her gun arm slightly in case she needed to take out whoever was coming up on their flank.

Castello stepped into the hallway, followed quickly by Jeffers. She let out the breath she'd been holding, gave them a slight nod, then turned back to follow Luke as quietly as possible.

Holding up his fist to signal them to stop, as he pressed his ear up against the door.

She stood just behind his shoulder, straining to hear what was being said inside. A loud male voice was all she could make out, not what was being said. If that room was as huge as the one she and Luke had been in up the hall, the bed was too far away for them to make out actual conversation.

Was Brianna in there? Was she still out from the

drugs?

They heard something being smacked.

Luke motioned for Castello to stand on the far side of the door. When she moved to join the Marshal, Luke pulled her back behind his hip. Jeffers flanked her, his back to them as he kept his gun trained down the hall. Luke pointed at Castello, then at the door, and held up three fingers.

Frank nodded.

Luke looked back over his shoulder at her and held up three fingers. Frank would kick in the door on a silent count of three and they were all going in.

She nodded, relaxed the hands on her gun then gripped it tighter.

"Please don't," Brianna screamed on the other side of the door.

Abby surged forward, but Luke held her back. With a pointed look at her he reached up and tapped his ear bud three times, then spoke into his wrist phone. "Utah, Utah, Utah."

The signal they were ready.

"Omaha, Omaha, Omaha," Jake said in their ears.

Luke held up one finger.

She exhaled.

Two fingers.

She inhaled and tightened the grip on her weapon.

Three fingers.

Castello's boot heel slammed into the door just above the knob, shattering the wood and forcing it open.

"Federal agents!" Luke yelled as he was first in the door, with Castello right behind him. Abigail came in third with Jeffers on her heels.

"Drop the knife!" Luke said, coming up behind Dylan Klein, who dropped the knife on the floor.

Castello had his weapon drawn on the bodyguard who had his hand in his suit jacket. "Ease that gun out slowly, big fella, and drop it on the rug."

"How dare you. This is a private home," Senator Klein blustered from the far side of the room.

"And you're all under arrest for human trafficking, Senator," Luke said as he secured Dylan's hands behind his back with a plastic zip-tie.

Not wanting to look at the bed until everyone was secure, Abigail focused on the people standing around the room. Master Lee had moved back against the wall, his female slave by his side.

"Ms. Whitson, let's get Ms. Mathews unbound," Luke said, forcing her to look at the bed.

She swallowed the bile that rose in her throat at the condition her friend was in. Yes, she'd seen it on the television downstairs, but up close and in real life it was even worse.

Quickly, she pulled the sheets back up over Brianna to cover her nudity, then retrieved the knife Dylan had dropped. Once she had the bindings cut, she lowered Brianna's hands to her side. Leaning in she smoothed the hair from Brianna's uninjured eye and whispered in her ear. "It's okay, Brie. I'm here. You're safe now."

A sob racked Brianna's body as she clutched Abigail's hand in hers. "Abby, I didn't tell them, I didn't."

"Abby?" Both Senator Klein and his son said.

Staccato gunfire sounded from outside the mansion and yelling could be heard downstairs.

"We're moving in. Secure the mansion. No one leaves." Jake's word filled their ears. *"Luke, I'm on my way upstairs."*

"That would be our task force securing the area, Senator. Your days of selling women have ended," Luke said, shoving Dylan to the floor.

"You bastards," the senator said. Moving quickly for a man of his age, a weapon appeared in his hand, focused straight on Luke's heart. "I'm not letting some lowly government grunt destroy what I've built."

He was going to kill Luke, the man she loved. She had to do something.

"Luke!" Abigail didn't pause, just threw the knife at the senator and herself at Luke.

A boom sounded in the room as the gun went off.

Searing pain and heat exploded in her side as she landed on Luke's warm body.

She looked into his beautiful hazel-green eyes and smiled at him. "I love you," she whispered.

Then everything went dark.

"Abby!" Luke cradled her to him even as he saw

Jeffers tackle the senator, clipping him in the jaw with his elbow and snapping the weapon out of his wrist.

"I love you," she whispered, then went unconscious.

Something sticky filled his hands and he rolled her away from him. His hand was bloody and the right side of her torso was covered in it. "Oh God, baby, no."

Someone pushed a towel in his hands and he pressed it against the side of her chest.

"Sami. Get in here now," Jake was beside him talking to his sister.

"Why'd you do it, Abby?" He pulled her in closer, keeping pressure on the wound, the bleeding slowing.

"Let's clear the room." Castello led Master Lee, his woman and the bodyguard from the room, while two of Jake's agents secured the Kleins who were both babbling about warrants.

"Please wake up, Abby. You know I didn't want this." Pain seared his chest so hard he couldn't take a deep breath as he stared down at the woman he loved. He cradled her against his chest, smoothing the hair from her head and feeling the side of her neck for a pulse. It was there, but it was fast.

"Luke, let me look." His sister-in-law Katie was there.

"She won't wake up."

"It's probably shock." She caught his hand in hers. "Just let me see where she was shot, so Sami and I can let the hospital know."

"I'll get an evac copter on the way, Luke," Jake said,

already stepping away to make the call.

Luke eased Abby down onto his thighs, and lifted the blood-soaked towel from her side.

"The bullet was meant for me. Why did she do this?"

Katie examined the spot, then placed a clean towel over the site, pressing his hand back down. "Keep the pressure on it. It's helping stop the bleeding. And she jumped in front of the bullet because she loves you. I'd do the same for Matt. Sami would for Jake."

"That's right. We protect our men," Sami said, breathless from the apparent sprint in from her truck. She squeezed in beside him. "Luke we need to stabilize her as best we can for transport."

"I can get her down to the truck, Sami." He started to gather Abby close once more, but his sister laid her hand on his shoulder.

"No, Luke. The medic and I will take Brianna in it. She's more stable than Abigail. It will be faster for her to go by helicopter to the closest trauma center."

That made sense, but there wasn't a helicopter here. He looked down at Abby's pale face. And there was so much blood. Just like he'd seen in his dreams.

"Luke, I need to get an IV in her and keep her blood pressure from dropping."

IVs. Sami knew what to do. She'd done it hundreds of times in the ER. Helped save hundreds of lives. She could save Abby.

"Luke, you have to let her go." His sister's eyes held both calm confidence and a gentle pleading.

Tenderly he lifted Abby off his legs and slid her to the floor, keeping pressure on her wound with his hand as his sister slipped a tourniquet on Abby's opposite arm and proceeded to insert an IV needle, which was attached to a bag of IV fluid.

"It's okay, sweetheart," he leaned in to whisper in Abby's ear. "We've got you. You can handle this. You're the strongest woman I've ever met."

As Sami worked to slip on the blood pressure cuff and check her vital signs, he continued to whisper to Abby, even after he heard the whap-whap-whap of the helo's blades outside on the mansion's lawn.

"Let me get a pressure dressing on the site, Luke," Sami said, nudging his hands off the towel he had pressed tightly to Abby's side. When they moved it, a soft moan escaped Abby.

"Easy, sweetheart," he whispered in her ear again. "I'm so sorry I let this happen to you."

He watched Sami and the medic work.

"The blood isn't coming as fast now. That's a good sign, right?" he asked.

"Could be." Sami said without looking up. "We won't know until she's been seen at the hospital. The gunshot wasn't a through and through."

"The bullet's still in there?" Damn, that wasn't good.

"Right. She's going to need surgery and God only knows what it nicked while it bounced around in there."

A litter was brought in and Luke stepped to the side as they lifted the limp body of the woman who had become so important to him on it. *Why wasn't she waking up?*

"Her BP is 80 over 45, pulse is 120," Sami was saying to one of the people in orange-and-brown flight suits as they moved down the hall. "We started an IV of Ringers and there's a pressure dressing to her right side, just under the ribcage."

"Estimated blood loss?"

"About five hundred to a thousand ccs, if I had to guess."

"Can I go with her?" Luke asked, numb with worry, hearing everything as if from a long distance.

"Sorry, sir. There isn't that much room inside," one of the young helicopter crew said. He'd introduced himself as a transport nurse and he seemed to know what he was doing. At least Luke prayed he did.

He followed the team, Sami and the medic outside to the waiting copter. As soon as they had her on board, he grabbed the young transport nurse by the front of his flight jumpsuit and stared straight into his eyes. "You take care of her, you hear me?"

"Yes, sir. We'll get her to the hospital."

"Luke, she's in the best hands," Sami said beside him, but still Luke didn't let go.

Castello stepped into his view. "You're wasting time that Abigail doesn't have."

His words cut into the pain and anger coursing through Luke. He released the kid and stepped back, watching as the helicopter took off.

"Let's go," Frank said. "The others can clean up this mess. You want to be there when that lady wakes up in the hospital."

He ran after Castello and jumped into the front seat of the sedan they'd arrived in just as Frank hit the gas, tearing across the grass of the estate towards the exit.

He just prayed she was alive when he got there.

"She said she loved me," he whispered.

"I know."

"I didn't get to tell her..." he swallowed, unable to finish.

"You will, kid. You will."

He prayed Frank was right.

CHAPTER 19

By the time Luke and Castello arrived at the hospital, the staff had already taken Abby into surgery. His ass was going numb from sitting on the damn fake leather couches in the waiting room. Castello had been the only one with him at first.

Thank God, Frank knew not to talk. He couldn't take useless prattle or meaningless reassurances. Not now. Not with the vision of all that blood Abby had lost still fresh in his mind. All he could think about was how she'd thrown herself in front of him and how he'd never told her how much she meant to him.

Slowly his family started to arrive. First Matt and Katie, who'd taken the time to get the women admitted to the emergency room to be checked out and help the local cops get statements from the ones less drugged from the ordeal.

Next came Dave, who handed him a coffee. "Drink it, you look like shit. Abigail doesn't need to wake up and see you looking like this."

Kirk F. Patrick arrived with a bag of sandwiches from the caterer, Paolo. He handed one to Luke, who took a few bites, not really registering what was in it, but wanted to prevent Dave from forcing it down his throat.

Sami and Detective Jeffers walked in next. They'd stayed with Brianna all the way to the hospital. She'd given them all the information she could about her attack in the condo, her torture and what she'd discovered about the slavery ring. She still hadn't told anyone where she'd hidden the flash drive she supposedly left for Abby. The hospital team had quickly sedated her upon her arrival so they could begin fixing her broken arm, nose and clean her various wounds.

Finally, Jake came in with a report on the senator. "He's going to need surgery to repair the torn ligaments and nerves from the knife wound. Abigail had one hell of an aim with that knife. It knocked off his aim and probably saved your life."

At that point Luke left the nearly claustrophobic waiting room to get some fresh air.

Lucky wasn't what he was feeling. Scared shitless was more like it. Guilty for not keeping her safe. Abby's actions might've saved his life, but if he lost her, would it really matter?

"She's one brave woman," Castello said from behind him.

"The bravest," he said without turning around.

"Smart, too."

"The smartest."

"Too good for you."

"Damn straight."

"Best to walk away and let some other smart guy have her."

"No way in hell." He turned and stalked into his friend's personal space, fists clenched and ready for a fight. "She's mine, and if she'll have me, I'm never letting her go."

A slow grin split the older man's face. "Good. I'd hate to have to kick your ass for being stupid."

Some of his anger and frustration dispelled, they went back inside just in time to meet the surgeon coming to talk with them all.

The doctor took off his green scrub hat and rubbed his hand through this thinning hair, then down over his haggard face. Luke's stomach sank and his knees went wobbly.

"As you know, due to HIPPA laws I can't really give you much information. The surgery went well and we did get the bullet out in one piece," the surgeon said, focusing on Luke. "For now Ms. Whitson is stable and in recovery."

"Can I see her?" he asked, desperate to see for himself that she was okay.

"Not just yet. As soon as she's in her room in the Surgical Intensive Care she can have visitors, but no more than two at a time."

* * * * *

Abby lay so still in the hospital bed.

Watching her chest rise and fall in a steady rhythm, Luke held her limp hand in his, running his thumb over her knuckles, wishing she'd grouse at him to stop.

At least her vital signs were steady as they beeped across the monitor screen above the bed. The surgeon, as well as Sami and Katie, had all reassured him that she was stable and that it would just take a little while for her to wake from the anesthesia. When he'd asked how long, no one could give him a damn answer.

And here he sat, finally at her bedside, waiting for her to wake up.

"Sometimes it helps if you talk to her," the nurse said, coming in to check the blood dripping into one of her IV's. Sami told him they'd had to start a second one to give her the blood, something about it not being able to mix with the other IV solution.

"Not really sure what to say." He knew what he wanted to say. He wanted to rail at her for getting hurt. He wanted to fuss at her for putting him before her own safety. He wanted to tell her he loved her, but not with an audience of medical professionals walking in and out of the room, and certainly not with Abby not awake to hear it.

"Talk about anything. It's the recognition of your voice that helps them muddle back to consciousness."

"Muddle?" He couldn't help the half-grin at her

terminology.

"Not a medical term, but patients often tell me it's like trying to walk through thick fog. So, muddle." She smiled back, a charming blush on her cheeks—a look that would've encouraged him to flirt with her just weeks ago—before Abby. He nodded without saying more, then focused once again on the dark-haired woman in the bed.

Just talk.

"Senator Klein may lose the use of his right hand. Seems someone threw a knife into his wrist severing the nerves and damaging a few ligaments. Couldn't happen to a nicer guy."

Nothing.

"Kirk F. Patrick brought cheesecake for all the nurses. Said his nana said they'd give you extra special care if we fed them. Had to run the kid off though, he kept trying to get hook up dates with the younger nurses."

He smiled at the memory, but Abby still didn't move.

"Jeffers stopped by. He's been in your friend's room all night. Said she had lots of details but still refuses to tell him where the flash drive is hidden. We need that evidence to cement our case. Of course the videos we found in the mansion and Babbette's injuries cover us for probable cause."

"*Brianna*," she whispered, her eyes still closed. "Her name is Bri-ahn-na. Why can't you get it right?"

She was awake.

Thank God.

He stood and kissed her on the forehead, smiling through his own tears when she slowly opened her eyes. "Because I didn't want you to ever think she was more important to me than you are, sweetheart."

"I already knew that."

"You did? How?"

She gave him a whisper of a smile, his heart swelling at the sight until he thought it would burst out of his chest.

"Because you dreamed about me."

"I did, but don't remind me. You still ended up covered in blood."

"And you bossed me around."

He leaned in to kiss her gently. "Someone had to protect you."

"And you love how my brain works."

"I do and if I live to be a hundred I'll never quit thinking how much you fascinate me." He kissed her again, then leaned back. "You scared me with all that blood. Why did you jump in front of me? You could've been killed, nearly were, in fact."

She pushed a button on the bed, slowly raising herself up to a forty-five-degree angle. "Because he had line of sight on your heart. Too many people would've been sad if you'd died. While I'm more expendable."

Expendable? What the hell was she talking about?

Before he could correct her misconception, a knock

sounded on the door.

It was Jeffers pushing Brianna in a wheelchair.

"Sorry, but she insisted she wanted to see her friend," Aaron said with a slight shrug of apology.

The smile that lit up Abby's face took some of the anger out of Luke's frustration over the interruption.

"Come in. I've just been catching Abby up on what happened while she was napping."

Jeffers wheeled Brianna right up to Abby's bedside and the two women clutched each other's hands and the tears started flowing.

Luke looked at Aaron, who appeared just as perplexed, then shrugged as if to say, *Women*. He nodded and shrugged, too. Apparently they had to cry before they could talk.

"You're going to be okay?" Brianna asked after a bit.

"Yes. It was just a little gunshot," Abby said and Luke coughed to cover up the choking sound at her description of her injuries. She cast him a slanted look and he moved to the foot of the bed as she focused on her friend once more. "Are you going to be okay?"

"The doctors fixed my nose and arm, but they think the damage to my cheekbone and eye socket might need more surgery once the swelling goes down." Brianna looked out the window a minute, then back at Abby. "I'm so sorry I dragged you into this, Abby. I had no idea how dangerous Dylan and his people were. I'd only wanted some advice on what to do with the information I'd found. Then, two men were attacking me in my home and…"

She choked on more tears and Abby reached out to stroke her hair.

"We know, Brie. I was so scared when I saw all that blood and the mess, I knew you were in trouble. But I never found the information you had for me."

"It was in the picture of me."

Abby laughed, then caught her side. "Dang that hurts."

Luke started to her, but she shook her head at him.

"Brie, there were dozens of photos of you all over the place."

"I know, but only one addressed to you. It was taped on the back. The cardboard backing hiding it from anyone."

Abby's eyes shot to his. "We had it all the time and didn't know it."

Luke nodded, then turned to Jeffers. "I'll have Castello get it to the station later today."

"Appreciate it," he said. "We'll be mopping this mess up for some time. All the information on that will help our case."

"I'd keep that profile up on those websites, too." Luke gave him a pointed look.

"You think there might be sharks out there we haven't rounded up yet?"

Jeffers was a smart man. "Could be. Might be worth a little fishing, don't you think?"

The nurse came in carrying a small IV bag and a cup

of medicine. "I'm afraid I have to break this up. Ms. Whitson and Ms. Mathews both need to rest."

Jeffers moved in behind the wheelchair again, but Brianna still clutched Abby's hand. "Thank you, Abby. Thank you for not giving up on me. And I never told them who you were, even when I realized they thought Abby was a church."

Anger shot through Luke. Brianna *had* told the Kleins about Abby, only they hadn't realized it. He knew she'd put her in danger, but Abby simply blinked and patted her friend's hand. "I would never give up on you, Brie. You're my forever friend."

"And you're mine," Brianna said as Jeffers eased her away from the bed.

After they left, Luke sat back down in the chair by her bedside, slipping her hand in his, threading their fingers together as the nurse hung the small bag of antibiotics, checked the end of the blood transfusion, marked down more of Abby's vital signs, then gave her the medication, warning her it would make her sleepy in ten or fifteen minutes.

He waited for the nurse to leave then brought Abby's hand up to his lips and kissed it. "You're wrong, you know."

"Wrong about what?" she asked, looking at him with those fascinating green eyes.

"About being expendable. If you hadn't made it through this..." he swallowed, fighting the lump suddenly in his throat. "If you'd died, a hole would've been left in my life. One I don't think I could ever crawl out of..." He paused again, kissing her hand. "I love you, Abigail Prudence Whitson and don't you ever put your life in danger like that again."

Tears slipped down her cheeks, but she smiled at him. "I love you, too, Lucas Edgars and I won't put myself in danger as long as no one points a gun at your heart."

"Stubborn woman."

"Bossy man," she said with a yawn.

"You get some sleep," he said, pulling up the covers around her.

"Will you be here when I wake up?" she asked, and the slight question in it reminded him how vulnerable she was, even to something as powerful as love.

He leaned in and kissed her, tenderly but with enough heat to promise more when she was up for it. Then he sat back down, her hand still in his. "Sweetheart, I will always be here for you."

The End

Thank you for reading THE EDGARS FAMILY NOVELS! Want to know more about my books and when new releases will be coming? Please consider joining my newsletter mailing list on my website at:
www.SuzanneFerrell.com
I only send out newsletters when new books are being published, so only a few times a year. I promise not to SPAM you. Your email will NOT be sold to other sites and is only to be used for the purpose of sending out my newsletter.

****

The Edgars Family Novels

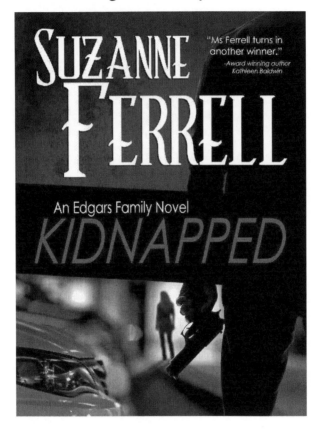

FBI Agent Jake Carlisle is in deep trouble. He's been shot and if he can't get help fast, two lives will be lost-his and that of the young witness whom he's sworn to protect. Desperate, on the run from both the police and the Russian Mafia, he kidnaps a nurse from a hospital parking lot.

ER nurse Samantha Edgars has been living in an emotional vacuum since the death of her daughter. Mentally and physically exhausted following a difficult shift, she's suddenly jolted from her stupor when she's bound and gagged, then tossed into the back of her car. Forced to tend a bleeding FBI agent and his injured witness, she's terrified. But Samantha quickly learns the rogue agent and orphaned boy need more than just her professional skills. Danger is bearing down on them, and she must learn to trust Jake – and her heart – if they're all going to survive.

****

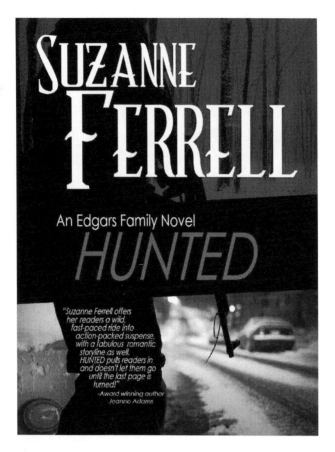

In one fiery explosion Katie Myers' witness protection cover is blown. Unable to trust the Marshals who've been responsible for her safety, she's on the run from the cult leader she put on death row. In desperation she forces a near stranger at gunpoint to help her hide.

By-the-book patrolman Matt Edgars is shocked when the woman he's come to rescue points a gun at him and demands he help her leave a crime scene. The stark terror in Katie's beautiful eyes has him breaking rules for the first time in his career.

With a hit man on their trail, Matt must break down the walls Katie has built to guard the secrets of her past. If not the cult leader will fulfill his prophecy and take the one woman Matt has ever loved to the grave.

****

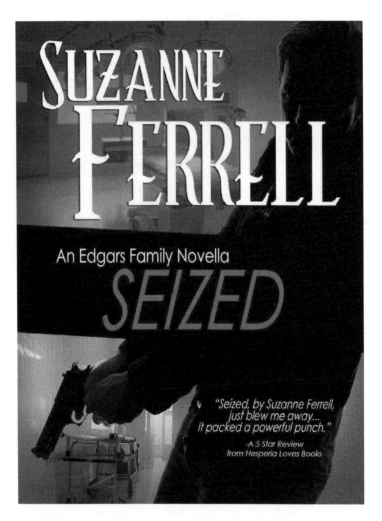

Dave and Judy Edgars have always loved each other – they've been married ten years and have three kids. But ever since Dave, a SWAT team member, was shot on duty Judy can't control the intense fear that grips her every time he heads out to work. It puts a strain on their relationship. Dave knows she's scared, but damn it she knew he was a cop the day they met. His patience is wearing thin.

Until the tables are turned...

One icy winter night, Judy, an operating room nurse, is called into work. She's taken hostage by a crazed gunman with an agenda. Now with Judy's life in danger and the SWAT team deployed elsewhere, Dave must face the same fear his wife does on a daily basis. Terrified he will lose her, he and his law enforcement family race to save Judy and stop her captor's plans.

****

This boxed set includes the first two Best-selling Edgars Family Romantic Suspense Novels, KIDNAPPED and HUNTED, along with the fast-paced novella SEIZED KIDNAPPED.

Other Suzanne Ferrell Books...

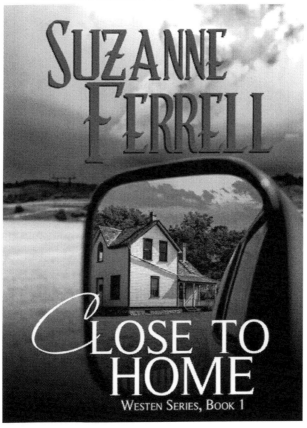

Emma Lewis has a lot on her plate. The single mother of two precocious twin boys and an aging mother who is having trouble getting through each day, the last thing Emma needs is a man in her life, especially a doctor. So when the town's doctor goes on vacation and his handsome nephew takes over, Emma is shocked to not only find him standing in her bedroom, but accusing her of being a neglectful parent.

Clint Preston came to Westen for the year to fill in as the town doc while his uncle took a long needed vacation. Clint also needed a sense of peace and calm to try to find his passion for medicine burned out by long shifts in an urban hospital's ER. Angered to find two boys in his clinic with broken wrists and no accompanying parent, he is determined to confront their mother. The feisty redhead he meets quickly dispels his belief that she's a neglectful mother, but he can see her situation is more critical than she wishes to face and finds himself volunteering to help care for her sons and the remodeling of her home.

As Emma and Clint forge a relationship among the slightly off-beat characters that inhabit Westen a menace from Emma's past threatens her and her sons. Clint and Emma join forces to prevent the loss of either boy and the love they've discovered in each other's' arms.

****

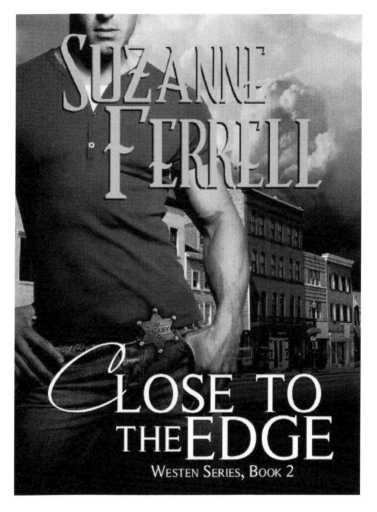

After facing death as an undercover narcotics cop, Gage Justice has come home to heal. His recuperation is cut short by his father's unexpected diagnosis of cancer and subsequent death. Now he's honoring one of his father's last wishes by taking over as the sheriff of his boyhood home, Westen, Ohio. Biding time until his father's term is finished, he fights boredom more than crime in the sleepy little town – that is until one sexy little teacher-turned-Private-Investigator literally falls into his arms.

Bobby Roberts is looking for adventure. After giving up her own dreams to raise her two sisters after the death of their parents, she's been trapped in a schoolroom for nearly two decades. The suffocating claustrophobia of the classroom has set her on a new career path. She arrives in Westen, complete with brand-spanking-new PI license, a handgun and a simple case – investigate a lien on property of a dead man.

Little does she realize her "simple little case" will lead her into the world of one sexy sheriff and the path of a murderer intent on keeping them both from discovering his secrets or stopping his plans that could destroy Westen.

****